the Singer of All Songs

POINT

SCHOLASTIC INC.

New York Toronto London Auckland Sydney
Mexico City New Delhi Hong Kong Buenos Aires

No part of this publication may be reproduced, stored in a retrieval system, or transmitted in any form or by any means, electronic, mechanical, photocopying, recording, or otherwise, without written permission of the publisher. For information regarding permission, write to Scholastic Inc., Attention: Permissions Department, 557 Broadway, New York, NY 10012.

ISBN 0-439-55479-9

Arthur A. Levine Books hardcover edition designed by Elizabeth B. Parisi, published by Arthur A. Levine Books, an imprint of Scholastic Inc., March 2004.

12 11 10 9 8 7 6 5 4 3 2 1   4 5 6 7 8 9/0

Printed in the U.S.A.   01

First American paperback printing, November 2004

for Alice

Contents

The Wall of Ice

Long before sunrise, even before the first faint blush of gold had touched the snowy peaks that ringed the valley of Antaris, the bells began to peal. The sky was still dark overhead, and the three moons sailed silver-bright between fading stars as the priestesses gathered under the cloisters. A hundred women shuffled and rustled in their yellow robes, their breath rising in puffs of mist into the cold air.

The sisters did not whisper to one another. Shivering, they drew their shawls over their heads and nodded in silent greeting. It was forbidden for any of the Daughters of Taris to use her voice on this day, unless to do the work of the Goddess. But the quiet footsteps of the priestesses on the stones of the courtyard and the swish of their robes made a kind of wordless murmur beneath the steady clang of the bells.

Slowly the sky began to lighten. By the pond, the ducks shook out their feathers; the goats bleated, rubbing their bony heads against their pens. Sunlight crept down the wooded slopes of the valley in a wash of gold, and the snowcapped mountains sparkled

I

pink and blue-white. But the orchards, the river and the walled gardens, the gray stone Dwellings where the priestesses lived, and the villages and cottages of the ordinary folk of Antaris, those who had no gift of chantment, were all in cold shadow.

In the courtyard, the sisters turned their faces upward to the square of pale sky that framed the three moons, strung like beads on some invisible thread. Steadily they breathed. The chilly air burned their nostrils and lungs, but they didn't falter. In and out, to the rhythm of the bells, they breathed together. Some closed their eyes and swayed a little, back and forth; others held up their hands as if to gather in the air and the power that it held.

Nine times a year, the three moons, the Lamps of the Goddess, sailed full in the sky; nine times the sisters set out for the Day of Strengthening.

The first time Calwyn helped perform the ritual, two years before, she'd stayed awake all night, too full of pride and nervous anticipation to sleep. But she was sixteen now, almost a full priestess, and the idea of a long day's walk and chantment, all on an empty stomach, no longer seemed as enticing as a festival. She wriggled her toes in the narrow strip of warmth under her bedcovers, calculating the last possible moment she could wait to get up before Tamen would notice her absence. Would it really matter if the Wall did melt away? She had never seen any attackers from the Outlands lurking in the forests.

Even the traders, who came every year to bring goods from the lands across the mountains, were far from being bloodthirsty invaders. Indeed, they seemed reluctant to be in Antaris at all, uneasy for every moment they spent within the Wall, always struggling for breath in the unfamiliar thinness of the air, jumping with fright at the sight of any yellow-robed sister. The only time Calwyn ever saw looks of happiness on the Outlander traders' faces was at the end of their stay. Last year she and the Guardian and some of the other priestesses had led them back to the Wall and had sung the spell of unmaking, to melt a gap in the ice through which they could squeeze themselves and their handcarts, laden now with precious honey, herbal medicines, and fine woven cloth. When the crack was sealed up again behind them, Calwyn heard a great pent-up rush of laughter from the far side of the Wall, the nervous laughter of those who have managed to escape from death and can't quite believe their luck. The memory made her smile. The Outlanders feared the magic of Antaris, and they were right to fear it.

As the last echo of the bells died away to silence, Calwyn threw back the covers and leaped out of bed. Pulling on loose trousers and a soft yellow tunic over her undershirt, she ran down the stone steps toward the cloisters, braiding her long dark hair into two plaits as she went. If she was lucky, she could slip into the back of the crowd without Tamen or Marna seeing her. Down the steps and out into the chilly courtyard she ran, with her boots still unlaced, stumbled, tripped, and cannoned into the tall, upright figure of Tamen herself, the Guardian of the Wall.

A warning finger rose to Tamen's lips as she gave Calwyn a cold glare and pointed silently to the throng of women who stood breathing as one, the cloud of their sighs rising toward the dimming moons and the slowly brightening sky. Calwyn bent to her shoes, glad to hide herself from that forbidding stare, and relieved that, for today at least, the Guardian was silenced by the ceremony. Perhaps by the time they returned at nightfall, Tamen might have forgotten to be angry, and she would escape yet another lecture. Perhaps.

Plump Gilly, one of the younger novices, nudged her and grinned. It was Gilly's very first Strengthening that day. Calwyn thought she looked as excited and scared as if this were her first Festival of Shadows, the one night of the year when the priestesses mingled with the men chosen from the villages, under the warm shelter of spring moondark. Although the novices took no part in that ritual until after their initiation, Gilly was already beginning to flirt and stretch her eyes at the lads who tended the fields and cut up the firewood for the sisters. Calwyn herself was to become a full priestess next midwinter, but when Gilly asked her who had caught her eye, she had no answer. There were plenty of handsome youths among them, but they were all so juvenile, so absorbed in skittles and kick-ball and bantering with the village lasses, that Calwyn had no time for them.

"They'll be lining up to dance with *you* around the fires, with your big black eyes and your long black hair!" Gilly had said more than once. "Though it *is* a shame you're so tall and skinny —"

"I'm not very good at dancing," was Calwyn's stiff reply. In truth, she wasn't looking forward to the Festival of Shadows. Now she gave Gilly a quick, distant smile and turned away.

Marna, the High Priestess, was standing on the wide steps, robed in the same regal dark blue cloak that Tamen wore, and holding the silver-topped staff of her office. She wore no jewels, but her silver hair was piled high on her head like a crown. She raised one hand and in her clear voice sang out the blessing of the Goddess upon them all as they set out to perform Her work. With heads bowed and hands clasped in their sleeves, the sisters listened, and then, as the last faint notes died away, they turned and began the steady shuffling march away from Marna, finding the paths that radiated out from the Dwellings in every direction toward the Wall.

As they walked, they began to sing. Calwyn heard the sweet, clear notes rising around her on all sides, a net of chantment that spread slowly out from the heart of Antaris toward the Wall, a golden mesh of magic woven from their voices, with her own voice one strand of gold among many. The sun was coming up, flooding the valley with light, and she could see the narrow path that her feet followed, winding away through the orchard and across the river. Already to her left she had lost sight of Gilly; she'd vanished behind the outbuildings. But she could still hear Tamen's strong voice on her other side and see her tall, unbending figure as she made her way along the neighboring path. These were not the everyday paths that the sisters used, broad and indistinct, blurring into the grass. The paths that were used only for this ritual were narrow as one foot's width, worn into a deep groove by generations of priestesses, back and back to the first days of Antaris.

Calwyn sang, and as she sang she felt her sleepy crossness fall away. As always the ancient song flowed easily, dreamily, from her lips, the words so old that their meaning shimmered just out of reach of sense. In the apple orchard, pale buds starred the branches where the trees were coming into blossom. The dark mounds of the beehives slumbered at the end of the orchard. Lately, Marna had decided to make the keeping of the hives Calwyn's special responsibility; Damyr the old beekeeper was too feeble now to turn the heavy frames, or even to walk as far as the hives without help.

The river ran slow and wide at the foot of the orchard. Gingerly, Calwyn crossed the narrow bridge that spanned it, careful not to slip on the dew-damp stone; as with everyone in Antaris, the dread of water and drowning ran deep in her bones. One of her earliest memories was the sight of a fish, plucked from the river, writhing as it choked on the bank. *As we breathe the air, so the fish breathe the water. And just as the fish die when they come into our world, so we perish when we enter theirs.* She couldn't remember who had delivered the warning, she'd been so young. But even now she tried not to look at the dangerous water as it swirled beneath her feet, and when the bridge was safely crossed, her song lifted in relief.

As she sang and walked through the woods and up the slope, the sun rose steadily higher, until at last she could glimpse the shimmer of the Wall ahead. The famed Wall of Antaris, smooth, impenetrable, stood as high as the height of three men, as wide as a river, vast and gleaming and slippery in the sun.

As she drew closer, Calwyn held out her hands for the ritual incantations, and almost at once she was aware of the chantment taking hold, the tingling in her hands that signaled the flow of power, and the sudden sharp consciousness of everything about her as her voice rose and fell. Up and down the Wall, the sisters were all singing the same words, summoning the same magic, calling on the Goddess to make the great Wall solid and without flaw, to strengthen the ice barrier between Her daughters and the dangers of the lands beyond.

Calwyn's senses were so heightened now that she could almost hear the sunlight falling on the trees and the sweet grass and smell the scent of each tiny wild herb that grew in the moist shadows of the Wall. She could hear the unfolding of every leaf toward the light, and the gentle gurgle of the distant river, and far off in the orchard the familiar hum of the hives. And now, very faintly, she could hear the voices of the other priestesses joined in song, a shimmering web of chantment that rose and fell, circling the lands of Antaris. Now there was nothing else but the rush of power, making whole what was damaged, making strong what was weak, drawing together the humming of the morning into the fabric of song. There was no Calwyn, no Wall, no path beneath her feet, only the light and the song and the ever-shifting eternal bright movement of chantment.

Calwyn did not touch the Wall. The power that hummed and crackled through it was so strong that only the Guardian herself could lay hands on it safely. As Calwyn sang, she could feel in every fiber the pulse of the living, dangerous flow of magic between herself and the Wall that was the presence of the Goddess, called up by her voice and the ritual words she sang. The ice seemed to set before her eyes; in the places where the sun's growing warmth had produced a slippery sheen, the ice grew hard and brilliant once more. Calwyn began to walk slowly along the length of the Wall, the sun at her back, singing as she went. She walked with care; the path was uneven, a rough groove beside the towering rampart of ice, and she was light-headed from walking and chantment and going without her breakfast. The sisters always fasted before embarking on important rituals. She would not eat before sundown, when she returned to the Dwellings.

All morning she followed the path she knew so well, singing without cease, giddy with magic, methodically checking the surface of the Wall for any weakness or flaws. It sometimes happened that the earth shifted, or a rockfall from the mountains might crash against the Wall's far side and crack it. Even the digging of rabbits and burrowers beneath the Wall might weaken it a little.

She was just past the panna groves when she saw him.

Calwyn stopped in her tracks, and her song faltered on her lips. For the space of a heartbeat she thought she must be dreaming; the steady chantment she'd been singing without pause since dawn jerked almost into silence.

A young man was lying across the path. His eyes were closed: He was asleep, or dead. She could see at once that he was not a man of Antaris. His face was pale, and his hair was fair as straw, rather than dark and glossy. He was slightly built, not stocky like the men of the villages. His jerkin was too short, and his mud-stained cloak was too long. He did not belong here.

Her first thought was for the Wall; there must be some breach, some gaping inexplicable wound through which he had entered. It was her fault. This was her stretch of the Wall, the half-day's walk from the crest of Goats Hill to the river. She must have been care-less that last Day of Strengthening, in the depth of winter. There was a blizzard that day, the whirling snows so thick that she couldn't even see the Wall ahead. Priestesses had been lost in bliz-zards like that before, but this time the Goddess had watched over them all, and every one of Her daughters had stumbled back safely to the Dwellings. Could it be that she'd missed something in the blinding snowstorm, some crack, some crumbling, that had let this man inside their lands?

But the Wall was whole. There was nothing, no gap, no crack, not even a patch of roughness that might give toehold to a climber. It stood, shining, impervious, rearing up beside the path, as solid as ever. Relieved, she turned her attention back to the un-moving body of the stranger. She took a step closer, still singing the words of the chantment of strengthening. Its rhythms were so familiar, and she had practiced it so often, that she could sing it without thinking; she could have sung it in her sleep. The man did not move. Surely he must be dead. The Goddess had seen his presumption and struck him down. Calwyn could see now that his foot was injured, twisted back on itself, and there was blood on his boot. There was blood on his head too, from a great gash across his forehead, matting the straw-colored hair.

Still singing, Calwyn took another few steps forward and bent to study his face. He was older than she'd thought at first, nearer thirty than twenty. His features were boyish, but his nose was slightly beaked, giving him a hawklike look, and there were lines around his closed eyes, as if he'd stared long into the sun. He looked pale and peaceful, and cold, lying there in the Wall's shadow. Should she leave him here to rot in the woods at the mercy of the Goddess, or should she run back along the Wall and fetch Tamen? Tamen would know exactly what to do. Somehow it seemed wrong to leave the body of an Outlander untended, so close to the sacred Wall. But she couldn't move him by herself. She would have to go back to the Dwellings and bring a party of men to carry him —

Suddenly the stranger's eyes flew open.

Calwyn gave a little scream and was instantly ashamed of herself. But the Outlander was as startled as she; he struggled up on his elbows and tried to pull himself away, dragging his broken foot across the ground. His eyes, gray as a winter sky, were wide with dread. And then he did something that surprised Calwyn utterly. He began to sing.

It was a shaky chantment, to be sure, and the stranger stammered as he sang, but although the notes were low and growling, from deep in his throat, completely unlike the high, clear chantments she knew, it was unmistakably a song of power. Calwyn's hands began to tingle as they always did in the presence of magic. And then she felt the oddest sensation, as though someone had grasped the back of her tunic and tugged it firmly. She actually turned her head to see if someone had come up behind her, but there was no one there, only this invisible force pulling her backward, a force that came from the Outlander and his song.

She threw out her hands. She couldn't speak; she was forbidden to use her voice except for the Strengthening chantment until the day's ritual was complete. Yet surely even Tamen would say that to combat an Outlander was to serve the Goddess, the highest service there could be.

Calwyn made up her mind. The rule must be broken, for all their sakes. She breathed in deeply, as she'd been taught, raised her hands, and sang. She sang a spell of cold and ice, a chantment to weave a shadow of icy air all about the stranger, so that his hands shook and his teeth chattered. Still he managed to keep up his own song, growling it out through teeth clenched against the cold, and Calwyn felt the unseen hand at her back grow suddenly stronger, yanking her backward with unexpected force, and she fell onto the grass, breath and song knocked out of her. But then, just as suddenly, the invisible hand released her. She sat up, shaken and a little dazed; the Outlander, the last of his desperate strength exhausted, had collapsed back across the path, and there was silence.

Calwyn went to kneel beside him. It was obvious that he was at the very end of his strength; his eyes blazed with fever, he was thin and weak. Perhaps he had lain there helpless for days. When she tried to brush back his hair to look at the cut on his head, he pushed her away, but only feebly. "Get back," he croaked, and at once began to cough, fighting for breath as those from outside always did in the mountains.

"Peace," said Calwyn. "I won't hurt you." His foot was more severely injured than she'd thought; now she could see, through the torn leather of his boot, the gleam of crushed bone and the mangled flesh beneath. No wonder he couldn't move himself from the cold breath of the Wall into the warmth of the sun. He caught at her sleeve.

"I know you — you have not deceived me." His voice was only a whisper, but it was fierce and urgent. "You have not deceived me! I am not persuaded! I have found you out!"

"Very well, very well," Calwyn soothed him. Before old Damyr had taken her to be apprentice beekeeper, she had spent a year working with Ursca in the infirmary, and she had seen people delirious with fever before. This man was very ill and perhaps badly hurt. She knew that a cut to the head might bleed heavily and not be serious, or it might scarcely leave a mark and yet lead to death from bleeding inside the skull. She said, "Can you sit up?"

"I must get away from here." His voice was weak, but much more reasonable than before. "He will find me if I stay in the open for long." His voice had a stilted, foreign lilt to it, though it was not the accent of the traders from Kalysons.

"Who will find you?"

"*He* will. You know who I mean." He peered at her face. "Is it you? I am not sure of anything anymore — Who are you?"

"My name is Calwyn. Listen to me: I'll try to take you back to the Dwellings, the sisters there can help you more than I can. Do you think you can stand? Here, lean on me."

The Outlander struggled to his feet, wincing with pain and leaning hard on Calwyn's arm. Though she was tall and strong, and he was slight and barely as tall as she, his weight was heavy on her shoulder, and she staggered to support him. "I can make it easier, a little," he said, and from deep in his throat he began to sing another low, gurgling chantment. His crushed foot lifted off the ground, and it seemed to Calwyn that his weight on her shoulder did ease slightly. Slowly, very slowly, they were able to limp along together.

They didn't follow the sacred path beside the Wall, but cut back through the thin woods where the rabbits leaped and the berry bushes caught at them as they made their slow progress. At first the Outlander tried to keep up the chantment that held his broken foot from the ground, but many times he seemed to forget to sing, or even where he was, and more than once he half-fainted against Calwyn's shoulder, and she was forced to stop and revive him with water from the river or a chantment to cool his brow. Once she asked him, "How did you cross the Wall?" But when he

answered her, "I flew, I flew across it —" she knew that he had retreated again into delirium.

All afternoon they walked, and as the sun began to slide toward
the rim of the mountains, they spoke no more, only to say *Careful
now* or *Wait a moment*. His hand pressed hard on her shoulder; his
labored breath was the only sound in her ears. Calwyn thought of
the remainder of the Wall that she had not inspected, of the
chantment left unsung, of the lecture on neglecting her duty that
Tamen was sure to give her. Well, the Wall had lasted so long; it
would last a little longer without her help today.

But the nearer they came to the looming towers of the Dwellings,
the less certain she was that she had made the right decision.
Tamen would have left him where he was, she was sure of it. She
thought wildly of hiding him in one of the outer barns, or in the
Bee House, where no one came but herself, feeding him secretly,
until his foot healed, and then — and then what? It was impossible. He would be discovered. "Easy there," she said, holding his
arm as he stumbled by her side. His eyes were squeezed shut with
pain; he seemed hardly to hear her.

It was almost sunset by the time they reached the cloisters,
where Marna waited to greet the sisters as they returned. Calwyn
was the last; there was a flock of priestesses gathered there before
her, a murmuring throng in their loose trousers and long tunics of
pale yellow, some with their shawls drawn over their heads to keep
off the evening chill. First one, then another saw Calwyn ap-

proaching with the pale-haired, dark-clad stranger leaning on her shoulder, and then a wordless bewildered buzzing went up, as though the bees themselves had come out to greet her.

The High Priestess and the Guardian, both robed in blue, stood waiting on the steps of stone. Tamen's face was like thunder. Although as Calwyn had grown older she had learned to fear her less, it was still a difficult thing to walk steadily toward that stern stare while she led beside her a stranger, an Outlander, a dangerous enemy who had somehow, with powers unknown, managed what no one had ever done: crossed the Wall. She tried to keep her gaze fixed on Marna, who always had a kindly twinkle in her blue eyes for little children and errant novices alike. But Marna was not smiling now.

"In the name of Taris, our mother and our protector, I sing you welcome, daughter." The clear, thin voice of the High Priestess rang out in the ritual greeting.

"In the name of Taris —" Calwyn faltered the response. She could not reply, as she should, *the work of the Goddess is done.* She had left her duty uncompleted. But Marna leaned forward to kiss Calwyn's forehead with her dry lips just as if she had responded properly, to conclude the ritual, and then stood back to survey the stranger, as if she hadn't noticed him before.

"Child, who is this man?"

"I mean you no harm," said the stranger faintly. "Please —" His grip on Calwyn's shoulder tightened, and his head drooped. "Have mercy," he murmured, so low that only Calwyn could hear.

"*You* will not speak!" Tamen rapped out the command. Both she and Marna were looking at Calwyn.

"Lady Mother, my Sister, I found him by the Wall. He is hurt, and I have brought him back for healing." Calwyn could hear how feeble her words sounded. She should have left him there, it was obvious now, she should have bound him securely and left the Goddess to finish the work She had begun. And yet the Outlander's hand was still heavy and hot on her shoulder, and she knew that she couldn't have abandoned him.

Tamen said sharply, "You brought him across the Wall?"

Calwyn shook her head. "He was within the Wall when I found him."

A ripple of nervous laughter ran through the assembled sisters. The stranger looked around wildly and cried out, "He is here, I know it! You will not hide him from me!"

"Be silent!" cried Tamen, but it was too late. The Outlander had finally let go of his grip on Calwyn's shoulder and collapsed fainting to the ground.

"Take him to the infirmary." Marna nodded to two of the sisters. "Calwyn, go to the dining hall and break your fast. I will speak with you later." She turned to the assembled priestesses and raised her hands for dismissal. "In the name of the Goddess!"

The murmuring response went up from the sisters. "In the name of the Goddess."

The priestesses began to move toward the great hall, eager to take dinner after the long day without food. Most of them looked sideways at Calwyn and moved on hurriedly without speaking; they wouldn't dare to question her before Marna had done so. Suddenly Calwyn felt very tired, almost as if she might faint too. Someone plucked at her sleeve. It was Gilly, her round face glowing pink with sun and exertion. "I'm glad it was you that found him and not me! Were you *terrified*?"

"No," said Calwyn thoughtfully. "No, I wasn't terrified."

"What will they do with him now?"

"I don't know."

"However did he get across the Wall? Is he one of the traders that came last summer, has he been hiding in the woods all this time?"

"Don't be a featherhead, Gilly. How could anyone live in the woods through winter? Does he look like a bear to you?"

"Well, he must be either a bear or a bird or a burrower to get inside the Wall!" said Gilly cheerfully. "Come on, I'm hungry enough to eat a whole goat."

A bear or a bird or a burrower. Or something even more strange, an Outlander with his own chantments. Slowly Calwyn followed the younger girl toward the great hall, until the smell of spiced stew and good, fresh bread filled her nostrils, and then she could think of nothing but dinner.

The High Priestess's rooms were small and plain, as plain as the rooms of any of the sisters. An ancient tapestry hung on one wall, stitched by the hands of long-dead priestesses, so frayed and faded that the picture could scarcely be seen anymore. A small fire crackled in the hearth. Through the narrow windows Calwyn could see the dying flames of the sunset on the snowcapped peaks, glittering with lights of rose and topaz and ruby. One silver moon was visible, sailing high amid a faint scattering of stars. Marna was sitting by the fire, and Tamen stood silently in the shadows, her hands thrust into her wide sleeves.

"Sit, child."

Calwyn drew up a low stool by Marna's feet. She had sat in this spot many times during the years of her training, reciting the long songs and repeating the spells for the High Priestess to hear.

"Tell me, child, where exactly did you find him?"

"Near the foothills of Two Teeth. Not far past the panna groves."

"I know the place," came Tamen's voice from the dark corner.

"Think carefully before you answer, Calwyn. No one will be angry with you if you have made a mistake. We have all made mistakes in our time. Even the High Priestess." Marna's voice was weary, but Calwyn could hear the smile in it now. "Tell me, child. On which side of the Wall did you find him?"

Calwyn felt like weeping. It was a terrible thing to be doubted by the High Priestess. Trying to keep her voice steady, she said, "I swear by the three moons and by the Goddess, he was within the Wall."

Tamen said sharply, "How?"

"I asked him that, my Sister, and he said — I think it was the fever speaking — he told me that he *flew*. He was lying by the path, I thought he might be dead at first. But then he —" She stopped.

"Go on," said Tamen.

"He sang a chantment. At least, it was a *kind* of chantment. I tried to go up to him, and the chantment held me back." Calwyn spoke rapidly, her eyes on the floor; when she looked up, the two older priestesses were looking at each other as if she were not even in the room.

"A sorcerer," said Marna softly. "Can it be?"

"He is no trader, that is certain," said Tamen. "But if he is a sorcerer, then what Power does he command that he could fly over the Wall?"

"Ironcraft, perhaps. Though it would be a difficult chantment. Perhaps he sang the clothes he wore up into the air and carried himself inside them. A risky spell, but not impossible."

Tamen shook her head. "He is too pale to be a Merithuran. Would he not be withered and burned by the desert winds? More likely he's a man of the islands, from Firthana or the Outer Isles, a worker of the winds, and sang up a breath to lift himself across our Wall. And a wind to hold *her* away, as she said."

"It didn't feel like a wind," said Calwyn eagerly. "It was as though a hand clutched at my tunic." But they weren't listening to her.

"Is he safe in the infirmary? If he is indeed an ironcrafter, then bars and bolts will not hold him."

"Ursca tells me he is deep in fever. I have warned her to be careful of him, but if he is a sorcerer we should take care to silence him."

"Surely he can't go far, in any case. His foot is so damaged he can't walk two steps without help," said Marna.

Tamen frowned. "Better to be too careful than not careful enough. I will go down to the infirmary myself and see what may be done to secure him."

"Very well."

At the door, Tamen turned back. "Calwyn, tomorrow you will go back to the Wall and complete what you have left undone."

"But Tamen, I must tend to the hives," said Calwyn in dismay. "I haven't even looked at them today."

Tamen's face was dark with anger. "The bees have survived without you for one day; they must manage without you for another. The Wall is more important than the bees. Proper care of the Wall is the highest duty of any priestess. Do you understand me, Calwyn?"

"Yes, my Sister," Calwyn whispered.

Marna leaned back in her carved chair and closed her eyes as Tamen swept out of the room, the hem of her robe brushing the stone flags. For a long time, Calwyn, who had not been dismissed, sat quietly on the low stool. The little fire with its sweet-smelling smoke glowed against her cheek; she shifted her stool out of the heat, and Marna's eyes opened.

"I'm sorry, Lady Mother, I didn't mean to startle you."

"Child, I had almost forgotten you were there. Stay, there is no need for you to leave." Far off, from the great hall, came the sound of the evening songs, all the sisters singing together, not weaving magic now but simply celebrating the end of a long day's work well done. The room was almost dark now, the last of the light fading fast from the luminous sky. "Light the candles, little daughter."

Calwyn fetched the branched candlestick from the table by the window and lit the beeswax candles with a taper from the flames. At once the room was filled with shadows and wavering golden light. Calwyn sat down again at Marna's feet. "Lady Mother, may I ask a question?"

"Of course."

"Is the Guardian very angry with me?"

Marna laughed a little. "No more than usual." She placed her hand lightly on Calwyn's head. "She is angry with herself more than with you. The care of the Wall is a heavy burden; the safety of all Antaris depends on the Guardian. Today she has failed in her duty. She tells herself that if she were more vigilant, if her gift were stronger, the Outlander would not have been able to cross the Wall. That is why she speaks so harshly."

"Tamen has spoken harshly to me before today, Lady Mother."

"Yes." Marna's voice was very gentle and sad in the flickering firelight. "At next winter moondark you will become a full priestess, Calwyn, if the Goddess wills it. There are certain things you are old enough to hear. Tamen is not easy with you. Partly that is because she fears you."

"Tamen fears *me*?"

"She knows that your gift is stronger than her own. When I am gone, most likely it will fall to the two of you to govern this land. Tamen is not ready for that day to come. I tell you this, Calwyn, only so that you may understand her better. You two must work together, not be enemies. Do you understand me?"

"Yes, Lady Mother." Calwyn stared into the flames; her heart was beating very fast. She had never dreamed that one day she might be Guardian, or even High Priestess. She could never be as wise as Marna or inspire such awe as Tamen. Hesitantly she said, "I am not ready for that day either."

Marna laughed. "Taris willing, it is a long way off yet."

"Lady Mother, you said that was part of the reason why Tamen seems always angry with me. What is the other part?"

Marna was silent for a time, then she said, "My daughter, you have never been an obedient novice. You have always been willful, more eager to ask questions than to listen, and more keen to look over the Wall than to go about your work inside it. Tamen, and others among the sisters, are afraid that you will end as your mother did."

"My mother?" All Calwyn knew of her mother was that she had died of a winter fever when Calwyn was still a baby.

"Calida, your mother, was very like you, always wild and restless, always staring over the Wall. She used to go to the same place you like to go, Calwyn, up to the top of the western tower, and gaze out across the forests, and dream."

Calwyn took a breath. She had thought that the western tower was her secret place, that no one even knew she went there. But Marna was still speaking.

"When your mother was only a little older than you are now, just after she had been made a full priestess, she left us. She ran away from Antaris. To this day I don't know how she crossed the Wall. She simply — disappeared. We mourned her — oh, we grieved for many years. And then one day, toward the end of winter, we heard the beating of the gong the traders use to tell us of their arrival. Some thought it must be the winds, or that a tree had fallen over against the gong, but some said, no, we must go and see. And so we went, across the snow, and sang the spell of unmaking. And when the Wall opened, there stood Calida on the other side, with a babe in her arms."

"Me?" whispered Calwyn.

Marna nodded. "It was you. It had taken all her strength to bring you back to us. The Goddess took her that very night. We swore that we would raise you as a priestess and keep you safe among us. But as soon as you could walk, you were climbing the trees of the orchard and running away from your lessons to follow the goats. There have been times when we despaired of you, Calwyn. We thought that it might suit you to be apprenticed to Ursca in the infirmary and learn herb lore and healing."

Calwyn smiled. "It bored me," she admitted.

"Yes. You were more restless than ever. We held a council about you. Then old Damyr said, give her to me, to learn bee-keeping. Perhaps if she is outside in the clean air, singing like the bees, she will learn to be content. And you have seemed happy among the hives."

Calwyn did not know what to say. It was true, she was happier now than she had been when she was shut up with Ursca, but the restlessness that Marna spoke of was still inside her. She said nothing, feeling the weight of the High Priestess's hand on her head, just as the hand of the stranger had weighed on her shoulder all afternoon.

"Lady Mother, what will happen to the Outlander?"

"Ursca says he may not live." Marna sighed. "Poor man. You did right to bring him back to the Dwellings, sorcerer or no." She removed her hand from Calwyn's head. "Go to bed, little daughter. You must be weary."

But as she left the room, Calwyn thought that Marna was the one who seemed tired. And with so many things to think about, she knew that she would find it hard to sleep that night.

The next day, she did as she'd been bidden and set out on the long walk to the Wall for the second time, still weary from the day before. It was hard to give the chantment the attention that she should. Her mind teemed with images: her mother trudging through the snow with her baby girl in her arms, Tamen's haughty stare, the wild gray-green eyes of the Outlander as he scrambled away. But again and again as she followed the shining length of the Wall, she came back to the thought of her mother as a girl, climbing the western tower and gazing out over the forests, filled with longing. Did she dream, as Calwyn did, of seeing the fierce ocean? *She was braver than I am. She did more than dream.* Where had she gone, what wonders had she seen? How had she climbed the Wall? It was strange; Calwyn had always thought herself Antaris-born. But her father had been an Outlander; why, she was *born* in the Outlands! Now she knew why some of the older priestesses looked at her in the way they did.

Calwyn stumbled and hastily drew her mind back to the chantment and the Goddess's work. She passed the place where she had found the Outlander; the Wall stretched on either side, slippery, unblemished, smooth as an egg. However he had crossed it, he had left no mark. She tried to imagine him flying over the great rampart like a bird. Did all sorcerers travel that way? Had he flown across the seas and plains and mountains all the way from the Isles, or from Merithuros?

Dutifully, but without joy, she managed to complete the long day's ritual. Her section of the Wall ended where the river cut through the ice; swollen by the spring thaws, the water foamed and tumbled, racing away through the trees. Calwyn lingered there for a few moments, half-scared and half-fascinated by the roaring water, and then she turned and began the long walk back to the

Dwellings. If she hurried, she would have time to visit the hives and check that all was well before the bells began to call the sisters to the evening meal.

"Calwyn! Where have you been? Ursca has been searching for you all day. She wants you to bring some queen's jelly to the infirmary."

Calwyn wiped her mouth and slid off the long bench. She was so tired she had almost fallen asleep over her bowl. All she wanted was to crawl into bed and pull the covers over her head. But everything that came from the hives was her responsibility now. The bees gave the sisters wax for candles and polish, honey for cakes, and many things that were used in healing: queen's jelly and honey and the glue that the bees used to seal the hives from wind and rain, even the venom from their stings, all had their uses in the infirmary. A little honey on a cut helped it heal, and bee-stings were good for the pains in the joints that troubled many of the older people in the cold weather. Calwyn had other novices to help her tend the hives, but the Bee House was her domain, and no one else knew where she kept the precious store of queen's jelly.

When she arrived at the infirmary with a small pot of the rich, creamy substance in her hand, Ursca came trotting up to greet her. The infirmarian was a dumpy, fussy little woman; when they'd been shut up together day after day all through the long winter, she had driven Calwyn halfway to madness with her nervous, fidgety ways. Every setback was a calamity, every slip a disaster, met with wringing of hands and cries of despair. Yet when she was with someone who was ill or hurt, Ursca was transformed into a model of quiet calm and kindness, and no one among the sisters knew more than she did about healing and herb lore. Now that she was free of her brief apprenticeship, Calwyn was happy to see her, and happy to be back in the infirmary with its familiar smells, its rows of pots and jars and boxes, and its bunches of dried herbs hanging from the roof beams.

"Dear child, I have been hunting you all day long! Hunting you as well as I could without setting foot out of these rooms. I sent my messengers off in all directions, and they all came back without you. Is she at the hives? No, she's not there! Is she taking a lesson somewhere? Oh no, there's no sign of her! Perhaps she's at candle-making? Though it's not the season for candle-making, but Calwyn must always be doing things in her own way, stubborn creature that you are, as well I know. But back they came, no, no, she's disappeared, off to one of her hiding places again, run away up the valley to fish, no doubt."

"I wasn't fishing!" said Calwyn indignantly.

"Ah well, never mind, never mind. But I hope you had a good catch!" Ursca gave a knowing wink, whisked the pot of jelly out of Calwyn's hand, and bustled away before Calwyn could argue. That was the most exasperating of all the exasperating things about Ursca; once she had an idea in her head, nothing could budge it.

Calwyn followed her to the other end of the infirmary and watched as she carefully spooned out a little of the queen's jelly and stirred it into a bowl of smooth junket. "Is the Outlander any better?"

"Ah, poor man." Ursca shook her head. "I've done what I can for his foot, but the bones are crushed. He will be lame as long as he lives. And as for his wits, I fear they are truly addled. He starts at every little sound; he's sure we are all out to harm him. None of us can come near him except when he sleeps!" She put her mouth to Calwyn's ear and whispered, though there was no one about to hear. "You know he is a sorcerer?"

Calwyn nodded.

"Tamen would have me tie a gag on him, but I told her no patient of mine will be bound or gagged while I'm infirmarian! The man's ill, chanter or not. Besides, he's too exhausted to do any harm, his body and his mind are both worn out. But perhaps the jelly will help him, it's good for sickness in the mind. Do you remember me teaching you that, Calwyn? Good for wandering wits and confusion."

The Outlander was lying in the farthest cell, a stark, white-washed room with one small window on to the walled garden where Ursca grew her herbs. He looked paler than ever, propped up on pillows, his eyes closed, and a bandage across his head. "It's good that he's sleeping," whispered Ursca. "Sleep is the best healer of all."

But even as she spoke, the stranger's eyes flickered, then opened wide.

"Peace, peace," said Ursca at once, in the soothing tones she kept for frightened children. "Here, see what I've brought you — sweet junket."

"Stay back, woman!" cried the Outlander, hauling himself upright and thrusting out a hand to ward them both off. For the first time his gray eyes seemed keen and unclouded. His thin face was like a hawk's, hungry, alert. "I know you," he said slowly, frowning uncertainly at Calwyn.

"I was the one who found you."

He frowned again, then his face cleared. "Yes. I remember." He leaned back against the pillows. "You may come in. But the other one must stay outside."

"Taris bless him!" exclaimed Ursca. "Listen to him order us all about, as if he were the emperor of Merithuros!"

"Merithuros? Are there Merithurans here?" he asked quickly.

"No, you are in Antaris," said Calwyn. She took the bowl of junket and the spoon from Ursca and offered them to him. "Are you hungry?"

He poked the spoon about suspiciously through the curds and began to eat, tentatively at first, then with real hunger. Watching from the doorway, Ursca clasped her hands together in delight. "Well done, well done! Ah, very well, if I'm bothering you, I'll go away. It's time the lamps were lit!" And she hurried off through the gloom to see to it.

The stranger stared after her. "She seems harmless enough," he said, half to himself.

"More than that, she's been very good to you! She's dressed

your wounds and set your foot and fed you. You should be thanking her, not ordering her away," said Calwyn.

"I must be careful," said the Outlander, and Calwyn noticed again how he pronounced his words oddly, and with stilted precision. He glanced apprehensively toward the door.

"You're safe here, you are within the Wall of Antaris."

"If I could cross your famous Wall, then the one who seeks me could do the same."

"And see what the Goddess brings to those who presume to trespass in Her land." Calwyn indicated the foot, swollen with bandages, that protruded from under his bedcovers. It was something that Tamen might have said.

"Yes," said the stranger after a moment. "Your goddess has had her revenge, and I hope she is well satisfied. But I charge you to be on your guard, you and all your priestesses, for the one who pursues me is strong, and he is dangerous, and he won't give up the hunt. Do you hear me? He will not give up. Perhaps he is already here —" In his agitation, the Outlander seemed about to throw himself from the bed and begin searching for his mysterious pursuer. The bowl and spoon clattered to the floor.

"Calm yourself," said Calwyn in alarm. "There's no one here!"

"I am perfectly calm." The brief effort had exhausted him, and he fell back, his face ghostly in the gathering dusk. He whispered, "Who rules this place?"

"Ursca is the infirmarian."

The stranger gave a faint smile. "Antaris, who rules Antaris?"

"Our High Priestess is Marna."

"Tell Marna that she must be vigilant. Tell her that one is hunting me, one who would be the Singer of All Songs. Can you remember that?"

"The Singer of All Songs," repeated Calwyn in puzzlement.

"Swear that you will tell her." His hand shot out and seized her sleeve, and Calwyn jumped. "Swear it! He brings great danger, not only to Antaris, but to all Tremaris." He began to cough. "If she does not understand, send her to me."

Calwyn smiled despite herself at the idea of this imperious stranger ordering about the High Priestess as well as Ursca and herself. "I will tell her."

"Thank you." He let his hand fall from her arm. "And tell her that he has the power of seeming — What do they call you?" he asked abruptly.

"Calwyn." The question took her by surprise. "And you?"

"My name is Darrow." He touched his fingers to his lips and then held up his palm toward her in what seemed to be a salute of greeting. After a pause, Calwyn awkwardly returned the gesture. He seemed satisfied; his eyes closed, and a moment later, to judge from his breathing, he fell asleep.

"You see! I always said you had the gift of healing," whispered Ursca from the doorway, "in spite of everything."

"I hardly think so," said Calwyn ruefully. "He was happy to see someone he could recognize, that's all." A huge yawn split her face, reminding her of her own fatigue.

"Take yourself off to bed, child, your day's fishing has worn you out."

"I wasn't —" Calwyn stopped; she was too tired to start arguing. She let Ursca bustle her out of the infirmary and press a little pouch of dried herbs into her hand, to slip under her pillow. And whether it was the scent of the herbs or her own sheer exhaustion, she never knew, but she fell into a sleep as deep and dreamless as the Outlander's own before she had even finished unlacing her boots.

The orchard was white with apple blossom, as though the ancient trees held heaped armfuls of snow in their gnarled, low branches; the bees hummed their contentment, and the novices who were taking their turn to help Calwyn with the hives trotted about as sunny as strawflowers in their yellow tunics. One of them pulled off her big veiled hat to fan her forehead, squinting in the sunshine. "Calwyn, look!"

Calwyn looked up and was surprised to see the slight, blue-robed figure of Marna making her way slowly across the grass. "Lady Mother!" She hurried to offer her arm, but the High Priestess waved her away. "They told me you were unwell."

"Well enough for a stroll in the orchard, as you can see." With a slight grimace of discomfort, Marna settled herself on a low bough; a shower of petals fluttered to the grass. "It is too long since I came to see the hives. All is well here, I trust?"

"Yes, Lady Mother. But Amara hive is preparing for a swarm, though it's so early in the season."

"Is that why you came to see me this morning, Calwyn?"

"No." Calwyn hesitated and looked about at the little group of novices clustered nearby, each with a basket or a scraping knife in her hands, each staring wide-eyed at this unaccustomed visitor. She lowered her voice. "I have a message from the Outlander. Likely it's only the ravings of his fever, but . . ."

"Very well." Marna's voice held the trace of a smile. "Send the little girls away."

Calwyn shooed them to the hives at the end of the orchard and warned them not to return until she came to fetch them. Once they were safely out of hearing, she settled herself cross-legged at Marna's feet and recited what the stranger had told her. ·

"The Singer of All Songs?" repeated Marna. "You are certain that's what he said? Those were his exact words?"

"Yes, Lady Mother. And he said to tell you that he has the power of seeing *something*, but he never finished what he was saying."

"The Power of Seeming," said the High Priestess under her breath. "No wonder he jumps at every shadow." For a moment she stared out across the river, toward the gleaming mountain peaks, lost in thought, then turned her pale blue eyes back to Calwyn.

"What does it mean, Lady Mother?"

"The Outlander's enemy has the Power of Seeming. That

means he can wear any face he chooses, and conjure up illusions that appear as real as this bough under my hand. Imagine wandering alone through the mountains, never certain if what you see before you is real or a dream. It's no wonder the poor man's wits are strained."

Calwyn had taken off her broad-brimmed hat; now she pleated its protective veil between her fingers. "And the Singer of All Songs?"

Marna was silent while the bees in the next hive, readying themselves to swarm, buzzed with their high-pitched furious humming. She was silent so long that Calwyn feared she was never going to answer, but at last she spoke.

"Once you have become a full priestess, my daughter, you will learn more of these matters. It is not fitting that I should tell you too much while you are still a novice. But you already know that there are other Powers of chantment besides our own. You have heard, you have seen this sorcerer yourself, and you know that the magic he practices is not the same as ours."

"Yes, Lady Mother." Calwyn felt suddenly very solemn and serious. Usually during lessons and lectures she felt only a fierce desire to be elsewhere or an irresistible urge to fidget, but now she sat as still as a statue, sensing that what Marna was about to tell her was more important, and certainly more interesting, than herb lore or weaving patterns.

"You know already that in the beginning of the world, the Ancient Ones walked the lands of Tremaris. And you know that long ago, the peoples of Tremaris were divided by the gods, each against the others, into their different lands. But now I will tell you something that you haven't yet learned. In the beginning of the world, there were nine Powers of chantment, and the Ancient Ones were masters of them all. They had gifts beyond our imaginings, and they practiced marvels that we cannot even dream of. And when the peoples of the world were divided up, the Nine Powers were divided too. We of Antaris, the children of our Goddess Mother Taris, were trusted with the second of the Powers, the craft of ice-call, and we wear her mark in token of it." Marna lightly touched the ice-brand of the three moons that every priestess carried on the inside of her wrist. "The secrets of the other Powers were given to other peoples."

"Ironcraft — is that one of the other Powers? And windworking?"

Marna nodded. "Ironcraft is the chantment of Merithuros. And the people of the Isles possess the gift of windworking."

"And the others, Lady Mother?"

Marna's voice took on a dreamy, singsong tone as she counted off the Powers on her fingers. "Ninth is the Power of Tongue, which commands all speech and language and song. Eighth is the Power of Beasts, which commands all animals that creep and run and fly. Seventh is the Power of Seeming, which makes illusions visible and hides what is real. Sixth is the Power of Winds, which governs winds and waves and weather. Fifth is the Power of Iron, which commands any object that belongs to the earth, excepting any living thing, or air, or water, or fire. Fourth is the Power of Becoming, which holds the secrets of quickening and growth and change. Third is the Power of Fire, which commands all that is light and all that is hot. And there is our own craft, the Power of Ice, the power of our Goddess, who commands everything that is cold: ice and snow and freezing. And it is the power of all that is dark: shadows and night and the blackness that lies in the deepest caverns and between the stars. And it is the power of all that is dead."

A thrill of dread ran down Calwyn's spine. This was the lore she would learn after midwinter moondark; this was the shadowed face of the Goddess that only the initiated were allowed to glimpse. "But Lady Mother, that comes to only eight Powers."

Marna smiled. "All the lessons you've missed haven't harmed your arithmetic. Can you not guess the first of all the Powers? It is the greatest power of all, that which moves everything that is, and everything that is not, the Great Power that is unknown and unknowable, the mystery that lies beyond our understanding. It is the Goddess."

Calwyn said quickly, "But the Goddess rules over the Power of Ice —"

"That is the face she turns toward us here. All the chantments, all the gods, are but aspects of the same unknowable mystery, just as each face of a jewel strikes light in a different direction. Our Great Mother Taris is the name we call her here, but she has other faces and other names in other places." Marna placed her hand lightly on Calwyn's head. "You will understand it better in time. These are matters that have occupied the greatest priestesses for generations. You cannot expect to know it all in a heartbeat." Stiffly, she got to her feet and tugged a fold of her long robe free where it had caught on a twig. "I am too old to perch in the trees; let us walk by the river."

The ducks squabbled on the water; hoping for scraps, they crowded up to the bank and quacked for attention. Marna looked up and sniffed the air. "There will be rain tomorrow."

Calwyn would not be so easily deflected. "Is Darrow a priest of iron, then?"

Marna gave her a strange look. "So he has told you his name? It's said that sorcerers are superstitious about giving out their names. . . . Perhaps it's not true. But no, he is no priest. A sorcerer is different from a priest or priestess. The sorcerers of the Outlands do not serve their gods in the same way that we serve our Mother Taris. They use their chantments for themselves, not as we do, for the good of us all; their power is corrupted. You know that an Outlander cannot be trusted. An Outlander sorcerer can be trusted least of all."

Now it was Calwyn's turn to be silent. At last she ventured, "I think this sorcerer can be trusted, Lady Mother. He is — not respectful. But I think he is honest."

Marna smiled. "We shall see."

"He told me to tell you, if you didn't understand what he meant when he spoke of the Singer of All Songs, that you should ask him, and he would explain himself."

Marna said drily, "I understand well enough. Outlander arrogance! We may be shut away from the world here, but we are far from ignorant."

"May I ask him to explain it to me, then, Lady Mother?"

"No, you may not!" Marna quickened her pace, and Calwyn thought she had made her angry. But then she said in a quiet voice, "You are like enough to your mother to frighten me, child. Sometimes I think she ran away from us because no one would answer all her questions; that is why I have tried never to turn away any child's question, no matter how foolish it may seem."

It was true. Thinking back, Calwyn couldn't remember a single time that Marna had laughed or been impatient, however tiresome the novices' questioning became. She said, "Is the Singer of All Songs a person who wants to become as the Ancient Ones were, masters of all the chantments?"

The High Priestess shook her head. "Even in the time of the Ancient Ones, there was no chanter who was master of each and every field of chantment. But there is a tale, as old as the Ancient Ones themselves, that one would arise who has that gift: to sing all the chantments, the high notes and the low, the swift rhythms and the slow. And this person would be more powerful even than the Ancient Ones were, as powerful as the gods themselves."

Calwyn drew in a sharp breath. "What if he does find Darrow here? We would never be able to protect him!"

"Peace, child. It's a hearthside story, that's all, a fable, not a true prophecy. No one person could ever master all the chantments. No voice could ever be so supple, able to sing the highest of high notes for ice-call, the lowest of low for ironcraft, and all else in between. Think of it. It's impossible. No man's voice can reach all the notes we sing in our chantments of ice; that is why Antaris is ruled by priestesses, not by men and women together. In other lands," she added a little sadly, "it is different, no doubt."

Calwyn remembered the growling notes she had heard Darrow singing by the Wall. Could she ever learn to sing deep from her throat like that? It did seem unlikely. "Then there's nothing to fear," she said.

"I did not say that." Marna's voice was troubled, and she turned and began to walk back the way they had come. "Any man, any sorcerer, who is deluded enough and proud enough to think that he can achieve such a feat is dangerous indeed, perhaps even deranged. No, we must be on our guard, in case the Outlander's hunter does come seeking him. But this is nothing that should worry you, child," she added, as if she only now recalled that Calwyn was still a novice, not a full priestess, almost as if she regretted speaking so openly. She patted Calwyn's sleeve. "Go and see to your bees, my daughter. I think I hear the song of the swarm you have been waiting for."

With an exclamation, Calwyn broke away and ran back toward the hives. A cloud of bees was pouring from Amara hive in pursuit of their queen, streaming toward a settling place high in the branches of one of the apple trees, a thousand restless creatures swirling thick in the air. Calwyn could see some stragglers emerging from the old hive, small golden dancers looping in confusion. Softly she sang to them, an ancient soothing song that Damyr had taught her, persuading the strays to join their sisters in the swarm, and one by one they obeyed her.

When she thought to turn back to help Marna across the long grass of the orchard, it was too late; the High Priestess had already gone.

The Silver River

Marna was right. The next day, the spring rains began. For Calwyn, it was almost as bad as winter. Except for her brief morning and evening visits to the bees, she was trapped in the weaving rooms with the looms and spindles and the incessant shrill chatter of the other women.

She had been excused from spinning long ago on the grounds that her thread invariably came out in lumps, but her weaving and stitching were not much better, so she knew, when Tamen stopped by her loom, that it would not be to praise her work.

The Guardian stared down her long nose at the misshapen cloth. "It's lucky we're not relying on you to keep us in warm garments, Calwyn. There's a hole here I could put my finger through."

Gilly, who was sitting beside her with a lap full of mending, tittered, then hastily lifted her own work to her face and pretended she hadn't heard.

Tamen paid her no attention. "No matter. I have another task for you, if you are willing. I should like you to visit the Outlander in the infirmary and speak with him."

41

"Gladly!" Calwyn pushed back her stool with relief.

Tamen drew her aside, out of hearing of the others. "Ursca tells me that he trusts you more than anyone. I would like you to watch him. Talk to him, find out if he has another purpose here, if he has come to spy for Merithuros or another land. Can you do that?"

"If you wish, my Sister," said Calwyn, taken aback. "You don't believe his story, then?"

Tamen snorted. "Only a child would believe such a fantastical tale. He must take us for fools, or else he is truly mad. See what you can discover."

The Outlander did not seem particularly surprised, or pleased, to see her. He was out of bed, and the bandage on his head had been reduced to a thin strip of linen, but he was still shut inside the tiny cell at the end of the infirmary, his broken foot propped on a stool. Outside, the rain was coming down in silver sheets onto Ursca's garden; he stared dourly at the falling water, as though it were the cause of all his troubles.

"You gave them my message, then," he said, by way of greeting. "I have had a visit from your High Priestess, and the other one — the Guardian. At least they gave me that courtesy, though not the courtesy of believing what I had to say."

"I think Marna believes you," said Calwyn. "Tamen —" She hesitated. "Tamen has a skeptical mind."

He shrugged impatiently. "It doesn't matter. I'm finished in any case." He gestured toward his injured foot. "I am a wounded duck that's fallen into the swamp. All that remains is for the hunter's dogs to find me and rip me to pieces."

"They don't teach courage in the Outlands, then," said Calwyn tartly. "Your foot is hurt, but not your tongue. Instead of complaining that you can't run, why not stand and fight?"

"Fight *him*? With chantment?" He gave a bitter laugh. "What a fine idea. I should never have thought of that."

Calwyn was silent for a moment. Then she said, "One of the gardeners here was born with a crooked foot, and one leg a whole handspan shorter than the other. He has built himself a shoe with a thick sole, and he carves walking sticks that are marvelous to see."

"What a clever fellow," said Darrow acidly.

Slowly she said, "Perhaps it's easier for him to bear, since he's had his whole life to grow used to the idea. Perhaps if it had come upon him suddenly, like this, he would have been as angry and unhappy as you."

The stranger's face became still. Only his gray eyes flickered as he stared out at the rain; the whisper of its falling filled the tiny room. He was bitter indeed, but she liked his bitterness; he was different from anyone she had ever known.

At last she ventured, "Perhaps it's better to be angry and unhappy than to be mad."

Darrow's mouth twisted in a smile. "Is it? I wonder."

After that they did not speak for a long time. Calwyn drew up another stool, and he did not tell her to go away. So they sat together and listened to the music of the rain.

The next time, she brought him one of Tuw's sticks, and he sat, turning it over in his hands.

"I know you're not ready to use it yet. But I thought, if you had it waiting, it would be easier."

"It is a fine piece of work. I had some skill in carving, once, a long time ago."

"You talk like an old man whose life is nearly over!"

His face went still as he fingered the pattern of growing leaves and berries that Tuw had wound about the stick.

Calwyn could have bitten her tongue. She rushed on, "Tuw was glad to give it to me. He sits by the fireside all winter long, making them. He has too many to use them all for himself."

"Did you tell him it was for the Outlander?"

Her hesitation gave him his answer, and he smiled. "I thought not."

"If you like," she said, to change the subject, "I can bring you a knife, and some wood. It might pass the time for you, until . . ."

"Until I am brought to slaughter?"

"Until your foot is healed."

"Ursca says it will never heal." His voice was light and bantering, but there was pain in his eyes.

"In time, it will heal enough to bear your weight. And then I can show you the orchards and the hives. I'm the beekeeper here."

"Yes, I know." She stared at him in surprise, and he looked away, flushing. "I have been asking questions about you," he admitted shyly. "It seems I am indebted to you twice over: once for bringing me from the Wall, and once for supplying the jelly that restored my wits."

"You have the bees to thank for that, not me. And Ursca says your wits would have returned even without the jelly."

"In any case, I thank you," he said quietly, and he laid the stick carefully against the wall, like a precious thing.

Tamen would not permit him to have a knife.

"If he wished to harm us, my Sister, he could do so easily enough without a whittling knife!" exclaimed Calwyn.

"I am aware of that. If I had my way, he would be bound and gagged even now. You will not give him a knife."

Do not be her enemy. Do not be her enemy. Calwyn took a deep breath. "What if I watch him all the time and take back the knife when I leave?"

"No," said Tamen curtly, and walked away, her heavy, black-and-silver plait swinging down her back.

But in the end, Calwyn did give him her own small knife. "It's meant for taking wax from honeycomb, not for carving wood," she apologized. "I fear you'll find it too blunt."

"No matter." He turned over the little knife in his long, thin fingers and tested the blade. Then he sang from his throat, very quietly, so that Ursca, bustling about in the infirmary, should not hear. Calwyn felt her hands tingling and her head grow light. His chantment was brief, but when it was finished, Calwyn reached out swiftly and touched the blade. Its edge was so keen that she didn't feel the cut until she saw the red line spring across her thumb.

"Careful!" said Darrow.

"Too late," she said ruefully. "I'll put some honey on it."

And then he did something he had not done before: he threw back his head and laughed.

One day, not long into summer, but sooner than she had expected, she saw him limping slowly through the orchard toward the hives, balancing himself carefully with Tuw's stick. She waved, but he was concentrating too hard to wave back; as he came closer, she saw that his lips were moving. He was using chantment to keep the weight of his bandaged foot from the ground, as he had done on the first day.

When he reached the tree closest to the hives, he used Tuw's stick to lower himself painfully to the grass. "Well," he said, "that was a little more difficult than I expected."

"You shouldn't **have** tried such a long walk for your first time."

He waved his hand dismissively. "I have been shuffling around the infirmary for days already, it was time to give Ursca a rest from me. But my other foot is stiffer than I thought. And my voice also," he added.

Calwyn was silent, frowning.

"What? You don't approve of chantment? We were told always that Antaris was the one land where chantment was cherished and respected, not hidden away and feared as it is everywhere else in Tremaris."

"It's not that. But we're taught not to use chantment for trivial matters. Tamen tells us that every breath of cold that we make may grow and grow until it's a storm in the Bay of Sardi, and a hurricane by the time it reaches Doryus."

"Perhaps it is true. There was uncommon bad weather last time I sailed through the Great Sea." He stretched his leg in front of him. "Sing up a snowstorm now, I pray you, and it might hinder Samis from pursuing me."

Samis. He had never before spoken the name of the one who hunted him.

She asked, "What is sailing?"

He looked startled. "Sailing — in a boat — a craft that floats on the sea."

"We have no — no *boats* here." She pronounced the word carefully. "How do you dare? What would happen if you fell into the water? You would die."

"I can swim a little." Seeing her blank stare, he made motions with his arms. "Swimming. Moving through the water."

"Can sorcerers breathe in water?" Her eyes widened. This was a wondrous gift indeed, beyond all imagining.

"Indeed," he said solemnly. "Shall I show you how?" But he could not keep his face straight, and they both laughed. "Even without breathing water, it's possible to keep afloat," he said. "Have you never learned to swim?"

She shook her head. The idea was incomprehensible. "Did you *sail* all the way from Merithuros?"

"I have sailed all across the Great Sea, and back again, and north, too, as far as the Outer Isles."

The names meant little to Calwyn, but she was impressed all the same. *As far as the Outer Isles.* The words were as magical as any chantment.

Darrow picked up a green apple from the grass and frowned at it. "This is early fruit. In Kalysons, the trees bear apples only when the summer is nearly gone."

"Our summer is so short, perhaps our trees have to start the season sooner, or they wouldn't have time to bear fruit at all before winter returns."

"Hm." Darrow unfolded Calwyn's little knife and began to carve patterns onto the small green globe, whistling between his teeth.

"You're very cheerful today."

"Traveling makes me cheerful always, even if it is only the journey from the infirmary to here."

Calwyn watched as the point of the busy knife dug into the apple. Darrow took great care with his patterns, but they made no sense to her; the lines were not even, they meandered around the unripe globe. At last he was satisfied; he held up the apple on the palm of his hand. "Behold Tremaris!"

Calwyn dropped down eagerly beside him. "Show me!"

"Where I had my schooling, they teach that Tremaris is a sphere, just as the moons are." He pointed at the lines he had carved into the apple's green skin. "Here is the shoreline of Kalysons, and the Great Sea." He spun the fruit on its stalk. "Here is Merithuros —"

"Where is Antaris?"

"Here. At least, I believe so. And there are the Wildlands beyond, the forests and the untamed lands — all this half of the apple, blank and unnamed."

Calwyn reached out for the apple, but Darrow held it away from her and made as if to devour it with one bite. "Stop!" she cried, half-laughing, half in earnest, and caught at his arm. Their eyes met, then Darrow smiled a wry smile.

"At least there is one Daughter of Taris who is eager to save the world." He tossed the apple to Calwyn. Her face was flushed; embarrassed, she fixed her gaze on the globe, spinning it around and around, tracing the carved lines and notches with her fingertip.

"I've never seen a model of Tremaris like this before." She looked up. "If it is a question of saving the whole world, and not just your own skin, you should be even more determined to defeat him. Samis, I mean." She spoke the name lightly, not looking at Darrow.

"I have explained to you already, I cannot defeat him. He is ten times the sorcerer I am."

There was a flicker of pain in his eyes, but Calwyn was too

impatient to see it. "Well then, if you can't defeat him alone, there must be others who can help you. You could band together —"

"Band together!" He roared with laughter. "A band of sorcerers, indeed! Have you never heard the saying, that shutting two sorcerers in a room is like locking up two wild roancats in a box? They would tear each other to pieces."

"No," said Calwyn crossly, "I've never heard that saying. But I know that here in Antaris the priestesses help one another with their chantments, and we make more powerful magic that way than one chanter ever could alone."

"The rest of the world is not like Antaris," he said flatly. "It's a pretty idea. But it will never happen." He fell silent, and the sunlight dazzled through the leaves, dancing with every shift of the breeze. Calwyn put the carved apple gently on the grass.

"Marna said that no one man's voice could ever span all the forms of chantment. She said that no man could ever sing high enough for the spells of ice-call."

Darrow's mouth twisted in a smile. The gash on his forehead had healed now into a silvery scar that dragged across one eyebrow, giving him a quizzical look that made it difficult to tell when he was serious. "Your Marna is wise, but she does not know everything. The chantments of seeming are higher than yours, yet Samis can sing them. We were — he has learned tricks to stretch his voice. Like this." He sang a note in falsetto. Calwyn began to laugh at the unnatural sound, but at Darrow's sober look, her laughter died. He said, "It is true, mastery of the Nine Powers has never been achieved by any sorcerer, but Samis is no ordinary sorcerer."

"What is he, then?" She sounded more flippant than she'd intended.

Darrow stared at her gravely. "He is a prince of the Merithuran Empire. Do you know anything about the royal court of Merithuros? No? I thought not. There is one emperor, but there are many princes. Too many for them all to find favor. Samis is a minor prince. In spite of this, all his life he had thought that his gifts would earn him the title of heir to the emperor."

"Do you mean his gifts as a chanter?"

Darrow shook his head. "No. Those powers he kept secret. I have already told you, chantment is not prized in other places as it is here. No, he set store by his wits and his strength of purpose. But that was not enough to win him the prize he sought. The emperor chose another of his sons. So now Samis has decided, in his greed and his pride, that to be emperor of Merithuros is a paltry ambition, not worthy of his talents. He has decided to make himself emperor of all Tremaris."

"All Tremaris? *All* the lands?"

"Why not?" Darrow's voice grated harshly; there was no hint of teasing now. "It will be a simple enough feat for the Singer of All Songs. Already he has learned two crafts; why not three, or five, or nine?" He plucked up the apple and tossed it high into the air, so that it spun in the dappled sunlight. "All Tremaris will become his plaything, to torment or destroy or enslave at his whim. He will work on the world as a child works on a lump of clay. And no one will be able to stop him. No one." He bent back his arm and threw the apple in a high arc, so that Calwyn lost sight of it against the dazzle of leaves and sun. She heard the faint splash as it landed in the river. She could picture it, a small green bobbing globe, seized by the force of the current, dragged helplessly away, on and on, toward the distant sea.

Darrow saw her disappointment. "It would have rotted before long."

"And so might the real Tremaris, if what you say is true." She sat up very straight and stared at him. "Darrow, have you never thought, if this Samis is truly so powerful, then why would he bother to chase you?"

"In Merithuros, he's famed for his skill as a hunter. This time his quarry is a man, that's all. It will amuse him to hunt me down, at the same time as he hunts down the forms of chantment."

"No, no! Don't you see, he must be afraid of you — at least a little. There must be *some* way to overcome him. And he must know it."

With painful slowness, Darrow dragged himself to his feet and stood leaning on his stick, staring down at her. Suddenly he seemed much older than the playful young man who had been bantering with her earlier. His gray-green eyes burned with a cold anger. "Calwyn, Daughter of Taris, do not speak to me again about this matter. You know nothing. Your ignorance shames you." He turned his back and limped away with slow, unbending dignity.

Stricken, Calwyn jumped up. "Darrow!" She wanted to run after him, to shout and argue and shake him by the shoulders. But some force held her back; it was as though his chantment gripped her again by the scruff of her tunic and held her where she stood. At last she turned away.

The next day, Calwyn was at the hives not long after sunrise, glad that the novices would be busy at their lessons and she would be alone. She would not go to see Darrow in the infirmary; she told herself that she'd be too busy, but in truth she was still angry with him for his stubborn determination to be defeated. If *she* had a mortal enemy, she would never give up. She tugged at her gloves and jammed on her hat. She would fight and fight, until the breath left her body.

The bees that had swarmed were not happy in their new hive; all day they buzzed discontentedly. Twice she was stung by a bee that crept under her veil. Perhaps it was as Damyr always told her, that the bees could sense their keeper's mood. If she was restless, then so were the bees; if she was unhappy, then the hives would be unhappy too, and unhappy hives did not make good honey.

At last Calwyn pulled off her hat and gloves and sat on the riverbank. The silver-green leaves formed a whispering roof above her head, and crickets chirped in the warm air. Somehow she was not surprised to hear Darrow's voice behind her.

"Beekeepers work hard in Antaris, I see."

"I'm no good for the bees today. I should leave them alone for a while."

He cleared his throat. "I — I have something to say to you. I was wrong to speak so harshly yesterday." He spoke with diffidence, like someone not used to making apologies. And at once he added defensively, "You think I am too quick to give up the fight. But you don't know how long I've been fighting and running and fighting. There's a long, long history between Samis and me, longer than you can imagine. I am — very tired."

Calwyn bit her lip. He was right; she knew nothing about what might have happened between the two sorcerers in the past. It was as Marna said, she was too hasty to decide what was right and what was wrong. She should be apologizing to him, not the other way about.

But he didn't seem to think that she needed to say anything. "So. Shall we talk of something else? Will you explain the habits of your bees to me?"

"I would rather hear about your travels." She paused, not knowing where to begin her questions. "I want to hear about it all. Tell me *everything!* Tell me something about — about Merithuros."

His laugh crinkled his eyes and gave him a boyish look. "What shall I choose? Merithuros is crammed with wonders. Would you like to hear about the Black Palace of Hathara? It rises from the desert sands, as sheer as glass, without gates or windows, and so smooth that even the birds can find no place to perch."

"Yes," said Calwyn. "Tell me about that."

After dinner and the evening rituals of breath and singing were over, Tamen stood waiting for Calwyn just outside the door of the great hall. "Come walk with me, child, in the rose garden."

Though Calwyn couldn't see her face, shadowed under her hood, Tamen's voice was stern, and she stood more upright and unbending than ever. Heart sinking, Calwyn fell into step beside her.

The rose garden lay inside the Dwelling walls, an enclosed courtyard that caught the summer sun. A rich perfume of roses filled it in this season; trapped within the sun-warmed walls, the scent was overpowering. Velvety dark red roses drooped in the moonlight while the furled buds of white roses glowed like silver candle flames. The pair walked slowly along the paths. It was the time of Falling Petals: the largest of the moons just past full, and the two smaller ones silver crescents on the black velvet of the sky.

Tamen said, "You have been speaking with the Outlander almost every day." Her voice was deep with disapproval.

"My Sister, it was you yourself who asked me to speak with him!"

"I told you to discover his purpose here, not to befriend him. Have you found out anything, in all your conversations? Where is he from? Who does he serve? What are his chantments?"

"He is an ironcrafter, as our Lady Mother thought. He has traveled much." Calwyn hesitated. After all the time she had spent in the orchard over the past days, asking Darrow about his journeys and the marvels he had seen, she was still not sure in which land he had been born.

"What do you speak of?"

"He asks me about the bees. And he tells me about his voyages."

"You should not be speaking to him about such matters. It is not fitting for a Daughter of the Goddess, a priestess next midwinter, to have her head filled with wild tales."

Calwyn was silent for a moment as they walked. The roses hung bruised from the shining bushes, and their scent pressed on her, sweet and stifling. She said, "Where is the harm in talking to him about the world beyond Antaris?"

"Everything that should concern you lies within the Wall. I know Marna has told you what happened to your mother. Was that not enough warning for you? Do you want to end as she did?"

After a pause, Calwyn said, "I am sorry if my behavior was unseemly."

"That is well. But I charge you to be careful."

"I am careful."

"I hope you are not growing fond of him."

"No, of course not, my Sister." Calwyn's face grew hot; she hoped Tamen couldn't see.

"In any case, he will not be with us for much longer. At midsummer eve his stay here will end."

Calwyn missed a step and recovered herself. "His foot still gives him trouble. I don't know whether he'll be able to make the journey through the mountains so soon."

In the moonlight, shrouded in her long cloak, the Guardian was tall and forbidding, and her voice low. "That is of no matter. The road to the sacred valley is not long."

Calwyn's mouth was dry. They were to send him to the sacred valley. He would be sacrificed to the Goddess, his blood poured out at the foot of the blazetree, his bones lifted high into the branches for the birds to feed on. She had heard whispers of such sacrifice, a terrible punishment for terrible offenses against the Goddess. There were stories told at midnight when the older novices wanted to frighten the younger ones, but it had never happened in her lifetime, and she had come to think it was no more than something to scare the little ones. She stammered, "Surely if he were to be banished, that would be enough?"

"Banish him? So that he can fly over the Wall again? Think before you speak, child, and you will not appear so foolish. We must be rid of this Outlander; we cannot have him here forever, prying about. His foot will be healed enough that his offering to the Goddess will be no insult; at midsummer he will go to Her, and that is an end to it." Tamen's hand descended in an iron grip on Calwyn's shoulder, but her voice softened a little. "This seems harsh to you, I know. But those in high positions must make difficult choices, and the sooner you learn that, the easier it will be for you when your time comes."

Calwyn said nothing; her feet dragged on the paving stones. If this was the kind of decision that High Priestesses and Guardians had to make, she wanted none of it, not now, not ever.

Tamen released her shoulder. "Go to your bed now, and think about what I have said."

"Yes, Tamen," Calwyn whispered.

She glanced back once as she climbed the steps from the courtyard and saw Tamen standing still in the moonlight, a hooded pillar; all around her the roses stained the silver stones, dark as splashes of blood.

At first, Calwyn wasn't sure what had woken her. Was it the soft sigh of a cloak brushing the cold stone floor of the corridor, or a flicker of flame? Jolted awake, she lay for a moment breathless and confused in the panic of nightmare, her heart hammering in her ears.

Then she saw it: the fleeting light under her door that sent shadows flaring briefly up the wall, and the sound of a heavy cloak dragging, slow and deliberate, along the flags.

In an instant she was up and pulling on her clothes in the darkness, her fingers clumsy with sleep. She threw her winter cloak across her shoulders and slipped out of the room, stealthy as a roancat. It was the dead of night; all Antaris should be hushed in sleep. Something was wrong.

Whoever had passed her door was gone from the corridor. Calwyn stood still, listening hard. There: a footfall, an echo of a footfall. Someone was walking along the gallery that overlooked the central courtyard. Clutching her cloak, Calwyn crept along the corridor, down a handful of steps, and ducked into the shadow behind a pillar. There, on the other side of the gallery, a hooded figure moved, carrying a lantern, a huge wavering shadow thrown up behind. Calwyn could not see its face.

Suddenly the figure halted, turned its head. Calwyn shrank back. The light went out. Calwyn pressed herself against the cold stone, blood roaring in her ears. All the gallery was in darkness now, broken only by shafts of moonlight. Holding her breath, Calwyn peered out. There was no one. The shrouded figure had vanished.

For a long moment Calwyn did not move. Perhaps she had dreamed it all. Perhaps it was only Tamen, moving about the Dwellings, as she sometimes did at night, in solitary ritual. But Tamen never used a lantern; she was guided by the moons, the Goddess's light.

Calwyn waited. Gradually her breathing and her heart steadied. And then she heard it: a faint keening, at the very edge of hearing, as though an insect had strayed into the courtyard and was trapped within the walls. Calwyn shook her head to clear the misty confusion; her fingers were prickling with a familiar sensation. There was chantment here.

She looked out again along the empty gallery, striped with silver where the moonlight fell between the pillars. There was no one to be seen. Hesitantly she stepped out from the shelter of the shadows. Then she saw something from the corner of her eye, a whisk of movement, the slightest scuttling shadow of a shadow. She wheeled around. Someone was there, someone she could not see. The faint keening noise was louder now, louder and nearer. Every fiber of her body strained with fright; she longed to run, as fast as she could. But she must not. She must let this being, this unseen creature, think that she was deceived. Her mind worked quickly now. She rubbed her eyes and yawned, as if half-asleep, bewildered by dreams, and began to walk, very steadily, toward the steps that led to the kitchen yard.

How many times had Tamen and Marna told her to control herself, to be restrained, to walk when she wanted to run, to be silent when she felt like shouting? This was the hardest test of all. She couldn't tell if she was followed or watched; she must not turn her head. She made her way to the well that lay outside the kitchens, and forced herself to dip a cup of water that she did not want, and slowly drink it to the last drop. She listened hard, as hard as she had ever done. The shrill noise had ceased, the prickling in her fingers had disappeared. She had not been followed.

Then, and only then, she began to run, as swift as lightning. Samis — *he was real, he was here in Antaris* — might be a prince, and the most powerful of sorcerers, but he did not know the Dwellings as she did. She ran past the great hall, through the rose garden, up the steps, and then she was letting herself into the High Priestess's rooms.

It was Gilly's turn to attend the High Priestess; she sat up, blinking with sleepy surprise, in the cot outside Marna's door. "*Calwyn?* What do you want?"

"I must speak with the High Priestess!"

"Wait, you can't just barge in!"

But Marna was already standing in the doorway, her hair in a thin plait over one shoulder. "What is it, child?"

The words tumbled out. "He is here — the one Darrow spoke of — he's here! He's in the gallery — he made himself invisible, but I saw him."

"How could you see him if he was invisible?" asked Gilly, sturdily practical even in the face of midnight panic.

Marna held up a hand to quieten her. "You're certain? This is no dream, no mistake?"

"No, no, I am certain!" Calwyn was almost weeping with fright and relief.

"Gilly, go now and wake Tamen. Bring her here. Be quick and quiet. Calwyn, warn the Outlander to wait where he is and hide as best he can. Quickly now!"

Out again in the darkened corridors, Calwyn scurried, her cloak drawn over her head, keeping always to the deepest shadows. Twice she thought she felt a breath behind her or glimpsed movement where there should have been none, and she shrank back against the nearest wall, heart pounding. He might be anywhere, unseen, waiting to leap out, to catch at her throat or her ankle; any of these shadows might conceal a shrouded figure. And when she reached the infirmary and saw a light burning in Darrow's window, her breath caught in her throat. She was too late. He was lost.

But Darrow was sitting in his chair, knife in hand, carving by the light of a candle. He was dressed; it was clear that he had not gone to bed but had been sitting there, wakeful, all night. He looked up as she entered, and saw at once what was wrong.

With hands that shook a little, he folded the knife and put it in his pocket, together with the lump of wood he was carving. But when he spoke, his voice was steady. "So. He is here."

Calwyn nodded. "I saw him. He's searching for you."

Darrow reached for the stick that he kept always close at hand, and stood. "Very well."

"Marna knows — she has sent for Tamen. She said you were to hide yourself here, but I know a better place." She was thinking of the western tower, with its narrow, curved stairs and its views over the Dwellings. But Darrow shook his head.

"I have run too far already; I would rather face him."

"But —"

At that moment there came a distant sound, a single piercing shriek and then a low, unearthly cry. Without another word, Darrow pushed past her and loped through the infirmary with his crooked stride, swinging his stick, quick and grim. Calwyn heard another terrible cry and began to run.

At the archway to the courtyard, she caught one brief glimpse of what lay within before she cried out and fell back. Marna and Tamen were there, standing high in the gallery, hands clasped and raised, singing out across the enclosed space. The courtyard whirled with flurries of snow, as if a thousand pillows stuffed with goose down had burst open, and icicles dripped from every archway, gleaming like silver swords. Samis was there too, at the center of the storm, a dark shape with his arms raised high. The faint shrilling chantment that Calwyn had heard before was coming from him, but much louder now, piercing enough to make her stagger with the pain in her ears. And now she screamed, for the ground was writhing with snakes and serpents, and when the cold flakes of snow whirled against her face they were transformed into the sticky legs of beetles and spiders and crawling things that crept into her nose and mouth, and tangled in her hair so that she beat at her head, blind and terrified. And she was dimly aware that other sisters, old and young, woken by the commotion, were crowding along the gallery in their pale nightdresses. Their white shapes were darkened by the crawling, creeping things, and the stones of the Dwellings were alive underfoot, wriggling and slithering. The screams of the sisters mingled with the piercing shrill of the sorcerer's chantment until Calwyn clutched at her head and screamed in desperation to drown out the sound, and she was drowning, suffocating, she couldn't breathe, and the snow and the beetles whirled about her head, choking her, choking her —

A hand fell on her shoulder and she leaped away, trying to tear free. But she was held firm, and a calm voice spoke very close to her ear: "Be still. It is illusion. Do not be persuaded. Calwyn, hear me. Be still."

Darrow turned her away from the courtyard, pulling her hands from her head, and she opened her eyes, shuddering and sobbing for breath. "See, see, it is not real. Look at the ground — there is nothing but the stones." He held her shoulders with his strong hands, shaking her gently. She forced herself to stare down, wincing as the ground shivered with vague twitches. "Do not be persuaded, Calwyn. You can see past the seeming, if you try. See clearly. Do not fear." Darrow's voice was as steady as if they were sitting in the orchard in the sunshine, not in the deafening chaos of this night. The wheedling chantment of Samis bored into her skull; she would not listen to it, she would not! She stared at the ground, and it seemed to grow still. She could hear, through the wails and the clamor, the clear, sweet chantments of Marna and Tamen, strong and sure. She would listen to their music, not to the other, which twisted her mind and clouded her eyes. The stones swam up clear and sharp into her sight, and she saw a cloud of snowflakes drift across her feet, white as apple blossom; the writhing creatures were gone. She took in a deep breath, swung around to face the courtyard, and began to sing, adding her voice to the others, helping to weave a blizzard to choke the sorcerer into silence.

Beside her, Darrow was singing too, a chantment of ironcraft, and she saw, through the whirling snow, that icicles were breaking off and flying with deadly swiftness toward the center of the courtyard, where the hooded figure stood. But Darrow's aim was not good; none of the missiles reached their target. The sorcerer did not falter in his chantment; indeed, he seemed to grow stronger with every moment that passed. Calwyn had to close her eyes to concentrate on keeping her song true and clear; the screams of the other women, the flying snow, and her own fear all distracted her. She wished she were standing on the gallery with Marna and Tamen, their strong voices beside her and their hands firm in hers, instead of hidden away in this corner! But there was no time to run to them.

Another scream, more dreadful than any that had gone before, and Calwyn saw one of the white shapes on the far side of the gallery rise up above the rest. One of the sisters, maddened by confusion and terror, had climbed up onto the low wall. For one long, appalling moment, she hung there, a pale shape against the shadows, blurred by the flying snow. And then she fell.

In that heartbeat of time, Calwyn heard Darrow beside her change his chantment, frantic to hold the falling girl suspended in the air. But there was no time. She smashed onto the stones with a sound that Calwyn never forgot. Then there was silence.

Snow settled around the dark, unmoving figure of Samis, still with his arms raised high, but singing no longer. He was like a raven with wings outstretched, a black shape stamped on white snow, his head too large for his body. His back was to her, and she could not see his face. Someone on the gallery began to cry.

Then came a sound, dreadful as it was, that she rejoiced to hear: a moan of pain from the fallen girl. "She is alive! Thanks be to Taris!" That was Ursca, who pushed blindly past Calwyn and trotted across the snowy expanse of the courtyard to kneel beside the crumpled white shape. Whatever danger there might be, Ursca would let nothing stop her trying to help someone who was hurt.

Tamen's voice rang out into the terrible quiet. "The one you seek is in the infirmary. Take him, do what you will, but leave us be!"

Calwyn gasped. Marna cried out, "Tamen, no!" but her voice seemed weak and frail.

Samis lowered his arms; bloodred light flashed from a jewel on one hand. "Show me the place." His voice was deep and powerful; it seemed impossible that the shrill wheedling chantment of seeming had come from his throat. Perhaps Darrow was right; perhaps this man could indeed master every chantment.

Tamen was standing tall and straight, high in the gallery, her face pale against the darkness of her cloak and the shadows behind. She said in a low voice, "I will take you there." Then she was gone, swallowed up by the dark.

Calwyn whirled about. Darrow was slumped against the wall. She seized his arm. "Quickly, come with me!" An idea was half-forming in her mind; perhaps there was still a way out. Darrow grasped his stick and followed her past the outbuildings and the animal pens, darting as swiftly as he could manage from one pool of darkness to the next. When they reached the orchard, he said, "It's no use. He must know that I was in the courtyard."

"But he doesn't know where you are now —"

"He will find me wherever I hide. And it will be worse for you if he knows you have helped me. Go back."

Calwyn pressed on. The apple trees were gnarled silhouettes against the silvery grass; ahead she could see the hives, slumbering by the river. But Darrow had stopped.

"Go back. Calwyn, please! I will not have another life on my conscience."

"And I will not have your life on mine."

They stood facing each other for the space of five breaths; then Calwyn said, "I'm going on." She walked steadily past the hives and across the bridge, and after a moment she heard the awkward scrape of Darrow's boots on the stones as he followed. She was deep in the woods before it occurred to her that she ought not to be leading an Outlander along the sacred path; but then she remembered what Marna had said about the different faces of the Goddess. Surely Darrow too, whatever stars he was born under, was one of Her children.

"Listen!" called Darrow. He was some way behind her, limping up fast on his stick.

Calwyn stopped. A deep rumbling came from the Dwellings. "What is it?"

"Samis," said Darrow.

Calwyn shook off her cloak and pulled herself into the branches of an ember tree. She climbed fewer trees now than when she was a little girl, but she hadn't lost the knack, and ember trees were easy climbing. She swung from one bough to the next until she could see down into the valley, where the Dwellings spread out in the moonlight. She paused there, clinging to the rough bark. It wasn't hard to guess where the noise had come from; in the place where the infirmary ought to be was a pile of rubble and a great cloud of dust. And now came the sound of its final collapse, rippling out across the valley: a cracking, creaking roar of destruction.

After a moment, running figures appeared: the folk of Antaris, hurrying from the villages to investigate the commotion. Already she could hear faint shouts of horror echoing through the woods as the news spread.

She climbed down. Darrow said, "The infirmary?"

She nodded. "Perhaps he thinks he's killed you."

"That would be better luck than I deserve. More likely he is showing the sisters what a sorcerer of Merithuros can do." Darrow's face was grim. There was nothing else to say. Silently she picked up her cloak and they went on.

So painfully slow was their progress that it seemed to Calwyn they had been walking half the night before they came to the shining bulk of the Wall. She'd never seen it by moonlight before, immense and silvery-white. She could sense its dense chill near her skin, and for the space of a breath she felt almost afraid.

In a hushed voice Darrow said, "You will raise the chantment now?"

"I can't. Not alone."

"Calwyn, I cannot cross the Wall as I did before. I have not the strength. And if I was injured again —"

"You won't have to cross by chantment. There's another way." Perhaps the idea had been planted in her mind the first day that she and Darrow talked in the orchard, but she was certain now, as certain as if her mother's ghost had whispered it in her ear. She knew how Calida had done it all those years ago.

On and on she led him, beside the great curve of the Wall. Once or twice the eerie call of a night bird echoed above their heads, or a whirring of wings swooped from tree to tree, or a small shadow scurried across their path. Then Calwyn would hear Darrow stumble, and she would slow her pace a little. They passed the grove of the bellflowers and the place where Darrow had lifted himself over the Wall. On and on they walked, until at last they came to the place where the roaring river cut through the ice. The sky was beginning to pale after the long night; the dawn birds were singing.

Calwyn halted at the water's edge. This must have been where her mother had stood, so long ago, realizing it was her only way out. "The river flows quickly here, and the Wall doesn't cross the living water. You must let the river carry you out." She hesitated, trying to recall the word. "You must *swim*."

She had wondered if he would scoff, or argue, but he did not. Instead, he took off his cloak, his boots, and his jerkin and tied them up in a neat bundle around his stick. But when he was ready, he lingered by the bank, poised unsteadily on his crooked foot.

"Will you go back to the Dwellings now?"

"Yes." She hardly dared to think of what awaited her there: the infirmary in ruins; one of the sisters badly hurt — who was it? she did not even know; Tamen running about to Samis's bidding. She said with sudden passion, "I can't forgive Tamen for betraying you."

He shook his head. "Tamen's first duty is to protect Antaris. She did what she thought was necessary. Do not judge her too harshly."

"But she was going to send you to the sacred valley on midsummer eve, to be sacrificed under the blazetree, if you had stayed."

Darrow raised an eyebrow. "A scorpion under one foot, a snake beneath the other," he said. Then his face twisted in a half-smile. "Perhaps she was unwilling to carry out that duty, Calwyn. Why else would she tell you what she planned? She must have known that you would warn me."

"Perhaps," said Calwyn doubtfully. "But she was still willing to hand you over to Samis."

Darrow reached into his pocket and drew out the object he had been carving earlier in the night. He threw it to Calwyn and, startled, she caught it. It was a small wooden ball, the kind that the village boys used to play skittles. But Darrow had begun carving it into a map of Tremaris. "It's not finished," he said. "But I thought you might like it."

Calwyn cupped the ball in her hands. No one had ever given her a gift before, even at festival time.

Darrow said quietly, "Thank you for all you have done for me, Calwyn. Perhaps we shall meet again someday."

She could not speak, but nodded silently, pressing the wooden sphere hard between her hands. For a moment Darrow seemed about to say something more, but then he turned toward the river. She watched him plunge into the water, holding his stick above his head. Already the river had seized him in its current; soon he would be carried beyond the Wall and into the Outlands. Once more he would roam the world, and sail the wide seas in those boats of his, while she was locked inside the gray walls of Antaris, watching the moons wheel overhead and the seasons come and go, every day the same as the one that had gone before. And she would never see him again —

Abruptly she thrust the little globe deep into her pocket. "Wait!" she cried, stumbling down the slippery bank.

And then she was in the water.

The shock tore the breath from her lungs. She hadn't expected the water to be so icy, nor the current so strong; cold and terror clutched her heart. This river was alive, and freezing, and it wanted to drag her under. Her head dipped once, then twice; she inhaled a mouthful of water and came up choking. Now she was facing the wrong way, pulled along backward by the churning water. She struggled to turn, but couldn't balance; the weight of her clothes and her boots dragged her down as if strong hands seized her ankles and held them fast. She sobbed for breath, flailing against the current and the forces dragging, dragging her under.

Then a strong hand cupped her chin, and a commanding voice spoke above the tumult of the rushing water. "Be still — the water will carry you. I won't let you sink." Darrow was pulling her toward the center of the stream, where the current ran more slowly. Calwyn thrashed once and gasped wildly for breath, then lay still and allowed him to guide her. It was true. Once she stopped struggling with the water, she floated more easily; the current swept them both past the curving banks and the trees that trailed their leaves in the water. Darrow's head moved easily beside her, almost as though he were walking calmly along the bottom of the riverbed. His hair, still dry, gleamed pale as hay in the growing light.

They had left the Wall far behind; she could see it, shining white, through the trees. This was the *outside* of the Wall, which she had never glimpsed before. But there was no time to wonder at that. Darrow seized her shoulder and pulled her with matter-of-fact strength toward the bank. He sang one of his gurgling chantments, and his bundled cloak and stick flew through the air and landed on the grass. Then he was guiding her, not to the riverbank itself, but to a fallen tree that sprawled in the water, its branches catching leaves and twigs and other flotsam. Now it was to catch Calwyn herself; she saw his plan and reached out her arms to clutch a sturdy branch. The wood was slippery, but she wrapped her arms firmly around it and clung on. The black water churned past, but for the first time she was still.

She held her head out of the water, gulping air, and watched as Darrow pulled his lean legs up the bank as easily as an otter, and shook himself. Then he balanced on the tree trunk, gripped Calwyn's hand, and hauled her toward the bank with such force that she thought her arm would be wrenched from its socket. Was he singing a chantment to help lift her clear? She could hear nothing but the roaring of the water. Her leg scraped against the tree, but she didn't feel it; with a cry of relief she collapsed on dry land and huddled there for a moment, sobbing for air, clutching solid earth.

City of Cheesestone

Calwyn held out her tingling hands toward the fire. Darrow had made her run about the grove, to gather wood and warm herself, before he lit the fire with his flint. Only then did he let her sit down, wrapped in his dry cloak. Apart from the crackling of the flames, there was silence. It was almost dawn now; only one moon remained, shining pale above the dark mass of the trees. All around them, birds had begun to stir at the approach of morning, first one tentative call, then another, until the forest rang with their twittering.

Calwyn blinked and sniffed hard. She *would not* cry in front of Darrow. But it was too late; he was frowning at her.

"What is it?"

In a muffled voice she said, "I'm ashamed."

Darrow seemed at a loss. He poked another stick into the heart of the fire, and sparks shot into the air. "There is no shame in being afraid to drown when you have never been taught to swim," he said at last. "They say that children of Penlewin can swim before they can walk. Between the sea and the marshes, they have little

74

choice. But I'm sure there is not one among them who can tame a swarm of stinging bees without flinching."

Her teeth were chattering so hard that she had to force the words out. "I would have drowned if not for you."

"Ah, well." He cleared his throat, embarrassed. "Then I owe you my life only twice now, not three times over. But all the same, you'd better learn, and quickly. I wouldn't want to fish you out a second time."

She gave a shaky laugh. "So you will take me with you?"

He stared into the fire, not meeting her eyes. "I hadn't thought to take an apprentice. But I can hardly send you back. And I suppose I'm still in your debt."

This was not the hearty welcome Calwyn had hoped to hear. "You'll need my help in the mountains; you know yourself that your foot isn't mended yet." With a sudden flare of temper she added, "And I don't want to be your apprentice. I have my own power; I am your equal in chantment."

"Though not in swimming," said Darrow gloomily.

Calwyn's indignation was so great that her tears vanished. "If you think I'll hinder you, then I'll go on alone," she flashed, and started to her feet.

Darrow said mildly, "Then I'll thank you to return my cloak." And Calwyn saw a smile in his gray eyes. "Come, dry your hair, don't waste the fire. I would like to get some distance between us and Antaris before we rest again."

Obediently, Calwyn knelt and spread out her hair with her fingers before the flames, glad of the dark curtain that hid her face and the sudden smile of wild joy that she couldn't suppress. For the first time since she was a baby, she was outside the Wall of Antaris; who knew what wonders and terrors lay before her? At her side, the river gurgled, as though it were laughing with her, and the whole forest sang with birds.

Presently Darrow covered the fire with earth, and they began to walk again. This time there was no path to guide them. They followed the river as closely as they could, though trees clustered thickly along the bank. Darrow pointed toward one of the mountain peaks. "We must head that way, to the peak shaped like a hawk's head. There's a pass that will lead us through to the lands of Kalysons. That's how I came here."

"We call that mountain the Falcon. That's the way the traders come."

Calwyn was tired, her clothes were still damp, and it was not pleasant to walk in wet boots. She thought longingly of the breakfast of warm bread and honey that she would have had if she'd stayed on the other side of the Wall. But all the same, as the sun came up, touching the tops of the sparse trees with gold, she wouldn't have wished herself back in her narrow cell for anything in Tremaris. She breathed deeply. "The air tastes like — like queen's jelly!" she exalted. Had her mother felt like this at the start of her adventures?

After a time she asked, "Do you think Samis will follow us?"

For a moment Darrow did not reply. "I think he will stay in Antaris for now. Having come so far, he won't wish to leave without the chantments of ice-call. True, he will be disappointed to lose his quarry. But it is the hunt he loves above all, and the hunt is not over."

"He might never find us," suggested Calwyn buoyantly; anything seemed possible this morning.

"Maybe not," agreed Darrow, with the shadow of a smile.

By afternoon, Calwyn was dropping with weariness. Darrow noticed it.

"We should sleep now," he said abruptly, when she yawned for the third time, "while the sun will still warm us. We can walk by moonlight." He pointed with his stick toward a sunlit glade. "That looks comfortable enough."

Calwyn thought he must be teasing her again, but he scraped together a heap of leaves and lowered himself to the ground. Hesitantly she stood and watched as he rolled himself in his cloak. She chose a spot a little apart from his and lay down with her back to him. Tired as she was, she was painfully conscious of Darrow's presence only a handspan away, and the sound of his quiet breathing. It was lucky they were sleeping by day, she thought drowsily; at night they would have been too cold to do anything but huddle together. . . .

Her eyes flew open. Was *that* why? Was he as shy as she was?

But she was too exhausted to ponder such mysteries for long, and soon she was asleep.

* * *

It was true that traveling made Darrow cheerful. In all the days of their long trek eastward, he was in better spirits than Calwyn had ever seen him in Antaris, joking and teasing her, singing and telling stories.

It was not an easy journey. Darrow's foot was still not completely healed, and though he used his stick and his chantments in equal measure, he was always in pain. There were days when they covered hardly any ground. All too soon they emerged from the shelter of the woods and found themselves in a different kind of wilderness. Cruel spires of rock thrust toward the sky, as if in imitation of the towers of Antaris that they had left behind, and the path skirted precipices that fell away so steeply they couldn't see what lay at the bottom. It was grim country, gray and stony, and by night Calwyn shivered as the wind moaned between the crags.

In truth, the traders' path was scarcely more than a track. If not for the age-old campsites that they passed and sometimes used, Calwyn would have feared that they'd lost their way. But the blackened rings of ancient campfires, the shallow caves the traders used for shelter, and the odd scraps of cloth and piles of bones were some reassurance that they were not wandering blindly in the desolate landscape.

Then one day they had to scramble for cover as the traders themselves passed by. Hidden behind boulders, Calwyn and Darrow listened to the grumbles of the men and the rattling of the handcarts they dragged behind them, piled with cooking pans, silk threads, and spices. It seemed a long time before the line of clanking carts disappeared up the track.

After they'd gone, Calwyn said, "I wonder who will open the Wall for them this year."

"Perhaps Samis himself will do it," said Darrow with grim humor. "*That* would give them a tale to tell."

Even at the height of summer, the mountain passes were colder than the valley; mostly they walked by moonlight and slept by day, grateful for the sun's warmth on their cloaks. And even in this empty, barren place, there were birds and rabbits. Calwyn used small chantments to catch them, as she'd been taught, and Darrow would roast them over the fire. For the first time she was glad of all the long, dull lessons in herb lore she had endured, for there were many edible mountain plants that Darrow did not know. In turn, he showed her how to line her boots with palewood leaves to prevent blisters, and he cut her a staff to help her balance on the steepest paths.

Every night Darrow scanned the faint stars and pointed out the ones that they should follow. He told her the names they were given in Merithuros and in Kalysons and in Gellan, and she would tell him their names in Antaris. It was strange to think that every land had its own names and stories, that the constellation she knew as the Tree was called Tasgar's Lantern in Kalysons, and the Shoe in Merithuros.

By night, his hawk's face shadowed against the starry sky, Darrow seemed remote from her, more like a teacher than the easy, whistling companion of the day. Sometimes he did not seem to know what to say to her, and if they rested, he held himself aloof, lost in his own thoughts.

One day, out of nowhere, he said, "I've not had much to do with women." He was walking ahead of her, and she couldn't see his face. "Before I came to Antaris, I don't know that I'd ever spoken more than ten words to a woman. I have always thought them strange creatures."

"And now?" she couldn't resist asking.

"Now I think them much the same as men," came the reply, and she didn't know whether to be glad or disappointed.

Gradually the steep, stony ground gave way to gentler slopes, where the trees grew more thickly. The air was hotter every day, and Calwyn found that breathing made her giddy.

"The air is not so thin here as it is in the mountains," Darrow told her. "You will find that you can walk longer and endure more than the people of the plains, for you can better use your breath."

They walked now in the cool of the morning and evening, and took their rest at midday and the middle part of the night. At last there were signs that people had touched these lands: a stump where a tree had been cut down and hauled away, a broken-down hut, the remains of a stone wall. The track grew wider and easier to follow, and there was crumbling earth under their boots now, rather than skidding stones.

The first time Calwyn saw a distant farmhouse nestled between the folds of the hills, she strained forward eagerly, like a beast catching a scent, and she would have broken into a run if Darrow had not held her back.

"Calwyn, we must not be seen," he said urgently. "These people will not welcome us, believe me. And when we reach the plains, where there are soldiers patrolling from Kalysons, we must be even more careful to keep hidden. And never, never, let anyone see that you are a chanter. Do you understand?"

"I understand." She was disappointed; she had hoped for a meal with bread and cheese and spices, and perhaps a warm bed, from some friendly farmfolk. But she was beginning to realize that Outlanders were just as wary and suspicious of strangers as the people of Antaris, shut inside their great Wall. Somehow she had expected it to be different, outside.

They traveled through the hill country and then on to the wide plains, sleeping in barns and windmills, foraging for whatever food they could find along the way: wild berries, vegetables scrounged from the fields, duck eggs found beside the streams that crisscrossed the flat country, linking one farm to the next like a fine mesh of netting laid over the dusty land.

One whole day they spent resting and catching fish. Calwyn stripped to her undershirt, and Darrow gave her a swimming lesson. He didn't laugh as she spluttered and coughed, but coached her patiently until she could kick herself along for several strokes. Then she spread her hair over her shoulders to dry in the sun and showed him how to tease a fish into his hand and flick it out of the water before it even knew it was caught.

"I think I prefer my rod and baited string," he said, taking a hasty step back as Calwyn tossed a fish clear and splashed his feet. "Your method is so *wet*."

Calwyn sat up on her heels and laughed. "But it's so much simpler to use your bare hands!"

"Very well. I take your challenge." He threw his line into the stream. "Let us see who's quickest to catch the next fish."

"Done!" cried Calwyn, and when she held up her catch in triumph a few moments later, her happiness was complete.

That day stood forever in her memory as a golden time: sitting in the sun with Darrow, feasting on fish so hot from the flames that they tossed it hand to hand.

"I've never eaten a finer meal," sighed Calwyn, licking her fingers.

"There is a saying in Penlewin that hunger is the finest sauce," Darrow told her.

"That's the second time you've quoted me a saying from the marshlands." Calwyn looked at him sideways. "Is that the land where you were born?"

"The people of Penlewin have a stock of wise sayings. But that's not reason enough to claim kinship with them."

And her curiosity had to go unsatisfied again. No matter how often she asked him about his past, he never would give her a direct answer. But he had finished carving all the lines on her wooden globe now, working at it while they rested, and he was happy to tell her the names of every land he knew, and the stories of each place. Though how he had ever learned the stories of any people at all when he was so determined to hide himself, and dive off the road at every passing stranger, she did not know.

They saw few people on the roads — perhaps a farmer's field hand or herder, walking from one farm to the next with a laden goat-cart — and they always concealed themselves in a ditch before they could be seen, pulling their cloaks over their heads until Calwyn thought she would stifle in the heat. Once, from the shelter of the hedgerow, they saw a patrol of soldiers from Kalysons, with swords and clubs slung over their backs. Calwyn watched, hardly daring to breathe, as they went by; a miserable-looking youth shuffled in their midst, his hands and ankles bound loosely with rope.

"They are taking him back to Kalysons for judgment," whispered Darrow.

"What has he done?" she whispered back.

"He might be a thief. There is great hunger in these lands. Perhaps he took some eggs from a pantry or cheese from a dairy shed."

Certainly the youth looked thin and wretched as the guards jostled him along. "What will happen to him?"

"If he's lucky, not much. The patrol will beat him and let him go, to find his own way home. If he's unlucky, the Proctors will sell him as a slave on the Gellanese galleys, or banish him to Doryus."

"And what if we were captured?"

"If they found out that we're chanters, the same," said Darrow, staring with narrowed eyes after the dust cloud that marked the passage of the patrol. After that, Calwyn didn't complain when Darrow told her to move off the road and hide.

Every day they heard the ululating songs of the farmers echo across the plains as they drove their goats and oxen and called to their ducks. "Are they songs of chantment? Is this the Power of Beasts?" Calwyn asked, but Darrow shook his head.

"Once these lands held the secrets of the beasts, but now the animals obey no longer. The songs that the farmers sing are a shadow of the old chantments, but without the same power. You can see how thin the oxen are. And look —" He plucked a handful of grain from the field and crushed it in his hand; the hot wind blew a cloud of dust from his fingers. "The crops do not flourish here. The life is drying up in everything; this land is pinched and mean."

"The people too?"

Darrow gave a crooked smile. "Especially the people. That is why we ask for nothing and keep our heads low."

Calwyn said cheerfully, "If all the old chantments are forgotten, then at least Samis will never learn them."

"There is enough of the old knowledge left that he might be

able to piece it together, perhaps. But not enough to let the lands prosper. You saw how the farms in the foothills have been abandoned. Every season the farmlands shrink a little more, and there is less food for the farmers to sell to the city."

"Is that why there are so many soldiers?" The closer they came to the city of Kalysons, the more frequently they had to hide from the patrols. "To frighten the farmfolk into handing over their produce?"

"Perhaps." Darrow was silent for a breath or two, and then Calwyn heard the low growl of chantment that meant his foot was giving him pain, and she asked him no more questions. But she thought often of that hungry youth, and the hopeless dragging of his feet on the dusty track.

They had been traveling for many days, a full turn of the moons, before at last they set eyes on the city of Kalysons. They paused under a windmill at the top of a low hill and gazed down at the sweep of the plain and the city nestled below them. Unlike the blue-gray stone of Antaris and the mountains, the earth of the plains was a greasy yellow-gray. Kalysons looked like a city built from blocks of lard.

"Cheesestone," said Darrow briefly.

Except for the little hillocks raised for the slow-turning windmills, the drab and dusty land was as level as if it had been pressed with a flatiron, like a ceremonial robe. The mountains that hid Antaris were the faintest smudge of gray on the distant horizon in the west. But Calwyn was not looking at the mountains, nor at the city below. For behind the city lay the sea she had so often dreamed of seeing: the broad curve of the Bay of Sardi, glittering emerald in the sun, a bright ribbon that spanned the horizon. Her heart sang as she drank in the sight of the shining ocean: so vast, so beautiful, so terrifying.

"Come." Darrow was already limping down the hill. "If we make haste, we can be with my friends in time for dinner."

Calwyn's stomach growled at the thought of a rich stew and a cool cup of milk, and she hurried after him.

The sun had gone down by the time they reached the city gates.

"They're shut!" cried Calwyn.

The enormous metal gates, set into the thick wall of cheese-stone, were definitely, firmly, unmistakably locked. There was no one in sight, but she could faintly hear noises rising from the other side of the wall: the clatter and clamor of a city, the cries of street sellers, a murmuring hubbub. It was like the bees, Calwyn thought suddenly, the busy noise inside a hive.

"The gates are always closed at dusk. It's not important. We are not going to use the gates."

Darrow led her for some distance around the curve of the wall. It was not as beautiful and forbidding as the icy Wall of Antaris, and it was much smaller, thought Calwyn scornfully. Why, this wall enclosed only a city, while the Wall of Antaris stretched around all their lands. And she thought still less of it when she saw Darrow hold up his hands before the greasy stone and sing a

low chantment. One of the cheesestone blocks swung slowly outward to reveal a gap just big enough to squeeze through.

"What use is a wall that anyone can climb through?" she hissed
as she followed Darrow through the opening.

"Not anyone," said Darrow calmly. "Only an ironcrafter."

Once they were through, he sealed up the crack with a second
chantment. They were inside Kalysons.

Calwyn realized at once, to her chagrin, that Kalysons was
much, much larger than Antaris. From far away on the plain it had
looked small enough; now she could see that each one of the big,
square, squat buildings, which she had thought were the size of
farmhouses, was almost big enough to hold all the Dwellings of
Antaris. They were standing beside one of these buildings now,
hidden in its shadow; it rose so high that it blotted out the sky.
Darrow set off immediately, weaving his way through a maze of
narrow laneways and crowded squares, and over the humped
bridges that crossed the city's many canals.

Though it was long after dark, the air was still warm from the
heat of the faded day, and the streets were crowded with people.
It seemed to Calwyn that the walls exuded a greasy sweat, like a
cheese left too long out of the storeroom, and the sweaty odor
mingled with the pungent smells of fried vegetables and roasted
meats that wafted from the windows. Here and there in the dusk
were thicker clots of darkness; wavering lamplight from doorways
showed them to be groups of men, standing by the walls, muttering and watchful. "Be sure to keep your cloak wrapped tight,"

Darrow said in her ear, "in case anyone recognizes the garments of a witch-girl from the mountains."

At any other time, Calwyn would have protested at being described as a witch-girl, but now she felt very small and insignificant, almost frightened. She kept close to Darrow's side, and though clutching her cloak under her chin made her hotter than ever, it was a kind of comfort to feel the scratching of the familiar cloth against her skin.

Darrow led them briskly through the darkening streets, not allowing his lame foot to slow him; for once Calwyn had to hurry to keep up with him. When they turned into a street that was hardly wider than two arm-spans, with pallid tenements rearing up like cliffs on either side, she ventured to ask, "Where are we going?"

"To the harbor."

Calwyn quickened her pace. The harbor meant the sea; perhaps she might even be able to dip her hands in that shining expanse she had glimpsed from the top of the hill.

The streets grew yet more narrow and more winding, and the smell of salt told her that they were very near it. And then they turned a corner and saw the rows of boats swaying on the dark water and heard the soft slap of the waves.

Darrow led her past dark warehouses, sheds that stank of fish, and sailors' and fishermen's clubhouses that murmured with surly talk and the muffled clank of tankards. Little boats, the first Calwyn had ever seen, clustered by the jetties, riding the water like gulls resting on the waves. The smallest of the moons was rising, and the constellation she called the Tree was already visible in the crisp, clear sky. It had been very strange for Calwyn to watch the familiar stars come out every night, always the same, as she traveled farther and farther from home, but never so strange as it seemed this night, to see them gleaming over the dark, sighing carpet of the ocean. The stars seemed dimmer here than in Antaris; she did not know why.

Darrow was limping fast, swinging his stick impatiently, as he scanned each of the quiet jetties until he found what he was looking for. Calwyn caught up with him where he stood staring down at a trim little fishing vessel with cheerful but shabby paint. The cabin was all in darkness.

"They're not here." Darrow stared back toward the lights and faint noises of the city buildings. "They must be ashore, perhaps in one of those inns."

"Can we wait for them on the boat?" Calwyn was filled with hope; it looked so welcoming, bobbing gently on the dark water. But Darrow shook his head.

"I would not trespass on friendship by going aboard uninvited," he said. "Besides, the cabin will be locked." He saw Calwyn's look of surprise. "In Kalysons, people keep their houses and their possessions locked up. It is a more mistrustful place than Antaris. No, I will go looking for them. You had better wait here. The inns do not permit women to enter."

"But —" Calwyn opened her mouth to protest, then closed it

again. Perhaps it was best to do as he said at least some of the time, when it didn't really matter, and save her disagreements for a time when it did. Obediently she seated herself on a squat bollard, pulled her cloak tightly about her, and tried to look patient. "Very well."

"I will be as quick as I can." Darrow limped away, down the length of the jetty. Calwyn watched him disappear, then turned and gazed out over the endless dark, cold sea. She found herself thinking of the great hall in Antaris, and the sound of all the sisters singing and laughing together, and the cheerful swirl of the little girls dancing before the fire, the warm hubbub of the place. But there too she had sat apart and felt lonely and desolate; it was not so different here.

The single moon rose a little higher. She passed some time practicing the exercises that helped her to breathe and sing in one steady flow, without pausing to gulp for air. She did one round of the nightly exercises, and then another. Then she sang one of the hearth songs of the spring festival, the story of brave Si'leth and her doomed love for the dark hero Vereth.

She broke off her song abruptly, listening for footsteps on the jetty. Darrow had been gone a long time. What would she do if he never returned? Seized with panic, she leaped to her feet and began to hurry back down the jetty toward the lights.

She had no clear idea in which direction Darrow had gone. Raucous singing burst from the nearest of the inns; she couldn't quite make out the words. The door was open. Calwyn drew her cloak over her head and was about to slip inside when someone blocked her path.

"Where do you think you're going, missy?" A greasy-faced youth with lank hair leered at her.

Calwyn drew herself up as tall and proud as Tamen or Marna. "I am seeking my friend."

"Not in there, you're not. It's a private club, see? Not a member, are you?"

"Stay out here and talk to us, bright-eyes," came another voice, and Calwyn saw that there were three or four young men lounging about outside. One of them leaned over and spat close to her feet.

She stepped backward. "No, thank you."

"Where you from? That don't sound like a voice from our city."

Calwyn thought quickly. "I come from a farm far away on the plains — almost in the mountains."

They all sniggered. The greasy youth reached out and fingered the cloth of her cloak. Calwyn pulled away, afraid he might see the yellow of her tunic beneath. "Just being friendly," said the youth, and he gripped a handful of her cloak tightly in his fist.

"Come from the mountains, do you?" a voice drawled from the shadows. "Ever see any of them witches?"

"They're not witches." Calwyn flushed with temper. "They are priestesses of the Goddess."

"Hear that? I think she's a witch-girl herself!" The first youth looked to his friends for appreciation, then gave a tug on Calwyn's cloak to pull her closer. He put his face up to hers; his breath stank. "Sing a spell for us, witch!"

Calwyn was hot with fury. If they wanted to hear chantment, she would give them chantment. She drew in a quick, deep breath, narrowed her eyes, parted her lips, and sang.

Instantly, the youth who had been taunting her took a step backward, his hands flying to his mouth, his eyes wide with shock. He made a muffled imploring sound, as though he were gagged; frantically he tore at his mouth with his fingers, but he could not part his lips.

In a voice that shook with rage, Calwyn said, "Those who speak ill of the Goddess or Her servants should not speak at all."

The youth stared at her with wide, belligerent eyes, but there was terror there too. He shook his head dumbly from side to side, his fingers still scrabbling at his mouth. His friends had drawn back, gaping with shock and fright.

A sharp voice behind Calwyn said, "What goes on here?"

It was Darrow, striding along the cobbles with his uneven step, swinging his carved stick, his face set and angry. Behind him were two men, dressed in high boots and thick, short jackets.

"They have threatened a Daughter of Taris and received just punishment." Calwyn's fists were clenched at her sides; she stood tall and straight, staring hard at the youth who had mocked her. He turned wildly to Darrow, his hands clapped over his mouth, his face contorted with helpless rage.

Darrow was at her side now. "Whatever you have done, undo

it." His voice was low, but angry. Calwyn sang some notes, and at once the greasy youth tottered backward, released. His mouth opened wide; he felt his jaw gingerly with both hands and spat several times onto the street, as if getting rid of poison. Then with one final menacing yell, he and his friends stumbled away into the night.

"What did you do to him?" It was one of Darrow's friends who asked, half-admiring, half-amused.

"I froze his spittle in his mouth, that's all," said Calwyn. "It's done him no harm."

"Come." Darrow turned with a sweep of his cloak. Calwyn hurried to walk beside him. His profile in the moonlight was hard and hawklike; presently he looked sternly across at her. "That was very foolish, Calwyn."

"I didn't hurt him. And he deserved it."

"No doubt he did, but that's not the point. I have told you over and over again that chantment is feared and abhorred in Kalysons, that chanters are not welcome here. This is no place to play your tricks. What if those boys run about the town telling the story of how a witch of Antaris stopped one of their tongues with magic?"

"Don't lecture me as if I were a child! You should be praising me for using my wits." Calwyn's face burned with resentment and rage. "Those boys won't tell any tales, since they were the ones made to look foolish."

"I hope you're right," he said grimly. "But next time, try to hold your tongue."

Calwyn stalked along in a fury. Had she escaped the scoldings of the priestesses only to exchange them for lectures from Darrow? And to tell her off like that in front of his friends was unforgivable. Darkly she muttered, "At least in Antaris men don't behave as though women are there to do their bidding."

"Indeed," said one of Darrow's friends suddenly, coming up behind them. He was a short, curly headed man, a few years younger than Darrow, with bright, dark eyes, his face crinkled with lines of cheerful humor. He seemed to bounce along, ready for any mischief or merriment. He grinned at Calwyn. "I'm sure you've done a good deed tonight for all the young girls of Kalysons. Those louts will think twice before they tease anyone else." He held out his hand to Calwyn. "I'm Xanni. That miserable oaf is my big brother, Tonno."

The taller and burlier of the pair, still walking behind them, raised his hand in a brief salute. He was dark and curly haired, like his brother, but he had an ill-tempered, surly look, as if he had been dragged away in the middle of his meal, and his bushy eyebrows were drawn together in a permanent scowl.

"My name is Calwyn."

"And you come from Antaris. I can see that with my own eyes, even if Darrow hadn't told me." Xanni nodded down at Calwyn's yellow sleeve. "We'll have to get you some new clothes, you can't run about the town looking like that. It's not safe."

Suddenly Calwyn felt a pang of perverse attachment to her robes. It was true, they marked her out at once as a priestess, or a witch, for those who knew or had heard the tales, and yet she couldn't help feeling that to put the yellow robes away would be a kind of betrayal. No one would know that she was a sister of Antaris, a handmaiden of the Goddess. It would feel like losing part of herself.

They came to the brothers' boat. Xanni jumped down onto the deck, and casually, without making a fuss about it, extended a hand to help Darrow. Calwyn hesitated on the jetty; she had never set foot on a boat before. What would be between her and the deep, dark water? Only some thin pieces of wood, nailed together.

Tonno growled, "Jump down, lass, we haven't got all night."

Calwyn jumped, and staggered. Though the boat was still, she was certain she could feel the unsteady bed of seawater shifting beneath the soles of her feet. Darrow saw her uneasy look. "You'll get used to it soon enough. We shall make a sailor of you, never fear."

"You won't send me back to the mountains, then?" she said.

"Not tonight," he said gruffly. And he held out a hand to guide her to the hatchway.

Down below the deck, Xanni was busy with the lanterns, filling the snug cabin with a warm glow of light. The interior was as cozy as a tiny cottage, with a long table and cushioned benches on either side, storage cupboards and lockers, and a doorway to a lower cabin lined with bunks. Peering eagerly about, Calwyn squeezed herself into a corner behind the table.

But she had little time for staring before Xanni and Tonno rummaged in the lockers and produced some food. It was only hard bread, a cold leftover stew of fish and beans, and some dried fruits, but Calwyn fell upon it as gratefully as if it had been the feast she'd been dreaming of all day. "If we'd known you were coming, we would have stocked up the larder." Xanni grinned broadly as he watched Darrow tear off a large hunk of bread. "But Tonno will make you his *particular* hot potion."

Tonno was already at work over the little stove in the corner, and soon the cabin was filled with a delicious smell of ginger and spices. Presently the drink was slopped into four tin mugs, and Tonno shoved one across the table to Calwyn. "There's honey in that from Antaris."

She inhaled the sweet, clear brew with her eyes closed and shook her head. "Not from Antaris."

Xanni and Tonno exchanged glances, and Xanni laughed. "It was bought at the fair last autumn, and they swore blind it was best Antaris honey."

"We paid good coin for that," grumbled Tonno. "How do you know it's not mountain honey?"

"I should think I'd know the scent from my own hives."

"Calwyn was beekeeper to the sisters there," said Darrow.

"It's very good, all the same," said Calwyn hastily, but Tonno only grunted.

"And now that you have eaten badly and drunk well," said Xanni cheerfully, settling himself at the table across from Darrow, "I think it's time for the tale you owe us, my friend. How did you come by that limp?"

"How did you come by *her*?" growled Tonno from the steps, as he packed some dried leaves into the bowl of a pipe. Calwyn watched as he lit it, drew back, and blew the smoke out through the hatchway into the night air. The blue tendrils smelled of cherrywood and some other pungent scent she didn't recognize. She leaned back against the warm planks of the cabin wall and wrapped her hands around her mug. A pleasant tiredness was beginning to creep over her; dreamily she thought how easy it would be to fall asleep here, sitting up on this hard bench.

She closed her eyes and began to doze, half-aware of Darrow's voice as he wove the tale of his journey across the mountains, how he had injured himself crossing the Wall, how Calwyn had found him and brought him to the Dwellings, and how Samis had followed him there at last. Even the story of that final dreadful night seemed hazy and unreal, as if it had happened to someone else. Then he was telling how they had fled together down the river, floating and tumbling and drifting, carried farther and farther away . . .

She was woken by the sound of Xanni's laughter. "Fetch a pillow, Tonno, it would be a shame to wake her now."

"I am awake." Sleepily, Calwyn dragged herself upright and blinked in the lamplight.

"So," said Tonno, ignoring her. "You managed to escape him this time."

"This time. But perhaps we can turn the chase around and hunt the hunter." Darrow leaned forward eagerly. "I've been thinking about something that Calwyn said to me when we were in Antaris, that the best way to stop him from carrying out his plan might be to gather a band of chanters and face him together. I saw in Antaris, when all the priestesses sang together, how it weakened his powers."

"But he still defeated us that night," said Calwyn sharply. "And almost killed one of the sisters, besides."

"True, but most of his victories come more easily than that. You were right that day, Calwyn, though I wouldn't admit it." Fleetingly his eyes met hers, and he smiled at her astonished face, then looked quickly away.

Xanni began to laugh. "It will be the simplest of tasks! Look, we already have an ironcrafter and a priestess of ice-call. At this rate, by summer's end *Fledgewing* will be so heavy with chanters, we won't be able to move through the water!"

"*Fledgewing* is the name of this good boat," Darrow said to Calwyn, patting the warm timbers. "I hope it will take us to Mithates for the next stage of our quest. With its crew, of course. If they are willing." He raised an inquiring eyebrow to the brothers. Tonno merely grunted and glared at his pipe, but Xanni clapped Darrow warmly on the back.

"By all means! We haven't forgotten the promise we made to you in Gellan. We'll take you wherever you wish, and gladly, whether it be Mithates or Merithuros or anywhere in between."

"Steady," muttered Tonno. "He'll promise to sail you from one moon to the next if you let him."

"Mithates is the land of the guardians of the Power of Fire, isn't it?" said Calwyn hesitantly, struggling to remember what Darrow had shown her on the little wooden globe.

"It was so, once," Darrow corrected her. "But now chantment is outlawed, and the colleges of Mithates spend their days making weapons to sell to whoever will buy them."

For once Xanni looked serious. "Aye, they pride themselves on having no enemies. They'll sell spears to Rengan and swords to Baltimar, and call them both friend, and the two lands jumping to cut each other's throats."

"With friendship like that —" Tonno left his sentence unfinished and spat out of the hatchway.

"But if there are no more chanters in Mithates, why are we going there?" asked Calwyn.

"I said that chantment was outlawed, not that there were no more chanters. There are chanters in every corner of Tremaris, if you know how to find them."

"You think we'll find someone there to help us fight Samis?"

"I am sure of it. The Power of Fire is the third of the great Powers. If we can find a master of fire to help us, perhaps we will be almost strong enough."

"When would you have us sail?" Xanni ran an eager hand through his curly hair, as if he would be happy to start at once.

"As soon as we can be ready."

Xanni nodded. "All we need is one day to buy provisions. And find some clothes for the lass. We could be gone by nightfall."

From the steps, Tonno said, "Perhaps Enna's clothes will fit her."

"I was thinking the same thing." Xanni turned in his chair. "Enna was our sister. She was a tall lass too, like you, and not yet in skirts."

Calwyn had not seen a single woman in the city streets wearing a tunic and trousers like her own. In Kalysons, it was the custom for girls of marrying age to wear long, full skirts and aprons. Calwyn couldn't imagine what it would be like to walk or run or climb, dragging those cumbersome wide skirts.

Shyly she asked, "What happened to your sister?"

Tonno gave a grunt, tapped out his pipe, and abruptly hauled himself onto the deck. Xanni said, "Enna died of a fever when we were young. She wasn't even sixteen summers."

"Oh — I'm sorry —"

Xanni smiled sadly. "Aye, well, it was a long time ago. Tomorrow I'll go to the house of our aunt, where our childhood things are stored, and we'll make you look less like a priestess and more like a fisherman's daughter."

"Thank you." Calwyn's face was split by a sudden yawn she couldn't suppress.

"She is falling asleep where she sits," said Darrow. "You had better show her a place to lay her head."

Xanni laughed. "Never fear, my friend! We have quarters fit for your little priestess."

Calwyn had already glimpsed the lower cabin with its four

deep bunks, each screened by a curtain. But Xanni opened a small hatchway she hadn't noticed in the bow of the boat and revealed another tiny cabin. The space was cluttered with nets and coils of rope, which Xanni hauled out, clearing two more narrow bunks lying along the prow. "It's a long time since we had a cabin boy," he said. "We can tidy this better in the morning light." He stood aside to let Calwyn through the little hatchway. "I'm sorry it smells so strong of fish," he said doubtfully, but after nights of sleeping on bare planks or straw, with only her cloak for shelter, Calwyn was beyond caring. Rolled in a blanket, with the luxury of an old feather pillow beneath her head, her eyes were soon closing. Faintly she heard Darrow's cross voice say, "Not *my* anything," and the explosion of Xanni's laughter. But gently rocked by the boat, and lulled by the soft slap of water against *Fledgewing*'s sides, she was asleep before she had taken ten breaths.

When Calwyn woke, it was broad day, and Darrow and Tonno had already disappeared into the city.

"Gone to find someone who can tell us the best sailing to Mithates," Xanni said. "*Fledgewing* and Tonno and I know this side of the Bay well, and we have traveled north to Gellan, but we've never been so far west as Mithates."

They ate their breakfast on deck, perched on upturned fish baskets. As she sat in the sunshine and blinked at the light that gleamed off the mirror of the harbor, it was impossible for Calwyn not to be excited at the idea of sailing off toward that wide horizon.

She bit into her biscuit with a light heart. Xanni, who was never long without a smile, grinned at her.

"Tell me, Xanni, how did you become friends with Darrow?"

"Hasn't he told you that tale? We met him in Gellan last winter just after he quarrelled with Samis, and gave him passage back to Kalysons."

"Quarrelled with Samis? You make it sound as if they started out as friends."

"But they were friends." Xanni saw the look on her face. "He hasn't told you that, either?"

Slowly Calwyn chewed and swallowed, but the biscuit suddenly seemed to have turned to sand in her mouth. "No," she said at last. "I thought they had been enemies as long as time."

"Oh no. They were close as brothers when they studied together in Merithuros, even though Samis was a son of the emperor, and a good bit older. But when Samis told him of this plan of his to be master of all chantment, and the king of the world, Darrow wanted none of it. Samis stayed in Gellan to learn more about some kind of magic."

"Gellan. That's where he would have learned the Power of Seeming."

"Aye, that's right. And Darrow sailed south with Tonno and me. But Samis followed him and found him here, and said that he would rip out his heart and all manner of nonsense if he wouldn't help him, and Darrow took off for the mountains — but you know that already." Xanni wiped up the last of his porridge with a piece of bread. "It was a great sorrow to him to lose that friendship, aye, more than that, to have it turn so sour. Near broke his heart, I reckon. I've never heard him speak of any family or any other friend apart from Samis."

"But now he has you and Tonno."

"Aye, that's true. And you." Xanni looked at her shrewdly. "But I daresay you know by now he's not the kind to be sentimental. Especially not with business like this afoot."

"No," said Calwyn uncertainly. "I suppose not."

Xanni jumped to his feet. "Come on. If you're to be our deckhand, I'd better teach you how to do some hard work."

"I learned hard work in Antaris," said Calwyn indignantly, but as usual, Xanni was grinning.

There were many chores to be done aboard the boat, and Calwyn was keen to show Xanni that she was no spoiled and pampered priestess, but could work just as hard as he could. Willingly she scrubbed at the decks and swilled them down, and coiled ropes and folded nets, while Xanni told her the names of the different sails and riggings.

She eyed the brasswork around the portholes, which was stained with salt and green marks. "Do you have any beeswax for polishing?"

Xanni found her a rag and an old lump of soft wax wrapped in a cloth, and before long the first of the portholes gleamed softly as she rubbed at it. Xanni whistled. "I'd almost forgotten it could shine like that."

"The more often it's done, the easier it is," said Calwyn pointedly, pausing for a moment to wipe her forehead.

Xanni laughed. "I must go to the market and get us some supplies. And to my aunt's house, to fetch you some clothes. Will you come with me?"

The rest of the day passed in a flurry of errands. Though Kalysons was a less sinister place in the light of day, Calwyn still did not enjoy pushing her way through the crowded streets, even with Xanni for company, and she was happy to return to the wide space and bright air of the harbor, laden with bags and parcels and dressed in some of her new garments: plain trousers in dark colors, blues and greens, and jackets with fine embroidery in bright scarlet and yellow at the collars and cuffs. It felt strange indeed to lay off her yellow robes, but the other clothes were so soft and beautiful that she didn't mind as much as she'd expected. She stowed her new things in her little cabin and sank down on her bunk. Tonno was frying up the evening meal, and a delicious smell was creeping under the door. She would just close her eyes for a moment and enjoy it. Just for a moment.

Blacklands

Calwyn woke with a start. Something had changed, though she was sure she'd been asleep only for the space of a breath; there was darkness outside, and she was aware of a quiet creaking and gentle movement as the boat dipped through the waves. She scrambled up out of the hatchway into a fresh wind that whipped her long plaits against her face, and a wide expanse of sea lit up by the three moons and a canopy of stars. They had begun their voyage.

All was calm on deck. Xanni stood at the tiller; Tonno had lit his pipe and was leaning against the roof of the cabin. Darrow had his hand to a rope and his eyes on the sails, and his lips were moving with a low, rhythmic song of chantment. The only other sound was the rush of the waves as the boat ran forward through the water.

"Why didn't you wake me?" she cried.

"We thought you needed your sleep," said Xanni kindly.

But Tonno said, "Easier to let you be than fret about landlubbers getting underfoot," and Darrow laughed.

This was infuriating. "How will I learn to be useful unless you teach me?" she demanded.

Xanni laughed. "If you want to be useful now, you could brew up a mug of honey potion for the crew."

"I'll do it," said Tonno, and disappeared below. Plainly he believed no one else was capable of making the drink as well as he did, but Calwyn still found it maddening to think that he wouldn't trust her even with such a trivial task.

She turned and saw the lights of Kalysons spread along the harbor, a winking glow against the horizon, receding behind them. She held on tightly to the railing and tried to get used to the pitching of the deck beneath her feet. It was very different from the gentle rocking at the jetty. Now *Fledgewing* was truly alive, the water singing beneath her prow and the wind driving her onward.

Darrow broke off his song. "Not seasick, I hope."

"No, no." Calwyn hoped not too. "Are you speeding the ship, or is it only the wind?"

"I am helping her a little. The wind is not quite where we might wish it."

"I never thought of you using chantment to push *Fledgewing* through the sea. We will be in Mithates in no time!"

Darrow said, "I wish it were so simple. But it is harder to move something large than something small, and harder to move an object through water than through the air."

"Then move it through the air," said Xanni, with a wink at Calwyn. "Let us fly to Mithates, like a true *Fledgewing*."

Darrow gave a mock grimace. He was more lighthearted in Xanni's company than with anyone else, Calwyn had noticed with a slight pang. "That would take greater skill, and greater strength, than I possess. I can help us move a little faster than we might through the force of the wind alone. But only a little." And then the steady drone of his song began again, and Calwyn felt the ship surge beneath her feet as the chantment took hold.

Tonno brought up steaming mugs, two in each hand. Sipped out on the deck at sea, sailing swiftly through the night, the sweet spiced brew tasted even better than before.

Presently Darrow said to Xanni, "Let me take the tiller. You and Tonno should get some rest. You too," he added to Calwyn.

"I'm not tired," said Calwyn, and she was not. The blood seemed to sing through her veins just as *Fledgewing* sang through the foaming water.

After the brothers had gone below, Calwyn stood beside Darrow, leaning her elbows on the cabin roof. He said, "I am sorry we didn't have more time to teach you boat-craft before this, or I would let you take a turn at steering. But not tonight, I think."

Calwyn thought that it didn't look too difficult. And how wonderful it would be to feel the boat leap and turn at the touch of your hand. She would learn boat-craft; she would become as skillful a sailor as any of them. "I wish the sisters had taught me ironcraft or windworking instead of ice-call; then I could help you move the ship."

"There will come a time when ice-call will be useful to us, I'm sure. But you must be patient so that you can recognize that time when it appears."

"Now you sound like Marna." Calwyn knotted her plaits together so that they didn't whip across her face.

"Poor Calwyn. To flee so far and find the same lectures everywhere!"

Calwyn was silent. Since they'd boarded *Fledgewing*, she and Darrow had not had one moment's conversation alone. After all their days' journeying, she'd grown used to sharing her thoughts with him. And she'd believed that he was sharing his thoughts with her. She said, "Xanni told me that you and Samis were students together. He must have been a bad pupil. From what you've said, I can't imagine him listening to anyone."

"On the contrary. He was always exceptionally gifted." Darrow's voice was calm and even. After a pause he said, "I would have told you before long. But some things are not so easy to explain."

"It's not important."

"He was not always as he is now. At least —" Darrow hesitated, thinking as he spoke. "He was greedy always. But where once he was greedy for knowledge, now he is greedy for power. And he feels that he has been slighted and overlooked. He burns for revenge."

"Were you friends for a long time?"

Darrow gave her a swift look. "Yes. A long time." He stared straight ahead across the water as the wind blew his fair hair forward. After a moment he said, in quite a different tone, "Here,

Calwyn, hold the tiller for a moment. The wind grows stronger, I must trim the sail."

"But if the wind is stronger, won't we go faster? I thought we were trying to go as fast as we could."

"We must not try to go faster than the boat can stand, or we might be overturned. Balance, it is a question of balance, as everything is. That is one thing Samis has never learned."

Calwyn took the tiller, and Darrow showed her which star to aim for. As he loosed the ropes and brought in the sail, she felt the lively power of the boat surging under her hands. She sang softly to *Fledgewing* as she would have sung to the bees, a song of soothing and quiet, and she felt the ship obey her, and she thought that she had never been so happy.

But when Darrow came back to take the tiller, he was curt with her, in no mood for conversation. At last Calwyn went down to bed with a confused aching in her heart, sorry that she'd ever mentioned Samis.

For ten days and nights they sailed without sighting land, heading northwest straight across the wide expanse of the Bay of Sardi. Few ships sailed between Kalysons and Mithates, and those that did took a longer route, hugging the coast all around the Bay, always within sight of land. Out in the open water, they saw no other vessels.

"Not many sailors would dare to go this way," Xanni told her proudly. "But I'd wager *Fledgewing* against the Bay in any weather."

"Is it really so dangerous?" Calwyn looked about at the calm ocean on every side, the wheeling gulls that had followed them all the way from Kalysons, and the sunlight dancing on the gentle waves.

"It seems friendly enough now, I grant you, but the Sardi is deceptive as a Gellanese." Xanni sniffed the wind. "We may have a fog later, and then you'll see."

Darrow looked up sharply. "Do you smell fog?"

Xanni shrugged. "We may be lucky and outrun it."

Darrow gave a rueful smile. "Then I must work a little harder." His face was drawn and tired already from the work of pushing *Fledgewing* through the waves; Calwyn wished again with all her heart that she knew the chantments of iron, rather than ice, so that she could help him. He had explained to her that the craft of iron worked from the force of the earth, not from the water. "It is as if I had a long pole and pushed against the bottom of the sea. The water gets in the way, it interferes with the chantment."

"Can't you push against the water somehow, as if you had a pair of oars?" asked Calwyn, glad to show off her new knowledge of boating.

But Darrow shook his head. "Ironcraft does not work in that way." Day after day he sat at the stern of the boat, his eyes closed, his hands gripped so tightly that the knuckles showed white, his lips moving in a weary drone of chantment.

Calwyn asked Xanni, "What will happen if there is fog?"

Xanni shook his curly head. "No wind," he said simply, and went to take the tiller from Tonno.

Xanni was right. Later that afternoon, the air grew colder. Then the wind began to slacken; the sails, which had been taut, flapped loosely against the mast. With the mist thickening all around them, the world suddenly became silent. When Tonno called out to Xanni, his voice sounded oddly hushed, as though *Fledgewing* and all aboard her were inside a bubble of glass, and Darrow's song was smothered by the fog as soon as it had left his throat.

Calwyn couldn't see the sky; there was white mist everywhere. Even the top of the mast with its bright pennant had been swallowed by whiteness. Calwyn shivered as the fog's icy fingers crept up her sleeves and down her neck. The boat was still moving, but much more slowly than before, bobbing uncertainly through the water. The sun had vanished, leaving only a certain brightness in the blanket of mist that enclosed them.

Calwyn said, "How will we know where to steer?"

"That's the danger of the fog," said Xanni, as grim as she had ever seen him. "We're drifting blind now, until it lifts."

More and more slowly they moved through the silent, eerie whiteness, the touch of it cold and clammy on their skins, coating every surface of the boat with damp. Darrow had given up using his chantments to speed the boat; it was no use when they couldn't be sure in which direction they were sailing. Calwyn tried to think of some way to help. She remembered what Marna had said about the Power of Ice, how it commanded everything that was cold and dark. The fog was certainly cold enough. She went to sit by herself on one side of the boat and quietly tried some small workings of her craft. With one song she could make the droplets of moisture gather together until they splashed onto the deck like rain, and with another she could change them into snowy flakes that fell softly into the water. But try as she might, she couldn't lessen the thickness of the fog, nor clear a path through it.

All the rest of that day they drifted in the mists. They took turns to go below and sleep, so that after the fog lifted they could sail hard all night. They couldn't tell when the sun went down, but gradually the whiteness all around grew more and more shadowy, until the only light was the glow of their own lanterns, and there was pitch blackness in every direction. No starlight or moonlight could penetrate the thick wall of fog; it was like moondark, but the blackness seemed to press down even more heavily than it did on those nights, for there was no friendly starlight flung across the sky. Calwyn felt as though someone had taken a thick blanket and held it down over her head; she leaned over the side and gulped breaths of cold air, trying to dispel her growing panic. If she kept her eyes closed, it was not so bad. To lift her spirits, she tried singing one of the hearth songs from home, but instead of the sisters' cheerful, warm chorus, she heard only her own wavering, lonely voice, a thin thread of sound swallowed by the mists. She kept up the song bravely till the end, but when it was finished she felt smaller and more helpless than before.

The fog started to lift in the night. A light wind rose, and soon the mists began to thin and drift, and first one, then another of the moons appeared, shining through the transparent veil of the fog. It was the time they called in Antaris the Three Smiles of the Goddess, when all three moons were in crescent, and the name had never seemed so apt to Calwyn. Tonno called Darrow up on deck again, and the three sailors scanned the stars, trying to work out in which direction they were facing and whether they had drifted far off course.

The wind remained light, and Darrow stayed at his post in the stern all the next day, urging the boat forward, and would not go below even when Tonno threatened to kick him bodily through the hatchway. That made him smile, but it did not make him stir.

"We're not in such a hurry, are we?" Calwyn asked. "What difference will it make if we arrive in Mithates in eight days' time or nine?"

Darrow wouldn't even break off his song to answer her, but only frowned.

Slowly Calwyn said, "You think Samis will go to Mithates too? I suppose if he wants to learn the chantments of fire he will have to go there sometime. But Darrow, I'm sure he's still in Antaris, making Tamen teach him all our chantments." That was an uncomfortable thought, but better than imagining Samis sailing swiftly behind them.

Darrow said, "Yes, I'm sure you're right," and gave her a reassuring nod. But he didn't leave his seat in the stern.

As she lay sleepless in her bunk or leaned over the side with the breeze on her face, feeling the nose of *Fledgewing* dip and rise in the rhythm that had already become as familiar as her own breathing, Calwyn racked her brain to think of ways that she could be useful. She felt herself a mere passenger, unable to help much with the sailing, except to follow the occasional barked order to hold this rope or loosen that one, unable to use her chantment to make the boat go faster. She did what she could in the way of cooking and cleaning, but even in Antaris she had never been much good at those things, and she couldn't help noticing that Xanni and Tonno felt they could do better by themselves. As for Darrow, she was certain he was regretting that he'd ever brought her from Antaris, for he hardly spoke three words to her. Though she told herself he was exhausted, she still felt a pang of hurt.

It was late on the tenth day when Xanni cried out at last, "Land ho!"

Calwyn rushed to the side of the boat and shaded her eyes with her hand, dazzled by the low sun. After a long time she was able to make out a smudge of dark to the northwest. "The Elbow," Tonno said.

"The Elbow is the first sign of the approach to Mithates Port," said Darrow. "It juts out far into the Bay. We must sail along its flank to the harbor."

"We might even reach it by morning," said Xanni. "With luck and a lick of wind."

Slowly, the dark smudge grew larger, until just before sunset they were close enough to make out the flickering of lights from watchtowers perched on the clifftops. Eager to be helpful, Calwyn hurried to light their own lanterns in the dusk.

"No lights!" growled Tonno.

"There are archers in the watchtowers," said Xanni. "Their idea of fun is to set their arrows alight and rain them down on strange ships."

"I thought you said that the colleges of Mithates sold their weapons to whoever came calling? Flaming arrows are a fine welcome!"

"The towers have nothing to do with the colleges," said Darrow. "They belong to bandits who try to take tolls from every ship that passes. If we're careful, we can get by without their knowing."

Nearer and nearer they drew, gliding so silently in the darkness it seemed as though it was the cliff that crept toward the boat, not the other way around, a huge, hulking beast looming closer and closer, blotting out the starry sky. The lights from the watchtowers vanished as sheer black cliffs reared high above the boat. The water was deep and still here, and they made slow progress, Tonno steering carefully as they crept along. It was vital that they reach the safety of Mithates Port before sunrise, and Darrow still kept up his tired drone of chantment, though his song barely rose above a murmur. Even when Calwyn at last went below, she found herself tiptoeing about the cabin, as though the archers in the watchtowers might overhear a dropped shoe or a whispered *good night*.

Calwyn woke early to the sun flooding in through the fore portholes, and an unfamiliar sensation. She lay still for a moment, trying to work out what it was, and then she realized: *Fledgewing* had stopped moving. They were lying at anchor. For the first time in days, she could no longer feel the rush and dip of the prow surging forward. She dressed hastily and ran up onto the deck, blinking in the sunlight.

Fledgewing lay in a narrow inlet, flanked by the steep black cliffs they had sailed beside all night. The little town of Mithates Port clustered about the mouth of the river Amith where it met the sea; the cottages and inns were built from the same gleaming dark rock as the cliffs, as if they had all been carved out of the stone where they stood. Tendrils of smoke curled over the dark roofs and drifted out over the bay, where boats jostled in the shadow of the cliffs.

Tonno was leaning over the rail, packing his morning pipe, while Darrow and Xanni lowered *Fledgewing*'s tiny dinghy over the side. Xanni looked up. "We were going to wake you," he said guiltily. "Before we went."

"You were going to leave without me!" Calwyn cried.

"Someone should stay with the boat," growled Tonno, taking an extra pinch of tobacco from his special pouch. "This place is full of thieves."

"You will be safer here," said Darrow. "Mithates is a dangerous place."

Calwyn hardly knew whether to cry in frustration or stamp her

foot with rage. "I can help, you know I can! You can't leave me behind like — like a piece of old rope!"

"A piece of old rope would be useful," muttered Tonno.

"A piece of old rope will not burst out with a chantment at the
wrong moment," said Darrow, but there was the slightest crinkle
of a smile around his eyes.

"I *promise* not to sing any chantments."

"It's not possible," said Darrow firmly. "You cannot come with
us, it would hamper us very much. There are no women students
in the colleges." He saw Calwyn's eyes widen in indignation. "Just
as there are no men permitted to study icecraft in Antaris. Your
people are as bad as theirs."

She had nothing to say to that. She stood on the deck, lonely
and disconsolate, watching as the dinghy drew away. Xanni gave
her a cheerful wave, but she was too miserable to return it. It was
not fair. Had she come all this way, braved all these perils, to be left
behind on the boat just when the most important part of their
quest was beginning? Why, it had been her own idea to join together with other chanters, and now she was being left out. She
stared across at the shore, but *Fledgewing*'s dinghy was lost in the
crowd of other boats.

Mithates was half a day's walk from its port; Darrow had said
that they might be gone for several days. "You might practice
swimming," he suggested. "The waters of the harbor are calm
enough."

She scrubbed the decks and ordered the lockers, which were

overflowing with the provisions they'd bought in Kalysons. She cleaned out her own cabin until the last traces of the fishy smell had vanished, and found other places to stow the ropes and sails and nets. And she did practice swimming, cautiously at first, and with much splashing, securing herself with a rope that trailed from the bow. By the second day she was bold enough to swim round and round *Fledgewing* until her arms and legs ached, though she still couldn't quite bring herself to duck her head under the water. Then she practiced her chantments, the most difficult feats she could think of, singing up elaborate models of trees or castles of ice. Once she sang up a miniature *Fledgewing* from the sea, complete with masts and sails and little figures on the deck. But that reminded her that she was the only figure on the deck at present, and she hastily melted it again.

By the third day she was as bored and frustrated as she had ever been in Antaris. Now she didn't even have the bees to occupy her. And she was tormented by questions about what was happening to the others in Mithates. Had they succeeded in finding any chanters? Would they persuade them to fight against Samis? All afternoon she sat on the deck with her back against the cabin wall, rolling the wooden globe idly up and down, looking up hopefully whenever a movement on the water caught her eye, in case it was the dinghy returning. But every little boat she saw was bound for another vessel; no one came near *Fledgewing*.

The sun went down, the moons rose, and still she sat there, watching the smoke from the chimneys drift across the harbor and the lamplight glitter on the water. Then one by one the lanterns winked out. The town was folding itself into sleep. It was late; the others wouldn't be returning tonight.

She got up, stretching the stiffness in her limbs, and was about to go below, when she noticed a ship coming through the mouth of the harbor from the open sea, gliding silently across the moon-lit water. It was quite unlike the sturdy *Fledgewing* or any of the other boats she'd seen in Kalysons. This was a long, sleek vessel, barely rising above the level of the waves, with a prow shaped like a snake's head and long banks of oars that dipped and rose in a steady rhythm, gleaming at every stroke as water poured off them. Two masts rose from the center of the boat, but the sails were furled tight; clearly the oars were the power that moved the ship. This must be one of the Gellanese galleys that Darrow had spoken of, with a slave in chains hauling at every oar. Calwyn stared with horrified fascination as the ship moved slowly deeper into the harbor.

But then, as the ship drew closer, she saw that the benches where the slaves should have been sitting were deserted. There was not a sailor or a slave to be seen anywhere on that long, eerily silent boat; it could have been a ghost ship, gliding without a sound across the ocean. And yet the oars moved; without a hand to move them, they rose and fell, and now at last she could hear the whisper of their movement. Another sound came to her too, faintly, across the water: the sound of singing, low and strong, a powerful rumbling song that made her skin prickle. She knew these notes now; she had heard them from Darrow, day after weary day as he sat by the tiller, though this song vibrated with a greater power than he had managed to summon. It was a chantment of ironcraft.

And as she listened, pressing herself instinctively into the shadows, the oars lifted for one final time, and locked, and rested. The last throaty growl of chantment drifted over the water and ceased. Silence settled over the harbor.

Calwyn stayed in the shadows, her heart pounding. That sinister ship could belong to only one person: Samis, the captain of an empty ship, whose oars creaked and dipped through the water by the power of chantment. Though the night air was still warm, Calwyn clenched her teeth to stop their chattering. Could he have followed them here? She felt sick; only the friendly timbers of *Fledgewing* at her back kept her from sliding to the deck in despair.

Be strong, she told herself. The fact that Samis was here didn't mean that he had followed them. The Power of Fire was one of the great Powers; it made sense that Samis should want to master it as soon as he could. That was the very reason why they themselves had come here first. It was a coincidence, that was all.

But even as she argued with herself, doubts began to trouble her. What if Samis had come to Kalysons and heard the story of how a witch-girl in yellow robes had frozen the tongue of a young lout down by the docks? He would have learned from the sisters that Darrow had taken one of the priestesses with him when he escaped from Antaris. Darrow and Tonno had been talking with the old sailors around the harbor, asking how to steer to Mithates. If Samis had begun to ask questions, it wouldn't have been difficult to discover their plans.

It was her fault. He was here, and it was her fault.

Quickly, without pausing to think, she rushed down into the cabin and rummaged about until she found an oiled bag that Xanni used to keep their loaves dry. She shook out the bread and the crumbs inside, and shoved some clothes from Xanni's locker into it. A few moments later she slipped into the sea, holding the bag carefully out of the water, and then she kicked as hard as she could toward the shore.

The road to Mithates — the only road out of the port — ran beside the river, so that it looked as though two broad ribbons, one black and one silver, wound their way along the valley side by side. Calwyn tried to run, but the ground seemed to heave and swell beneath her feet; after so long at sea, she couldn't balance on dry land. And then the borrowed trousers threatened to trip her up at every step, and the cap that hid her plaits kept slipping over her eyes. She cursed the colleges that wouldn't allow girls within their walls, and cursed the treacherous road that refused to keep steady, and forced herself to go more slowly.

Afterward, she would remember that journey as a waking nightmare, stumbling through the barren valley, scorched by a thousand fires where the colleges had tested their weapons. Swirls of ash rose before every breath of breeze, and here and there the remains of a blackened tree twisted up through the stony ground like a ghastly figure of warning, pointing her onward.

It was almost dawn when she reached the end of the road. First she saw the black spires and thin towers rising like a small forest along the riverbanks, and then she turned a bend and saw the whole of Mithates spread before her: the twelve colleges, each with its bell tower and spire built out of the same dark, brilliant stone, and the narrow cobbled streets that threaded between. It looked just like Antaris, except that Antaris was built with gray stone instead of black. Her breath caught in her throat.

There was no defensive wall around the city. As the sun rose, she walked right down into the town without anyone to challenge her. But then she saw that the twelve colleges divided the place into twelve small villages all clustered together, each with its own high wall of stone. The streets were almost empty so early in the day; one or two frowning students hurried by in their soft cloth bonnets, a different color for every college, and a tired-looking woman with a basket over one arm and a baby in the other. There were no open squares, no markets, and no houses lined the streets. It was as though each college were an island, separated from the others, with the streets acting like rivers to keep them apart. There were many little iron gates set into the walls, through which Calwyn could glimpse green quadrangles, or stone stairs winding upward.

She had no idea how she was going to find the others and deliver her warning. Darrow had said that Mithates was the same size as Antaris, and she had vaguely thought that it would be set out in the same way. She'd expected to come across her friends soon enough, in a dining hall or a courtyard — one of the places where people gathered to be together. But there was nowhere like that here. Darrow and the others must be somewhere behind these high walls; there was only one way to find them, and that was to go inside the colleges one by one. Nervously she tucked her plaits up more firmly under her cap and tried the nearest of the little iron gates. It was locked; so was the second, and the third. Each gateway was topped with the carving of some beast or crest, an eagle or a leaping fish or a sheaf of wheat, the symbol of the college. There was a fierce-looking bee above the fourth gate she tried. She hoped it was a good omen, and sure enough, the gate swung open at her touch.

Calwyn plunged from the sleepy silence of the streets into a world of bustle and clamor. A babble of excited talk echoed through the cloisters as the students hurried between lecture halls, and bells were ringing to mark the next part of the day. Shouts and footfalls reverberated between the ivy-covered walls, and from somewhere far off came the sound of a muffled explosion, followed by loud cheers. With all this noisy activity taking place behind the high walls instead of in the streets and squares, it was as though the city had been turned inside out. Never at her ease in crowds, Calwyn ducked her head and pulled her cap a little farther down over her eyes, but no one challenged her.

She soon found that as long as she moved purposefully and

kept to the shadows of the cloisters, no one paid her any attention. She strode through the teeming quadrangles, across galleries and along bustling corridors, but she never saw or heard any sign of her friends.

By late afternoon, she had searched four of the twelve colleges without success and with growing apprehension. Surely Samis must be in Mithates by now; she was so tired and hungry, she had left *Fledgewing* unguarded, and it would all be for nothing.

At last she found herself where the wide, placid river cut through the center of the town, with a broad swath of green bank on either side. Spander trees spread their branches in a shady canopy over the grass, and she sank down beneath one of them. The declining sun sent shadows chasing down the narrow streets between the colleges, though the riverbanks were still golden with light. Perhaps she should go back to Mithates Port, Calwyn thought dismally; she was still scrutinizing every passerby, but now she was as fearful of seeing Samis as she was hopeful of seeing her friends.

Suddenly she was startled by shouts and hooting from the other side of the river. The strangest procession was approaching: a group of students running along, whooping and jeering, some brandishing sticks, others waving their bonnets in the air. Calwyn stared hard, but she couldn't see what was at the center of the parade. Then suddenly something broke away from the pack and began to cross the nearest bridge, moving quite fast, though unsteadily; she could just make out the head of a boy, a year or so younger than herself, with untidy brown hair blown back under his red bonnet, scowling with tremendous concentration as he skimmed along through the air, though still close to the ground. The rest of him was hidden by the bridge. The other students remained on the far side of the river, shaking their sticks and bonnets; some of them, bored, gave up the chase altogether. "Curfew's getting close!" Calwyn heard one of them call as he wandered away.

The flying student grew closer and closer, then suddenly he was across the bridge and in plain view, and Calwyn saw that he was not flying after all but was mounted on a strange contraption with three wheels, his feet pumping furiously, and dragging behind him a rickety cart laden with firewood. But she barely had time to take in this sight before the boy lost control of his machine. The front wheel wobbled mightily and plunged off the path, gathering speed as it hurtled down the slope. Calwyn gasped and leaped to her feet, certain that the boy and his machine were about to plunge into the river together. But with a desperate effort, he hurled his weight to one side and the machine collided violently with the trunk of a spander tree, flinging the boy to the ground, as limp as a doll. Firewood clattered over the grass. One back wheel spun slowly, whirring, in the air.

Calwyn hurried down the bank to where the boy lay unmoving. His eyes were open, and he was blinking dreamily up at the sky. "Steering pin must have come loose," he said. He sat up.

"Are you hurt?" cried Calwyn.

"Hm." He considered the question. "I don't think so." He put his hand to his face. "But I've lost my lenses." He began to feel around on the grass.

Calwyn spied something shining on the grass a little way off: two round pieces of glass, held together with a bridge of wire, with two long wires protruding from either side. "Is this what you're looking for?"

"Oh, thank you." The boy placed them on his freckled nose so that the long wires rested on his ears. A pair of vague blue eyes blinked at her solemnly through the glass. But he was more concerned about his machine; he bent over it gloomily, inspecting the damage, which was considerable. The front wheel was bent almost in half, and a piece of broken chain trailed forlornly on the grass. "I knew that chain would never hold. How will I get it back to my college?" He shook back his untidy hair and pushed the lenses up his nose in despair. "Look at that wheel."

"I can help you," said Calwyn automatically, but she was suddenly trembling. Perhaps it was the fright of witnessing the collision, but she felt she would like to sit down for a while beneath the trees. Her fingers prickled as though she were about to faint. She gave herself a shake and bent to straighten up the cart.

"They call me Trout, by the way." The boy held out his hand; it was filthy, and covered in burn marks and the scars of many small injuries, and there was a grubby bandage around one finger. It looked as though his clothes had also gone a long time without washing; his trousers were streaked with oil, there were various unidentifiable stains down his shirt, and he seemed to have been using his bonnet as a dishcloth.

"I'm Cal —" Too late, Calwyn remembered that she was supposed to be a boy. "Cal," she said firmly. Together she and Trout picked up the machine and piled the wood into the cart, though Calwyn's hands were still shaking. She hadn't eaten that day. Perhaps, she thought with sudden hope, this Trout might be able to give her some food, and maybe shelter for the night. With a little difficulty, they were able to balance the contraption on its one remaining good wheel, levering the front part between them and pushing it along, back across the bridge.

"Perhaps I should have used the horn. I forgot all about it." Trout pointed to a small, battered clarion fixed to the steering handles.

"Never mind that," said Calwyn. "The sight of you flying along on this thing was terrifying enough. What do you call it? I've never seen anything like it before."

"Of course not. This is the first one that's ever been built. I haven't named it yet. It's for transporting supplies swiftly on a battlefield —" He halted suddenly in the middle of the road and stared at her suspiciously. "Were you following me? Did your college send you to spy on me?"

"If you want to keep your inventions secret, you shouldn't ride them about in the street," said Calwyn tartly. Her head was throbbing; perhaps she had been walking in the sun too long.

A look of dismay dawned on Trout's face. "You're right. If the

Masters of the College find out, I'll be in trouble again. But I needed a long run, and there isn't room enough inside the walls."

Calwyn felt herself warming to him. "Are you in trouble often?"

"All the time, especially after the business with the explosion. Though it was the fire that really upset them. But that wasn't my fault. It got away from me."

"Yes, they should teach you how to control your chantments," said Calwyn absently, forgetting that magic was outlawed here.

Trout stared at her through the spokes of the bent wheel, as if trying to decide whether she was joking or serious. "*Chantments*? Where do you come from? Antaris? They still believe in magic up in those mountains, or so they say."

Calwyn didn't reply, struggling to wheel the machine straight along the bumpy, cobbled street. At last she said, "Supposing I were from Antaris. What would you say then?"

"Nothing." He gave a snort of laughter. "I don't believe those stories."

"What stories?"

"You know what I mean. The stories of the witches with their magical songs, who can raise up walls of ice out of nothing, and make a snowstorm on a summer's day. They're tales to frighten children, nothing more. Anyone with any sense can see that those things aren't possible. Only fools and babies would believe those stories. *Chantments!* You might as well believe in the gods!" He gave another derisive snort.

Calwyn was sorely tempted to sing up a flurry of snow to whirl about his head, just to prove him wrong, but then she winced as pain stabbed behind her eyes. All she wanted was to sit somewhere dark and quiet, and sip a cool drink of water until her head stopped aching.

"Here we are; this is my gate." They came to a halt below the towering walls. He said hesitantly, "Would you mind helping me a bit longer? My workshop's just inside."

Calwyn held the gate open while Trout clumsily maneuvered the cart inside; the gateway was so narrow that they couldn't both go through it together. Inside was a lush green lawn, dotted with spander trees. Trout led the way toward a cluster of low buildings that looked like sheds or stables. "They banished me out here," he said cheerfully. "After the fire."

Calwyn held the machine upright while he fumbled in his pocket for some keys. He unlocked the nearest shed, then he helped her wheel the cart inside. "Just drop it anywhere, it doesn't matter."

Obediently Calwyn let her side of the contraption fall, and looked around, her eyes adjusting to the shadows. Trout fumbled for a light, and the room suddenly brightened with a white glow from the brightest lantern that Calwyn had ever seen. The workshop was an incredible jumble of objects, bits of machinery, little cogs and wheels and gears like the inside of a windmill, and all sorts of things she couldn't recognize. There were tools and nails and screws, glass jars, lumps of rock with glittering veins of minerals running through them, rows of stoppered vials filled with different colored liquids, balls of string, flints, and coils of wire lying all over bench tops and stools and scattered on the floor. There was a large burned patch on one bench. She said, "It looks as though a storm has blown through here."

"Yes, people often say that." Trout gazed vaguely around the workshop. "Thanks for helping me. I should offer you something — something to eat." He looked hopefully along the workbench, but nothing remotely edible sprang to view.

"If I could just have some water —"

He fetched a jug and a beaker and watched as she gulped the water down. But the throbbing in her head and her fingers refused to go away.

Trout said suddenly, "Are you really from Antaris? Why are you dressed as a boy?"

So he wasn't quite as vague as he appeared, after all. Calwyn said shakily, "What a ridiculous idea. How could I possibly be from Antaris?"

Trout looked at her shrewdly. "I suppose you're right. I've heard that everyone from Antaris is kept locked away in the mountains and forbidden to leave on pain of death."

"You shouldn't believe everything you hear," said Calwyn. "I think there are a few who manage to escape. Those who want to see more of the world." She thought suddenly of her mother.

Trout pulled off his bonnet and rubbed his hands through his hair until it was even more untidy than before. "More of the world? No, thanks. I've got enough to keep me busy for a whole lifetime between these four walls." He tapped the bench with its odds and ends of machinery and strange tools. "This is enough of the wide world for me!"

"What about your machine? That could carry you far beyond Mithates."

He looked surprised, considering. "Yes, I suppose it could carry a traveler farther than he could go on foot. I hadn't thought of that."

Now it was Calwyn's turn to laugh. "Why did you build it, if not for that?"

"I told you, to carry supplies into battle. Or to carry messages more swiftly between a commander and his soldiers."

"Battle. Of course. Tell me, is everything you make here designed to help in killing people?"

"Of course not." His voice was indignant. "We have *loads* of inventions for defense."

He picked up a pair of pliers and bent over the mangled contraption. Calwyn leaned over too, and the buzzing in her head intensified. Something was calling to her, screaming to her, and all at once she knew exactly what it was. She reached out her hand to touch the battered clarion that dangled by a wire from the iron frame. At the precise moment that her fingers touched it, the screaming in her head cleared. She whispered, "What is this?"

Trout looked puzzled. "Just a little horn I found lying about. No one wanted it."

She could only nod dumbly. Now she understood what the throbbing in her head had signified; it was as though she had touched her flesh to the sacred Wall without knowing the power it held. This object, this small, battered instrument, immeasurably ancient, was an artifact so charged with magic that her senses had reeled from it until she comprehended what it was. The chanters of Mithates might have vanished, but they had left this precious gift behind them. And this boy Trout had tied it to his cart with a length of wire as though it were a child's toy! Trembling, her fingers fumbled to set it free.

"Please — may I have it?"

Trout shrugged. "I suppose so. Though I don't see what use —"

But he never got the words out. Even as Calwyn struggled with the last twist of the wire, the door of the workshop flew open. A figure stood in the doorway, outlined in the red light of the sunset.

Trout looked around, frowning. "Hey! Who's that? Mind the light — shut the door, will you?"

It was too late; the lantern guttered in the draft and went out.

"I'm sorry," came the voice from the doorway, and Calwyn's heart leaped.

"Darrow!" She flew across the workshop with a glad cry. To her surprise, Darrow opened his arms and gathered her into a rough hug. For that brief moment, with the cloth of his jacket pressed to her cheek, she felt so utterly safe and so joyfully relieved that nothing else mattered. Her head swam; she thought she might faint.

But now Darrow's strong hands were holding her away, and she struggled to see his face in the dusk. He said gently, "You have found something, little one. Give it to me."

"You mean the clarion? What is it?"

Darrow spoke low, barely louder than a breath. "It is the Clarion of the Flame."

The Clarion of the Flame

Calwyn could hear Trout fumbling to relight the lantern; there was a loud crash as it fell to the ground. He clucked in annoyance. "How did that happen? I hardly touched it. Cal, there are candles by the door, if you could throw one over."

"Cal — Calwyn," repeated Darrow softly. "Calwyn, my little runaway. Where is the Clarion?"

"Here, on the floor. I must have dropped it, I was so surprised." Her head buzzing with confusion and a faint unease, Calwyn dropped to her knees and blindly felt about in the wreckage of the cart. "Where are the others?"

"Waiting for us."

"If someone could pass me a *candle* — oh, never mind, I'll get it myself." Trout stumbled across the workshop and tripped over the pile of twisted metal on the floor. "Ow!"

Calwyn groped through the wreck of the cart. "Darrow, have you found any chanters of fire? How did you know about the Clarion?"

"Those who wield power know the objects of power. I followed its scent, just as you did."

"I didn't know what it was, until I touched it —"

On the other side of the workshop, by the door, Trout struck a flint to light a candle, and as the spark flew, Calwyn saw the glint of the small, dented trumpet. She pounced and held it aloft. By the candle's light she could see that its surface was etched with a design of leaping flames, flickering and shifting in the reflected light. The pattern was half worn away and tarnished, yet the Clarion shimmered and glowed with its own light, like the glow of embers from a fire that had burned for a thousand years. Held high in her hand, it seemed like a living thing. Calwyn caught her breath. There was no mistaking that it was an object of great power, more ancient than the stones and spires of Mithates or the towers of Antaris, steeped in mystery and infused with secret magic. How strange it was that this little battered horn, hardly bigger than her hand, should be the source of such immense power. It was as if the spark that Trout struck could light up the whole world like the break of day.

She stood up and held out the Clarion to Darrow. His back was to the light and she couldn't see his face, but she heard a soft *hah!* as his fingers closed around the horn. Yet Calwyn didn't want to let it go. Since Darrow first appeared, she'd felt a prickling of disquiet; now that feeling grew more definite. Something was wrong here. Holding firm to the Clarion, she was aware of a tingling in her fingers. Surely there was chantment nearby.

Could Darrow feel it too? Anxiously she sought his eyes as they stood there, each holding on to the warmth of the Clarion, joined by its golden fire. Then Darrow reached out with his other hand and gently caressed her hair. A thrill shot through her.

"Calwyn, Taris's child," murmured Darrow. "We can be together in all things now, and all the world will be ours: the mountains and the oceans, the islands and the deserts, the forests and the plains."

Softly, rhythmically, his hand stroked her hair. Her eyes closed. She couldn't move; with every gentle caress she felt weaker. His words flowed about her like honey, rich and sweet, intoxicating. To roam the world as she pleased, with Darrow at her side — Softly, softly, his hand moved over her hair.

"Tremaris needs a leader." Darrow's voice was as musical as the humming of the bees. "With the help of the Clarion, with your help, I will be the Singer of All Songs. And you, little Calwyn, will be my empress. All the peoples of Tremaris will bow down before you. They will obey you in all things, never question you . . ."

Never to be questioned, always to be taken seriously! At once a dozen voices flashed through Calwyn's head: *A piece of old rope would be more useful — Next time, try to hold your tongue — Think before you speak, child, and you will not appear so foolish — We have despaired of you, Calwyn —* How sweet, how sweet it would be to prove all those voices wrong.

"Excuse me!" Trout's voice broke into her reverie. "You can't just take that trumpet, you know. I mean, I'm the one who found it, after all. I'm not saying you can't have it, but it's only fair if we trade, isn't it? I'll tell you what —"

Darrow gave an impatient growl, and Trout fell silent as abruptly as if someone had clapped a hand, or a wad of cloth, over his mouth.

Calwyn blinked. She had fallen into a dream; now for the first time she truly heard what Darrow had said to her. Empress? People bowing down? Impulsively she tightened her grasp on the Clarion. At the same moment Darrow clenched his hand hard around it, and she saw a gleam of ruby light, a light that refused to be hidden, a bloodred light from the jewel of a square ring.

"Darrow?" she whispered. Then, "*Samis?*"

His hand shot out to circle her wrist, grasping it so tightly that her hand hurt. Now at last she recognized the chantment, as dense in the air as the shimmer of sunlight over a dusty path in summer. It was there in the tingling of her hands, the confusion in her head. Convulsed with horror, she wrenched at the Clarion, she twisted her wrist in his iron grasp, but she could not break free. She felt a scream rise in her throat. "Let me see your face! Let me see your face!"

"My face?" It was Darrow's voice: dry, amused, familiar as her own. The man who held her arm swung her effortlessly around so that the candle shone full on his face. And it was Darrow's face that gazed at her, a half-smile playing about his lips. He pulled her closer, so close that his breath was hot in her ear, and whispered, "Do you doubt me now, little one?"

She shook her head violently from side to side like someone struggling to wake from a nightmare. A voice cried out like a distant memory, "I am not persuaded!" This was not how Darrow spoke to her, this was not how Darrow acted. *This was not how Darrow looked.*

She whispered, "Your scar. Where is your scar?" She let go of the Clarion and reached out a fingertip to touch the corner of his eyebrow, the place where the silver scar should run.

Darrow's face contorted with rage; then, like a reflection broken up by ripples, his face wavered and dissolved before her eyes. There was no face, no figure standing in front of her: only a yawning space where darkness shifted and congealed. But the space that was shifting darkness still held her fast; she looked down and saw a band of clotted dark around her arm, as if it had been eaten. Somehow this was more horrible than anything else had been.

Frantically she yanked herself backward, but the sorcerer's grip was too strong. A voice came out of the faceless dark: "Join me, little priestess. In Antaris, they spoke of you as a healer and a keeper of hives. Help me to heal Tremaris. Help me to bring order to the swarms."

"Never! I will never help you!"

"Why do you fight me, little one? We are the same, your Darrow and I, we both strive for the same end. Yet only one of us will succeed. There is only one Singer of All Songs, and I am stronger than he."

"You're lying!" gasped Calwyn. "Darrow doesn't want to be Singer of All Songs, he has no wish to be emperor of — of anywhere —"

The wavering dark resolved itself, as if the surface of the water became still; once again Darrow's face was gazing at her, quizzical, affectionate, and it was his voice that spoke to her. "Why, little one! It was my own idea to collect the Nine Powers. It was only when I realized that Samis's gifts were greater than my own — far greater — that I turned against him. Make no mistake, beneath my soft words, I have the same ambition I have always had."

"It's not true!" cried Calwyn, and in desperation she began to sing a chantment, a song of icy cold to wrap about the hand that held her, a song to chill him to the bone. It should have made him drop her wrist in an instant.

A look of pained bewilderment crossed the face that was, and was not, Darrow's. "Little one, Calwyn, my heart, surely you don't mean to hurt me?" He didn't seem to feel her chantment any more than the pricking of a thistle; his clutch on her arm was tighter than ever. Calwyn sang on, but her voice was shrill with fear, the magic feeble. Wildly she kicked out, lashed out with her free hand, thrashed in his grasp like a roancat. She heard a snarl of chantment and felt her clothes drag on her like lead, pressing her inexorably to the ground. She screamed, "Trout! *Help me!*"

And then several things happened very quickly. Trout snatched up a spool of wire and hurled it toward Samis's head. The sorcerer at once raised a hand to ward it off and growled out a note of chantment. The spool halted in midair, then crashed to the ground; but he had loosened his grip on Calwyn's wrist, and his attention was distracted. It was only for a heartbeat, but that was all she needed. Instantly she threw herself onto the Clarion, seizing it with both hands and wresting it from the sorcerer's grasp, then she dived for the still-open doorway, clutching the little horn to her chest. Trout followed her, slamming the door behind them.

Quickly, quickly, fighting for breath, Calwyn launched into a chantment to block the doorway with a wall of ice, the same song they used in Antaris to build the great Wall. Her voice wavered; the spell would not hold. She was too weak, too slow.

And then all at once she felt it come right. All the notes of the song fitted smoothly together as they should, and the chantment was strong. The thin crust of ice might not stop him for long, but it would buy them a little time.

She grabbed Trout by the shoulders. "We must get away from here!"

"But it's curfew. Can't you hear the bells?" A steady, deafening clang pealed out from the bell tower above their heads. "We can't go out now. The guards —"

"We must go!" Calwyn cried. "Curfew or no curfew."

"Hold on! I don't like to see someone trying to kiss a girl when the girl doesn't want to be kissed. That's one thing. But breaking curfew —" He shook his head helplessly.

"Kiss me? Is that what you think? If we stay here, then you'll see him kill me!"

Trout stood in an agony of indecision, shifting from one foot to the other. At last he said, "All right, this way," and started to run along the high wall back toward the gate through which they'd entered.

"No, no." Calwyn caught at his sleeve. "We must get to the river. We must find a boat." If they could get back to the port, back to *Fledgewing*, they might be safe until the others returned. "Is there a quicker way out?"

Trout spun on his heel, then plunged off in another direction, toward the mass of buildings that made up the bulk of the college. Calwyn followed, tucking the little Clarion inside her shirt; she felt it glowing and warm next to her skin, like a living creature. Dodging through arched gateways, across courtyards, Trout led her through a bewildering maze of buildings and corridors, almost colliding with other students as they ran. "Hi, Trout! Careful there!"

"What's he up to now?"

"Who's that with him? Is that a *girl*?"

"Where are your wheels, Trout?" one boy shouted after them, but Trout had no breath to answer him.

At last they came to one of the low ironwork gates in the wall. "Through here," Trout gasped, thrusting Calwyn through it. Night had truly fallen; they emerged onto a darkened street, so narrow between the dark college walls that the moons couldn't light it.

"We must get to the river," urged Calwyn. "I saw boats by the bridge, near where you crashed your machine."

"I didn't crash it," said Trout indignantly. "The mechanism failed."

But Calwyn's sharp ears had picked up the sound of the river, and she was already running toward it. And then she heard another faint sound, weaving through the bells: a rumbling, menacing noise that drew closer and closer. Trout stopped and stared up at the darkening sky. "Can that be thunder?"

"No, it's Samis!" cried Calwyn, tugging him onward. "It's chantment."

"But —" Trout wanted to argue with her even now, but at the next moment a slate crashed down into the street from the roof high above, then another and another, until sharp-edged slates and tiles were raining down all around them.

"The river! We'll be safer by the river!" Calwyn gasped. Dodging the deadly hail as best they could, their hands over their heads, they stumbled onward, until at last they came out onto the green ribbon of gardens that flanked the river. Heaving for breath, Trout halted, listening. Calwyn could hear the noise of distant shouts and other heavy feet on the cobbles.

"You see? The guards are coming!" hissed Trout accusingly. "We're breaking curfew. They could expel me from the college for this!"

"Expel you!" snorted Calwyn. "That's the least of your troubles." She rubbed her elbow where a falling slate had struck her, while she caught her breath. Then she threw back her head — she'd lost Xanni's cap long ago — and began to sing, clear and loud and true. Her voice rang out across the town as she sang up a film of slippery ice to cover the cobbles of the narrow streets.

"What are you *doing?*" cried Trout. "This is no time to start *singing!*"

Calwyn broke off her chantment. "Find a boat! And hurry!" She could hear shouts of dismay and clattering thuds from the streets as the guards began to tumble, their feet sliding from under them. But ice on the streets wouldn't slow Samis for long. She had another idea. Drawing in a deep breath, she began a different chantment, this time to seal off the narrow streets with walls of ice, just as she had blocked the door of the workshop, so that the guards and Samis would be prevented from reaching the river. But she could only sing up one wall at a time, and it was impossible to tell where the greatest danger lay. Where was Trout with that boat?

There was shouting and clamor now all over the town as people rushed out of the colleges to see what the commotion was, the sound of running footsteps, the sound of bodies crashing down, cries of rage and fright and pain. *People will be hurt.* Calwyn faltered in her song, the Clarion burning next to her skin like a warning. She knew that this was not the way. She didn't know what else to do; she could have wept. Calwyn held out her hands imploringly to the moonlight, "Help me, Taris, Mother of the Dark!" And then she began singing once more, because she had nothing else. She sang up a storm of snow out of the clear sky, and she was sobbing as she sang.

Samis was coming closer. Through all the tumult, and the sound of her own chantment, she could still distinguish the background roar of his voice. Then she saw that the grass beneath her feet, the whole green length of the riverbank, was rising and falling, in small ripples at first, then in great unsteady dips and troughs like the undulations of a sea serpent. The spreading spander trees tilted and tossed, lurching as the ground convulsed as if someone were shaking it out like a blanket. With a cry she put out her hands for balance, and staggered, and lost the thread of her song; with every wrench of the ground, her breath was jerked out of her.

Then she heard a most welcome sound, and an unexpected one: the sound of Xanni's laughter. It rang out from somewhere nearby, from the maze of black walls, clear and gleeful. He shouted, "You must try harder than this, O mighty sorcerer! I am a sailor, I have braved rougher seas than this one." And Calwyn saw him leap out from between the colleges onto the riverbank that billowed before her eyes, surefooted as a goat, and she caught her breath in an echo of his laugh. She knew then, even before she saw Darrow and Tonno following behind him, that this was not a true earthquake, only another spell of seeming. She closed her eyes and trusted the feel of the earth beneath her feet, and she felt the ground stop its shaking and become firm under her boots. Snow swirled in the air, brushing cold against her cheek, and for a moment it seemed that everything fell quiet around her while the Goddess gently touched her face.

From the river, she heard Trout call out in alarm. Her eyes flew open. A figure stood there, powerful, dark, and forbidding, shrouded in a cloak. Calwyn blinked, and a chill ran down her spine. Was that Darrow, or Samis? Her vision blurred. No, this must be Samis. For the first time, she could see his face. His features were strong, almost ugly, as if carved from a slab of stone: a beaked nose; a long, cruel mouth; a shaggy mane of gray hair that sprang back from a high, broad brow. He was perhaps ten years older than Darrow. Without realizing it, she began feverishly to rub her wrist where his fingers had clutched her, as if she could rub the bruises away. She shuddered as she remembered the heat of his breath on her cheek and the touch of his hand, like a loathsome animal, on her hair. How easily he'd deceived her.

And it was only at that moment that she realized how badly she'd wanted to be deceived, to believe that Darrow did care for her.

Samis was not far from Calwyn, but he was not looking at her. His dark, piercing eyes were turned toward the place on the riverbank where Darrow and Tonno and Xanni were standing, frozen still. Why were they standing there like statues? And then she saw why: a flash of steel in the sorcerer's hand.

Calwyn heard the shouts of the guards, blocked from the river by the walls of ice she had raised. From the corner of her eye she saw the dim shape of a rowing boat close to the bridge, and a figure awkwardly waving an oar.

The dark figure spoke. "With one breath I can sing this knife into the throat of any one of you."

Darrow took a step forward. "Let them go."

"Do you know, there is some part of me that is glad to see you here, my old friend." The steel glittered, and the ruby ring winked with a dull red light.

"So you can have the pleasure of killing me, which was denied to you in Antaris?" Darrow's voice was taut, not with fear, but with a bitter anger.

"Is that what you think of me? I assure you, it will not be a pleasure. Only a sad necessity. Do not force me to it."

Trout's thin and desperate cry came from the river. *"Cal — Calwyn!"* And Samis turned his head a little, as if the sound reminded him of something he had forgotten.

"Give me the Clarion." His hooded eyes, and his knife's aim, were still fixed on Darrow, but his words were for Calwyn. "Give me the Clarion, and I will let you all go, and keep the guards from following. We will prolong the hunt a little longer."

Calwyn's hand flew to the warm little Clarion nestled inside her shirt. It seemed to beat under her hand with its own life.

"You've surrendered to me once already, my dear; I know you will do so again. Quickly, now. We have no time to waste."

Darrow said sharply, "Calwyn? What is it you have?"

"It's nothing," she said. "It's just a little trumpet." Slowly she drew it out; the Clarion of the Flame glowed golden on her palm with its own soft fire. Darrow gave a cry. Samis sang out a note of command, and the Clarion lifted from her hand and spun across the space between them, faster and faster, until it was a flat disc of shining light, making its own eerie humming song. Calwyn could hear someone's sobbing breath and realized it was her own. The

Clarion paused, still spinning, just out of reach of Samis's out-stretched hand, like a bird too wild to settle on someone's finger. Samis grabbed and caught it and held it fast, though a wince of pain flickered across his face as though it had burned him. As his fingers closed, its brightness dimmed, and its eerie singing faded away, so that it was just an ordinary little trumpet, a child's toy, lying dully in his hand.

And then, quicker than Calwyn could comprehend, he sang another note from deep in his throat, swift and harsh, and the knife flew from his other hand, a lightning bolt shooting toward Darrow. Xanni cried out and threw himself forward, knocking Darrow to the ground. Calwyn screamed. Something whistled next to her ear, and then suddenly the air was thick with lances and arrows tipped with flame. The patrols had broken through, the guards were upon them, shouting and hurling their weapons. Samis whirled around, lifting his hands, and sang out strongly, and the weapons twisted in midair and began to rain down on those who had thrown them.

"The boat, get to the boat!" cried Calwyn, shielding her head with her arms; she could see the others stumbling toward the river. She reached the rowing boat before them. Trout yanked her aboard and reached for the oars, but Calwyn stopped him. "No, wait — my friends —"

"We must go *now!*" Trout cried. But Tonno was there, hauling himself into the wildly rocking boat, dragging Darrow and Xanni after him. Darrow seized one of the oars from Trout and pushed him aside. Some of the guards ran up to the bank; one lifted his arm and hurled his lance, just missing Trout, who gave a moan of fright and threw himself backward so violently that he almost tumbled overboard.

"Keep *down!*" Tonno shouted, grabbing the second oar. At once he and Darrow splashed the oars into the water, unevenly at first, then with a smoother, stronger stroke, swaying forward and back in a desperate rhythm, sweat starting on their brows. If Darrow's foot was weak, there was nothing the matter with his arms, and he could pull on the oars as strongly as Tonno. They drew away from the riverbank into the current, moving downstream.

Somewhere there was a whistle, then a splash. The same noise was repeated several times before Calwyn realized what it was; more of the guards on the bank were flinging their long sharp lances at the boat. But none of them hit their mark, and thanks to Darrow's and Tonno's steady pulling at the oars, the little boat moved away faster than the flying weapons. She strained to see what had become of Samis; she couldn't hear his chantment any longer. Perhaps he had hidden himself in a cloak of darkness, as he had that night in Antaris, and stolen away to gloat over his prize — A sob broke from her throat.

"Calwyn!" said Darrow sharply. "Look to Xanni."

She turned around, startled, and saw that Xanni was crumpled in the bottom of the boat.

"Xanni?" She knelt beside him. "What is it, what's wrong?"

But she could see for herself in the bright moonlight the hilt of Samis's knife, and the dark sticky patch spreading at his side.

"Don't pull it out!" Tonno barked. "It'll bleed worse." Sweat streamed down his face as he yanked fiercely at the oars.

"I can slow the bleeding," said Calwyn. How she wished she had stayed longer in the infirmary to learn all Ursca's arts! But at least she'd learned enough to be some use. Xanni was groaning softly, his face pale and his eyes squeezed closed as he leaned against the side of the boat. Calwyn touched his shoulder. "Xanni, I'm going to sing a chantment to make you cold. It will help stop the bleeding, it will help you." He didn't answer her. She touched her hand to the wound and softly began the chantment.

Only once she lifted her head and shouted to Trout, who was crouched at the front of the boat. "Quickly, Trout, give me your shirt!"

Grimly, silently, Darrow and Tonno hauled at the oars, watching her as she tore Trout's shirt into strips. All the while she kept up the quiet chantment, as Xanni's skin grew colder to her touch.

Trout said, "Let me row for a while. I know how to do it."

He scrambled forward to take Tonno's place while Tonno knelt by his brother, cradling the curly head in his lap. "Easy, easy. We'll have you back on *Fledgewing* before you know it." He looked up at Calwyn. "Why is he so cold? You'll have him halfway to death. He's hardly breathing — we should warm him."

"That's not the way." Calwyn grasped the knife and gently

eased it out of the wound. "See, his heart has slowed, the bleeding is less. This is what we always do in Antaris." As deftly as she could, she washed Xanni's wound and bound it, but her hands were trembling.

Tonno struck her hands away from him. "I want none of your witch's craft near my brother!"

"Let her be, Tonno!" Darrow's face was pale and grim. "It was their witches' craft that saved me. Perhaps she can save Xanni too."

For a long moment Tonno and Calwyn stared at each other, then Tonno dropped his head, and Calwyn began her chantment once again, with a voice that shook at first, then steadied.

Darrow said, "We must have a lookout, or we will go into the bank. Tonno, you had better come back to the oar. You, what's your name? Trout, into the bow and keep watch."

Clumsily Tonno made his way to the center of the boat, and soon he was straining on the oars.

Trout pushed past him to the bow. He stared down the river, the silver path down which they were slipping, not quickly enough, toward the sea. "Pull harder, there's a fallen tree on the port side. No, not so hard." And then, "Hard to starboard."

Calwyn cradled Xanni's head. She remembered him sitting on the cabin roof of *Fledgewing* in the sun, teaching her the difference between port and starboard and laughing at her when she got it wrong. She blinked hard, then laid her hand across his cool brow.

"Rocks ahead," Trout called. "Easy there."

And all the while, beneath the soft murmuring of Calwyn's chantment, there came the long, groaning breaths of Xanni.

The journey downriver to Mithates Port was a far quicker one than the journey up the road had been, but it seemed to take longer. They couldn't pause at their rowing, for every moment they gained now would help their chances of escaping the port before Samis could follow them. Calwyn took her turn at the oars, though her arms were even weaker than Trout's. The scorched and blighted lands slid by in the quiet dark, on and on, until at last the river broadened, and they came shooting out into the mouth of the Amith and the little harbor.

They didn't bother to fetch their own dinghy; all anyone could think of was getting Xanni safely aboard *Fledgewing*. Darrow took both oars, and the rowing boat flew across the bay. Together Tonno and Darrow lifted Xanni aboard and carried him below, with Calwyn hurrying behind them.

Afterward, Calwyn tried not to remember the terrible night that followed. While she stayed below with Xanni, she was aware from the noises overhead that the others were hauling the rowing boat aboard, casting off and hoisting sail, and then she knew that *Fledgewing* was moving once more toward the open sea.

But these things were a dim background. The whole world had shrunk to the cabin and the bunk on which Xanni lay. She did everything she could think of to ease his pain, using honey and what herbs and healing potions she could find to dress his wound, as well as her chantments to cool his body as Ursca had taught her. But though the flow of blood slowed, she couldn't stop it altogether. She laid cold poultices around the wound to numb his pain. From time to time he seemed to look at her and almost smile, and once he touched her sleeve — the sleeve of his own shirt, which she had borrowed — and she thought that he winked at her in the old way, sharing the joke of her disguise. Tonno came below to sit with his brother, and took his hand, and talked to him, and Xanni seemed to hear him and squeezed his hand. Then Tonno had to go above to see to the ship, for although Trout knew how to row, he was no sailor, and Darrow couldn't sail *Fledgewing* alone.

Calwyn didn't know how long she sat beside Xanni, cooling his forehead and holding his hand. As well as the chantments, she sang him songs of the bees and lullabies from the House of Mothers, far away in Antaris. Presently, after *Fledgewing* had been sailing hard for some time, Darrow let himself quietly into the cabin.

Calwyn looked up. "I've done everything I can. I wish I had the craft of healing."

"I fear it may take more than craft." He touched the bandage lightly with his finger. His voice was grim, and he would not meet her eyes.

Calwyn said, "Do you think Samis will follow us?"

"I know not, and I care not," said Darrow sharply. He put his hand to his eyes for a moment. Then he said, a little more gently, "Take a watch above. I will sit with Xanni awhile."

In the doorway, she turned back. "I saw him. In Mithates. Before — before the river. He came after the Clarion. He — I thought he was you."

Darrow stared at her. "Samis spoke to you in my guise?"

She nodded. "He — he touched me —"

"He hurt you?" The question cracked like a whiplash.

Dumbly she shook her head. Xanni groaned softly, and Darrow turned back to lay a hand on his brow. His voice turned cold. "It is the hardest trick of seeming, to take another's face and voice, and stand before one who knows them well, keeping up the chantment all the while. He will be exhausted from it. That explains why he has not pursued us, even with the Clarion. He will need to rest. Hide and rest."

Hesitantly she said, "He told me — he said that it was *your* idea to collect the Nine Powers, that you wanted to become the Singer of All Songs. It's not true, is it?"

"By all the gods, Calwyn! This is not the time for such questions. Go now, leave us in peace!"

Alone in the cabin, Calwyn pressed her trembling hands flat on the table until the knuckles showed white. She hadn't realized how much she cared for Darrow. Samis had guessed it; she'd given herself away the moment she flew across the workshop into his arms. Now Darrow despised her, and no wonder. She was weak; she'd let

Samis trick her, she'd lost the Clarion, and Xanni . . . She swallowed hard.

When she climbed stiffly up onto the deck, she was surprised, in a dull kind of way, to see the faint haze of dawn beginning to lighten the sky. They were well away from Mithates Port, sailing east across the Bay of Sardi, toward the sunrise. She saw a blackened arrow sticking out of the cabin roof and another near the prow; the archers in the watchtowers must have fired at them, and she hadn't even known it. Tonno was at the tiller. He called her over. "Hold her steady. I'm going below. Keep her so that the flag points that way, and the sail like that."

At any other time, Calwyn would have been excited to take the tiller, especially with no one to watch over her, but now she hardly cared. There was no land for her to run into, after all. And she found that it was not so hard to hold the tiller firm and let the wind run the boat lightly over the waves.

Trout made his way toward her, holding on to the edge of the cabin roof and looking rather green beneath his freckles. Gingerly he took a seat beside her.

"Are you all right?"

"Seasick," he said briefly, and turned his head to let the wind blow full in his face for a moment. Then he said, "How is your friend?"

Calwyn tried to answer, but she found that she couldn't. Trout hesitated for a moment, then put his hand on her arm. "I'm sorry."

Calwyn nodded and blinked, gripping the tiller hard. There was a line of light now all along the horizon, and the white sail of *Fledgewing* shone with a pearly luster. She saw Darrow come up from below, a dark silhouette against the dawn, and make his way to the railing. He stood there for a time, not moving, with his face turned away from them. It was growing lighter all the time. The three moons still rode high among the few stars that remained, three pale globes in the pallid sky. The time of the Spilled Cup: one half-moon tipped over sideways, and the other two, small and clear and round, like droplets of liquid pouring out, frozen midway to the horizon, not yet fallen to the earth. Not yet, not yet.

Then she saw Tonno's head emerge from the cabin. She saw him pause at the top of the steps, at the place where he often sat to smoke his pipe, and then walk unsteadily to where Darrow stood by the rail. She saw Darrow turn, and Tonno speak, and then she saw Darrow lift his arm and grip his friend about his broad shoulders, while Tonno bent his head and wept.

Suddenly she found that blinking was no longer enough. But she couldn't let go of the tiller. She had to keep on steering, and so she gripped with both hands to keep *Fledgewing* steady on its course. She couldn't see the sail, or which way the little flag waved at the tip of the mast. But it hardly seemed to matter now which way they went. She just kept her face turned toward the light, and the nose of *Fledgewing* pointing eastward, sailing on and on through a mist of tears, blindly toward the sunrise.

The Troubled Sea

"I want to go home," said Trout.

He wouldn't meet Darrow's eyes, or Calwyn's, but stared obstinately down at the tabletop, where the remains of their last meal lay scattered. Since the morning that Xanni's white-wrapped body had slipped quietly beneath the green waves, no one had cared about tidying anything away. Tonno was not down in the cabin, but up on deck, steering through the night. He preferred it; he would not speak to anyone, but stood at the tiller, alone with his ship and the wild sea and the stars.

"It is no use bleating on the same refrain like a nanny goat," said Darrow impatiently. "How many times have I told you, we cannot take you back. Your life is forfeit to Samis as much as ours."

Trout turned a cup one way, then another. "You say he's your enemy. All right. I'm from Mithates, I understand hatred, I understand enemies. But his quarrel is with you. Why should he care about me?"

"Because you helped us!" Calwyn leaned across the table.

"Surely you can see that we can't turn back. We can't risk meeting him. *You* can't risk meeting him."

"You have defied him," said Darrow wearily. This was not the first time he and Trout had had this argument. "Samis will not let defiance go unpunished. That is one way to protect his power. Do you understand me?"

"No," said Trout. His mouth was a stubborn line. "I haven't seen anything of this *power* of his, I don't believe he has any *power*. I must get back to my studies. If I'm away too long, I'll fail the whole term. I'm going to be in trouble enough as it is, consorting with foreigners without the Masters' authority."

"How can you say that you haven't seen Samis's powers?" exclaimed Calwyn. "You were in the workshop when he changed his face. He stopped your mouth with your own shirt! And you were on the river when he made the ground seem to shake like an earthquake."

"I didn't see anything like that," said Trout, blinking his blue eyes behind his lenses. "All I saw in the workshop was an old man forcing himself on you. Not nice, but not magic. I got a mouthful of my collar in the dark. So what? And on the river I was busy managing the boat so you and your friends could run away, which you haven't thanked me for, by the way. I don't believe in these crafts you're always talking about, these *chantments* of yours."

"You need not believe in chantment to know yourself in danger," said Darrow. "It was cold steel, not magic, that killed Xanni."

There was a small silence. The timbers of *Fledgewing* creaked softly, and there came a faint, irregular murmuring from the waves creaming along the prow. Calwyn swallowed hard. Even now it was hard to believe that Xanni wasn't leaping about on the deck, that he wouldn't come whistling down the ladder at any moment. She swept some crumbs into a little pile with her hand and stirred them with her finger.

After a pause, Trout said, "Anyway, he will have left Mithates by now. He's got the little horn. You said that was what he wanted."

Abruptly Darrow got to his feet, knocking a spoon onto the floor, and limped up the steps to the deck. Trout stared resentfully after him. "I helped you," he said accusingly to Calwyn. "You said so yourself. I helped you, and now you won't help me. Take me back. *He* won't be there anymore. There's no reason not to take me back."

"It's too dangerous now," said Calwyn. "We can't go back yet. Not until —" She stopped. Until what? Their quest, which had been so urgent, seemed all but abandoned. Day after day, night after night, they sailed on to the east, but when Calwyn asked Tonno if they were heading back to Kalysons, he said nothing, but shook his head so fiercely that she didn't dare speak to him again.

Now Trout turned her own question back to her. "Then where are we going?"

"I don't know," said Calwyn sadly. "It makes no difference."

"It makes a difference to me," said Trout, and he went down to his bunk and yanked the curtain behind him.

Calwyn looked at the mess on the table, but there seemed no point in clearing it away. It would be time for breakfast soon enough. Why go to the trouble of putting everything into the lockers when they would just have to take it all out again? In any case, they weren't eating together, and no one was cooking proper meals; each of them took food when they pleased, and half the time ate it in their hands, on the deck. Dully she got up and shut herself in her little cabin in the bow and lay down on her bunk. She ought to practice her breathing exercises; the last time she'd gone through the nightly ritual was when she was alone on *Fledgewing* at Mithates Port, waiting for the others to return.

And that thought was enough to set off the accusing voice inside her mind. She never should have left the boat, never gone ashore, never met Trout or found the Clarion, never let Samis deceive her, never tried to fight him, never started the commotion that brought Darrow and Tonno and Xanni running into the streets. If she'd let Samis have the Clarion from the beginning, Xanni might be here now, clattering dinner dishes in the bucket.

Her heart was sore with misery and homesickness. She missed the sound of the bees in the hives. She missed the cold air of the mountains and the changing colors of the snowy peaks at sunrise and sunset. She missed Marna's hand on her hair and the echo of the sisters' singing in the great hall. She whispered into her pillow, just as Trout had done, *"I want to go home."*

Now she would never be made a full priestess. When midwinter moondark came, the others would go to the sacred valley, where the cold, dark pool and the waterfall would be stilled by the chantment of the priestesses, turned to black ice beneath the black sky. The silver stars, seen clearly only when the three moons were all in shadow, would be sparkling like icicles. The bare branches of the blazetree would be thrusting upward, lit by the leaping flames of the bonfire on the shore, and the thread of the chantment would rise up too, thin and clear in the cold air, as the novices who were to be initiated set out one by one across the sheet of ice, each girl alone holding up the surface beneath her feet. If her lone chantment faltered, if the ice cracked, she would be plunged into the freezing water, in the dark, to drown. But if, by the will of the Goddess, she reached the other side, to embrace the frozen column of the waterfall and return to receive Marna's kiss, then she would step onto the shore again as a full priestess.

This winter it would have been Calwyn's turn to step out across the black ice. But now the others would go through the ritual without her. Would they remember her then? Would Marna be thinking of her?

She ought to comb out her tangled hair and plait it again. In a moment she would get up and look for a comb. But she didn't move. Presently she closed her eyes.

The next day she went to stand beside Darrow at the tiller. There was not much wind; he turned the rudder this way and that to catch the breeze in the sails. Calwyn watched him. "Can I take a turn?"

"No. This is not a task that you are ready for."

"Then teach me."

"I am in no mood for teaching," he said grimly.

Fighting her misery, Calwyn looked away. It was the time of the Fingernail and the Quartered Apple; the third moon was a fine sliver, so delicate and pale in the highest reach of the sky that it was almost invisible. These were the days, at the turn of the season between summer and autumn, when the apples ripened and hung heavy in the orchard, and all the sisters turned out to help the men pick them, the older women holding the baskets to catch the fruit that the novices let fall from the higher branches. There was always much giggling and hilarity on the days of the apple harvest, the one time when it was permitted to climb the trees of the orchard, though no one ever questioned how the little girls had learned to climb so expertly, when it was officially forbidden for the rest of the year.

Calwyn said, "Perhaps Trout's right. Perhaps we should take him home."

"This is Tonno's ship," said Darrow shortly. "He sets the course, not I."

"He would change course in an instant, if you asked him."

"I don't think Tonno is inclined to do anything I ask just at present. It was at my asking that we went to Mithates the first time. I hardly think he will agree to go back there."

"But we must go back sometime. You still have to find a chanter of fire."

"There are no chanters of fire," said Darrow, and his voice was filled with bitterness. "They are all gone, every one. We were there for long enough to make sure of that. The chantments are lost beyond recovery. The only thing left of all that body of magic is the Clarion of the Flame, and Samis has that now. There is nothing for us in Mithates."

Calwyn was silent, shocked. Then she asked, "Does that mean we're giving up the quest?"

"By the bones of Ceb'atroth! What quest can there be? He has ice, and fire, and iron, and tongue, and seeming. He was strong enough to persuade you, in Mithates, that he was me, and he touched you —" Darrow broke off and took one slow breath. "If he had hurt you —" He left the sentence unfinished, and Calwyn's face burned.

After a pause, Darrow went on. "Did you not hear him by the river? *Let us prolong the hunt a little longer.* It's a game to him. He is more than halfway to his goal. It is finished."

Calwyn's heart was pounding. She reached out a hand to Darrow, but he flinched as if her fingers were made of ice. "Halfway is not the whole way!" she cried. "He still has to find the Power of Beasts and the Power of Winds. And the Power of Becoming. You said that nobody knows the chantments for the Power of Becoming, or even what people were entrusted with them by the Ancient Ones. He'll never find them."

"Depend upon it, there is some land, some people, in some corner of Tremaris, where those secrets are known. And he will find them. He is like a hunting dog to the scent of magic. If the chantments are there to be found, he will find them. Or perhaps the Powers he has already will be enough to draw the others to him, like ants to honey."

Calwyn stamped her foot. "I think you *want* him to become the Singer of All Songs! Why don't you just go back and help him? Why are you giving up so easily?"

Darrow rounded on her. "I? I give up too easily? You are a fine one to make that charge, Daughter of Taris! You who handed over the Clarion, our last hope, without so much as a whimper. Did he win you over with his fine words and his princely manners? How dare you speak to me of giving up!"

"What was I supposed to do?" Calwyn shouted. "Do you forget the danger you were in? How could I have borne it if he had killed you?" The words almost choked her, but anger swept her on. "You should be thanking me for saving your life! How many times is that now? Three, or is it four?"

Darrow said nothing for a moment, staring ahead at the horizon. Then he turned his gray-green gaze to her. "I would rather you had let me perish four times over and saved Xanni just once."

A sob burst from Calwyn's throat. Groping blindly, she pushed her way past Tonno along the length of the boat to the prow, where she hung over the edge as far as she could, so that the fine spray from the waves splashed at her face, and she could no longer tell the difference between the salt of the sea and the salt from her own tears.

Presently she became aware that someone had lowered himself

to sit beside her, and then she felt a hand on her shoulder. Roughly she shrugged it away.

"I am sorry for what I said."

But she didn't answer, and after a few moments she heard Darrow struggle to his feet again and limp away.

That night she was woken by the sound of voices overhead: Tonno's angry rumbling and the plaintive squeak of Trout. Moonlight streamed in through the little porthole above her bunk; she had forced it open to let out some of the heat that built up in her small cabin during the day, and now snatches of Trout and Tonno's argument were carried in on the cool night wind. She lay still for a moment, listening: *not too late to turn around — listen to what a pipsqueak like you says — not my fault your brother —*

Calwyn heard Tonno spitting onto the deck, and then an inarticulate roaring and desperate shouts. She rolled off her bunk and headed out onto the deck, clutching at the rungs of the stepladder as *Fledgewing* swayed beneath her. The boat was pitching more violently than usual; at first she thought they must have caught a stronger wind, but once she was up on the deck she saw that Tonno and Trout were wrestling over control of the tiller. Trout must have caught Tonno off his guard, or he would never have got a hand to it, but now he struggled breathlessly to hang on, pale and frightened but utterly determined. Tonno's face distorted with rage as he tried to pry Trout's hands from the tiller, but Trout kicked out and winded him so that he doubled over gasping.

"Stop! Stop it!" cried Calwyn, running forward. The wind knocked her sideways; the moonlight dimmed as if a lantern had gone out, and she missed her footing on the plunging deck.

"Get away, lass!" Tonno bellowed, staggering toward Trout, who was hauling recklessly on the tiller, trying to turn back. But that meant sailing against the wind; the timbers screamed, and the canvas of the sails cracked like whips, and the boat tilted onto its side, so that Calwyn had to grab at the cabin wall to stop herself from falling.

"Trout!" Darrow's voice was quiet, but somehow they all heard it over the roar of the wind and the fierce slapping of the waves. He was balanced in the hatchway, swaying with the ship. "Let Tonno have the tiller."

"No!" Trout clutched at the tiller with both hands, his body bent over the shaft.

"Give him the tiller, or we will all be drowned. There is a storm rising."

Calwyn looked up. One by one the stars were being eaten up by darkness; clouds gathered swiftly, blotting out the moons and the spangled sky. It was true. A storm was rising all around them, howling over the sea. She could hear someone's sobbing breath and realized it was Trout. His head was lowered, the bright discs of his lenses suddenly darkened. Calwyn heard herself whisper in agony, *oh be quick, be quick!* There was a distant, low rumbling of thunder, and she felt the first splashes of rain on her cheek.

"Come, Trout, be sensible." Darrow's voice was as calm and

unhurried as if Trout had the whole night to consider his answer, as if *Fledgewing* were not leaping up and down against the waves like a goat bucking on a mountain track. "If you wish, we can put you ashore at the next land we come to, and you can make your way back to Mithates."

"Aye, and perhaps we'll put you ashore too!" shouted Tonno, turning on Darrow suddenly. "You and your accursed chantments! Or mebbe I should put you overboard now and let you swim back to Merithuros where you came from."

"Tonno, *stop it!*" screamed Calwyn. "In the name of the Goddess, take care!"

Abruptly Trout let go of the tiller. At once *Fledgewing* twisted back under the force of the wind, and they all staggered. Trout fell to his knees and began to crawl back toward the hatchway, one hand blindly shielding his lenses from the rain that splashed down now in earnest on the deck. Tonno leaped for the tiller and bawled after Trout, "*Boy!* Stay on deck! We need all hands now!"

"Trout, Calwyn, with me." Darrow was still astonishingly calm. "Help me trim the sail."

Calwyn hauled on the ropes as Darrow directed her and fastened them as she'd been shown. Across the deck she could see Trout doing the same. For all their quarreling, now they must work together, like it or not. The mainsail was growing smaller and smaller, giving the wind less canvas to catch, and *Fledgewing* bucked less violently before the storm. Calwyn could sense how the tiller had eased under Tonno's big, sure hands. The boat moved more smoothly, but fast, so fast, through the water. The rain was driving down hard on her back and streamed into her eyes. Then Calwyn heard a noise she hadn't heard for many days: the deep, uneven boom of the sea crashing against rocks, somewhere ahead on the port side. She yelled out to Darrow, "Land ahead!"

"We are at the Mouth," he shouted back.

She nodded to show that she had understood, her hands still busy trying to fasten down the many tie points that held the sail in place, her fingers slippery and clumsy with the rain and the deck unsteady beneath her feet. Xanni had told her about the Mouth — it seemed a lifetime ago — the place where the Bay of Sardi joined the wide Great Sea beyond. It was a narrow and dangerous gap, flanked by cliffs, and the strait between them was dotted with treacherous rocks that sailors called the Teeth. Some of them thrust high above the water, but others lurked just below the waves. She glanced up, squinting against the rain, and saw one of the rocks slide past, silent and sinister, looming up out of the dark then vanishing once more. It was so close she could have touched it with her hand. But there was no time to feel frightened; already Darrow was calling to her to help him batten down the cabin where the water was getting in. She remembered with a pang that she had left open the porthole in her cabin too. All her bedding, all her clothes, would be drenched and damaged.

As she and Darrow struggled with the hatchway, she put her mouth close to his ear and yelled, "Will we be past the Mouth soon?"

"Not past," he shouted. "Through."

Calwyn gaped at him. "Into the Great Sea?"

He couldn't have heard, but he saw the movement of her lips and gave a nod. Then he was gone, hauling himself along the tilted deck to where Trout was struggling to stow some ropes that jumped and slithered from his grasp as though they were alive. Another of the great, sharp rocks loomed up out of the dark, then another; Tonno's face as he hung on to the tiller was set with a scowl of grim concentration. The storm was too strong for them to do anything but let it drive them through the Mouth. Tonno and Xanni had gone through the Mouth before; she had heard them speak of their voyage north to Nesca and Liminis, as far as Gellan. But they had only done it once before, and that was not in a storm, and not in darkness.

Suddenly *Fledgewing* was climbing a sheer cliff of water, flecked with white foam, rearing up and up; then they dived down the other side, skidding into a glassy chasm. Without warning, something smacked Calwyn off her feet and sent her sprawling to the deck, the breath knocked out of her. Helplessly she slid toward the edge of the boat and the yawning abyss of the waves, desperately scrabbling for something, anything, to cling to. But now *Fledgewing* rolled the other way, and she slithered back, cracking her head on the cabin wall, dazed and drenched and sobbing for breath. Tonno shouted at her to get up, to make herself fast, but she could only clutch the cabin railing as the next wave threw itself onto them. Above the scream of the storm there came the most terrifying sound of all: a tremendous creaking groan, louder than the nearest thunder, a noise that made the whole boat shudder from bow to stern. Calwyn heard Trout shriek, then the terrible *crack* as the mast snapped in two and crashed down onto the deck in a tangle of wet canvas and ropes. And then everything was chaos.

When the storm cleared, it was morning and they were adrift on the Great Sea. It had been morning for a long time, behind the clouds and rain, without their noticing. But now they were able to see exactly what damage had been done to *Fledgewing*, and to each other.

The top half of the mast was gone. There was a great gap in the coaming where it had crashed down, half-on and half-off the deck. With the mast had gone the mainsail, cut free and then washed overboard in the desperate panic to clear the Teeth. Trout had a gash on his forehead where he had been struck by flying debris. The others were all bruised and battered to varying degrees, and Tonno had difficulty breathing after a crack that had broken at least one of his ribs. But the greatest catastrophe was the loss of the mast. Until they reached land, and land where tall trees grew, they had no way to repair it. With the big sail gone, they could still limp along, but it would be all but impossible to turn and sail against the winds and the currents, back toward the Bay of Sardi.

Down in the cabin, Darrow and Tonno debated in low, fierce voices. No one had even begun to clear up the mess belowdecks; if everything had been properly stowed away in the lockers, it would not have been so bad, but food and plates and cups and clothing had been flung about and trampled in the confusion of the storm.

Darrow knocked a stump of candle from the bottom of his boot and hurled it across the cabin. "We must have a new mast. Without it, we are drifting, as good as helpless."

Tonno shook his head. "We must turn back to the west, try to run into the headlands of Kalysons."

"That will take too long. And even if we reach the cape, the currents are too swift there, we will never be able to land. Better to keep going east. We are bound to come across the Isles of Doryus before long."

"Finding the Isles is like finding one grain of sand hidden on a beach! I don't know these waters. We must go back," insisted Tonno.

"I have sailed this sea before, and I tell you the Isles are strung out across the Eastern Sea like the beads of a necklace."

"But who's to say we're in the Eastern Sea? By now we might have been swept into the Southern Straits, or even the Outer Sea."

"That's absurd —"

"Who's the sailor here, you or I?"

Back and forth they argued, while Trout and Calwyn sat up on deck, one on either side of the tiller. Calwyn grasped it firmly; it made little difference to the direction they drifted, but at least she felt as though she were doing something. She had no wish to join Darrow and Tonno's dispute. The brief truce of the storm had dissolved again; everyone was quarreling, worse than ever.

"Why don't we turn back?" said Trout. "We can't go on drifting like this, in the open sea."

"The current won't let us turn back. We have no choice but to go on."

"Go on into what?" Trout waved his hand at the vast expanse of empty ocean.

Calwyn didn't answer; she had no answer to give. She didn't know what lay ahead. Perhaps they would go on and on forever into the wastes of the sea, never touching land, until they starved or died of thirst, helpless and drifting. She tightened her grip on the tiller. "Darrow and Tonno will find a way."

"Your *chantments* don't seem to be much help to you now," said Trout gloomily, but with a trace of smugness.

"The ocean's too deep here for Darrow to use his powers," said Calwyn shortly. She had been racking her brain all day long for some way to use her own arts to aid them. But she could think of nothing.

"We could take what's left of the mast and splice it in half. Except it wouldn't be strong enough to hold up the sails. Or we could make a pair of giant oars. If we had anything to make oars with. Or we could catch a sea serpent, and it could tow us to land." Trout whipped off his lenses and polished them on his shirt, as he often did when he was agitated.

"Have you suggested any of these things to Tonno?" Calwyn could imagine his reaction.

"I *think* he was quite impressed with the idea about the sea serpent."

"How do you think we'd catch one?"

"I'm not sure, what do they eat?"

"People," growled Tonno, coming to take the tiller. "Why don't we tie a bit of rope around you and try some fishing?"

"Very funny," said Trout, but he edged away. Calwyn laughed; it was a long time since she'd laughed, and it was a long time before she laughed again.

Day after day they drifted on, caught in the swift currents around the cape of Kalysons, carpeted with farms and orchards and clear streams, all out of their sight and out of their reach. Sooner or later those same currents would fling them out into the unknown reaches of the Great Sea; they might carry them north toward the Isles of Doryus, as Darrow predicted, or farther south, toward Merithuros, as Tonno feared. *Fledgewing* was a little fishing boat, not built for long ocean voyages. The water barrels were full, but their food was running low.

The farther south they sailed, the hotter it became, as if they were drifting deeper into summer, even though by the reckoning of the moons they should have been feeling the first chills of autumn. Down in the cabin, the air was stifling. Calwyn took to sleeping on the deck, propped against a coil of rope; but Tonno grumbled that she was getting in the way and drove her below again, where she lay hot and sleepless and resentful, wondering what was to become of them all.

Tonno cast his nets over the side and managed to catch some fish, to eke out their food a little longer. They were not the sweet, fat fish that lived in the Bay of Sardi, but tough, lean fish that dwelled in the depths and tasted strongly of the ocean. Every day Darrow stood at the prow, trying his powers in the hope that he would be able to bring them closer to some shore. But every day he turned away with a bowed head. Every night Tonno stared up at the sky and tried to judge their position from the wheeling of the stars, and calculate how far they had come since the day before. It was never a great distance. Then each of them would turn away, retreating to their own private corner of the boat, so that the others would not see their despair.

"There must be a way," said Trout. "Can't we take the dinghy and row to land?"

But Darrow shook his head. "We are not near enough to the shore to try it. The risk is too great."

"But the risk now is that we'll go on drifting forever!"

"The Goddess will watch over us," said Calwyn.

"You and your goddess! I can see how carefully she watches," said Trout. "Since I came, there's been a wrecked ship, broken bones, soldiers chasing us. And your friend is dead."

At that Tonno stood up and walked away to inspect his nets.

"Unless you have something helpful to say, will you hold your tongue?" hissed Calwyn.

"And unless you can say something sensible, will you hold yours?"

"Peace, both of you!" Darrow looked up irritably. "We have troubles enough without quarreling."

"And yet you and Tonno spend more time quarreling than any of us," said Calwyn bitterly.

That very day, Trout began work on a device. He took a spare pair of lenses, slid them out of their wire frame, and fixed them one at either end of a narrow tube, which he held to his eye. "It's not as powerful as the one I made in my workshop in Mithates," he said, showing it to Darrow. "But it's better than the plain eye. Not *my* plain eye," he added. "My vision's no better than a mole's. But Calwyn's eyes are sharp. With this she could see land, or a ship approaching, long before the rest of us."

It became Calwyn's task to scan the horizon all day long, until she felt her eyes blur and she feared she'd become as shortsighted as Trout. But it was not until the third day after Trout had made the looking-tube that she finally spied something. "I think — I think I see a sail." She lowered the tube and blinked doubtfully toward the north.

Tonno grabbed the tube. "You're right," he said after a moment. "A square sail — two square sails."

"Two ships?"

"No, one ship with two masts. A large vessel, indeed. No ship that sails the Bay of Sardi is large enough to carry such weight of canvas. This is an ocean traveler, no fishing boat."

"Merithuran?" said Darrow quietly at his side.

Tonno shook his head. "Can't tell from its markings. But where else would it be coming from?"

"Most likely a trader, heading for Gellan."

"Will they help us?" asked Calwyn eagerly.

"If we can offer them something they value, we might bargain for a tow into the nearest port."

"They might take me with them," said Trout. "They might give me passage back to Mithates."

"They might take you as far as Keld," said Tonno. "But the Merithuran traders don't bother entering the Bay of Sardi."

"Keld would be close enough for me," said Trout fervently.

It seemed to take a very long time for the ship to come into view. "What if they can't see us?" said Calwyn, almost in agony. "I'm sure *they* have no looking-tube." And for a while it did seem that the other ship would sail past, oblivious to their plight. But at last the white squares of canvas became clearly visible on the horizon.

"They see us," said Darrow at last. "They've shifted their heading."

"Merithuran." Tonno slapped his hand on the railing. "No doubt of it. Look at the shape of her."

Now Calwyn could see the high-tiered decks of the other ship and make out the tiny figures of its crew swarming up and down in the rigging.

"A trader, carrying cargo in the hold, gold and silver and iron from the mines of Geel and Phain," said Darrow. "They'll fill with grain in Gellan and sail back again."

Trout was waving his arm in wide sweeps. "They can see me! They're waving back!"

"How can we be sure that they'll help us?" Now, when it was too late, Calwyn was struck with sudden doubt. "How do we know we can trust them?"

"Things are different at sea, lass." Tonno gave her a slightly scornful look. "Sailors help one another."

"For a price," said Darrow. "For a price."

Before long the huge ship hove to nearby, towering above them. The crew were dressed in short, ragged trousers, with bare feet, and wore close-fitting striped caps in different bright colors. Their skin was tanned brown, and their hair, where it stuck out from under the caps, was stiff and straw-colored, bleached by the sun. "Not Merithuran," said Darrow quietly at Calwyn's side. "Doryan. A Merithuran ship with a Doryan crew."

"They're lowering a boat!" Trout hopped from foot to foot with excitement.

Half a dozen sailors rowed rapidly toward them. One man in the dinghy did no rowing. His hair hung in a long, oiled plait down the back of his green coat, and there was a flash of gold at his throat and his wrists. "That'll be the captain," said Tonno.

At a word, the rowers shipped their oars, and the captain stood and hailed them. "Where are you bound?"

"North," called Tonno. "But swept off course by the cape-stream."

"Lost your mast?"

"In a bad storm at the Mouth, some nights back."

The captain's eyes flickered across them all as they stood in a row at the railing. *Like skittles*, thought Calwyn, with a sudden stab of unease. *Waiting to be knocked down.*

"What's your cargo?"

Tonno's eyes narrowed. "What's that to you?"

Trout gave a little anxious moan.

The captain raised a hand in appeasement. "I mean no offense to you or your crew. I'm only wondering what business a Sardi fishing boat might have out on the Great Sea."

Darrow stepped forward, and Calwyn saw him place a restraining hand on Tonno's sleeve. "We carry no cargo worth your notice. My friend takes me north on a voyage to visit my uncle, who lies dying in Gellan. I am anxious to be on my way with all haste. If you would be kind enough to tow us to the nearest land or port where we might replace our mast, then we will trouble you no further."

The captain was silent, stroking his beard. Calwyn could see threads of gold woven through the wispy hairs. He smiled, a wide, slow smile, and said abruptly, "Aye, we will take you under tow. Cast us a line and I will lend you one or two of my crew to help secure your craft to mine."

"I think not," said Tonno politely, though his big hands were clenched hard on the railing. "My crew is small, but we can manage whatever is needed."

"Ah," said the captain with equal politeness. "I fear I must disagree with you, my friend." And he swung around with a sudden roar: *"Seize them!"*

"Pirates!" shouted Tonno. "Ward off, for your life!" He whipped out the knife that always hung from his belt and brandished it with a fierce flourish. Already the crew of the other boat had drawn up close to the side of *Fledgewing* and were trying to clamber aboard. Darrow caught up a belaying pin and brought it down hard on the knuckles of any men who got a hand to the side of the boat. Calwyn made a desperate lunge over the edge, grasped hold of a wildly flailing oar, and swung it down, like Darrow, on the hands and heads of the boarding party. She saw Trout rush below, then stumble up on deck again, brandishing a saucepan in each hand. One of the pirates had managed to evade them all and had both hands and one foot over the gunwale. Calwyn gave him a sharp shove with the butt of the oar and sent him splashing into the waves below. But even as she turned to swing at the next invader, she was knocked off her feet, and the oar was wrested from her hands.

The crew of *Fledgewing* were outnumbered, and the invaders were strong and determined. One by one they were overpowered, their arms seized and bound behind them. Darrow was knocked into the edge of the cabin roof, staggered and fell, and lay unmoving on the deck. Too late, Calwyn opened her mouth to summon up her powers, but as if the pirates knew what she could do, a striped cap was thrust into her mouth and tied firmly in place to gag her. "None of your tricks, missy," hissed the sailor in her ear. Choking, her eyes smarting, she rolled over on the deck and saw Trout being wound around with ropes like a spindle wound with thread. Tonno held out the longest, sweeping his knife in broad arcs in front of him, but four of the Doryans, advancing slowly, backed him so far along the deck that his only choice was to dive overboard or submit. Even in this most desperate moment, he would never leave his ship; all four sprang at once and toppled him over. But Calwyn was savagely pleased to see through her tears that when they had finished trussing him up, each of them bore at least one bleeding cut from Tonno's knife.

The captain stood on the deck surveying the scene with evident satisfaction. "Easy as picking slava off the bush. And you say I make you work too hard!"

"The boat's worthless," complained the pirate whose cap was wedged in Calwyn's mouth. "A mastless, battered Sardi fishing boat. Not worth the trouble of towing her back to Doryus. Take whatever cargo they have, and the crew for slaves, and scuttle her where she sits."

The bound-up bundle that was Tonno gave a violent wriggle and a muffled roar of protest. The captain paid no more attention than if a wave had slapped against the side of the boat. "She's a neat enough little craft for shallow waters. With a new mast she'll do for an island fishing boat. I'll get a fair price for her." He nodded to the bareheaded sailor. "Throw the men below. You and two others stay aboard. I'll take the windworker back to our ship."

Calwyn watched the other three being half-kicked down the companionway. Then she was hoisted up over the shoulder of one of the pirates and unceremoniously dumped into the bottom of their dinghy. It was a long drop, and she bruised her knees and elbows in the fall. She managed to twist so that she could peer over the edge of the boat, and as it rose and fell with each stroke of the oars, she caught glimpses of *Fledgewing*, at first rising high above them, then moving farther and farther away. With a sinking heart she turned her head and saw the pirate ship on the other side, looming closer and closer.

At least they had not all been spitted on a pirate's sword. Not yet. But perhaps that might be preferable to being sold as slaves. *Windworker.* She pushed that thought aside and wondered how the others were faring. Tonno had seemed still lively enough, but Darrow was hurt. She didn't know what had become of Trout. Only that morning she had wished the others at the bottom of the ocean; now she longed to be back in the cabin of *Fledgewing* with them, tied up or not. All their futile squabbling seemed foolish beyond words. She felt she could have borne anything as long as they were all together — but here she was, alone. She might never see them again.

There was a soft bump at the side of the dinghy; the towering bulk of the pirates' ship blocked out the sun. One of the sailors looped a rope around her, and she was hauled aboard as carelessly as a sack of apples, smacking into the side of the ship with each heave of the rope. Dumped onto the deck, she fought to catch her breath. Someone said, "Another windworker. As much trouble as the other, no doubt," and spat on the deck beside her head. Then someone else hoisted her up and dragged her belowdecks, through a warren of close, stinking cabins, until she was finally shoved into one that seemed even smaller than the rest. She stumbled and fell, skidding across the floor until she fetched up with a bump against the far wall.

"Hey!" An indignant voice, a girl's voice, rang out above her head.

"A little friend for you. One of your kind," sneered the sailor who had dragged Calwyn there.

"This cabin ain't big enough for one, let alone two! You tell the captain —"

"Tell him yourself!" And already the door was slammed and locked fast.

"Son of a dog!" the girl shouted after him, but there was no reply.

Painfully Calwyn sat up, a difficult feat with her hands tied fast behind her. She was in a cabin not larger than a decent-size storage

locker, even smaller than her den in the bows of *Fledgewing*. There
was just room for two bunks, one above the other. The top one
was crammed with old sails and ropes and pieces of gear, and on
the bottom one sat a girl, one or two years younger than herself,
with the tawny skin and pale hair of a Doryan, who stared at her
with unabashed hostility in her golden eyes. Her skinny limbs
stuck out from a faded jacket and trousers that seemed far too
small for her.

"S'pose I'd better untie you," she said, almost to herself, and a
moment later Calwyn was spitting out the filthy cap that had been
choking her, and gasping while the girl wrenched at the knots that
still bound her hands.

"Thank you," coughed Calwyn as soon as she was able.

"Don't go thankin' me too quick. I'll get 'em to tie you up again
like *that*, if I want." The girl snapped her fingers under Calwyn's
nose; then she retreated to her perch on the lower bunk, drew her
feet up beneath her, and resumed her unblinking stare. There was
nowhere else for Calwyn to sit but on the floor, so she remained
where she was.

"My name's Calwyn. I was captured off our boat just now." She
struggled shakily to her feet and peered from the tiny porthole,
but *Fledgewing* was out of sight on the other side of the ship.

The girl shrugged. "I heard a racket, I thought they must've
found somethin' to chase after. But I can't see nothin', locked up
in here."

"You're a prisoner too? How long since you were captured? What happened to your ship?"

"I weren't taken from no ship. I'm their windworker."

Now it was Calwyn's turn to stare. "Your captain thinks I'm a windworker too."

"Ain't you? What else would they have a girl on board for?"

"Why shouldn't I be a member of the crew like any other?"

The girl snorted. "I guess your ship ain't from Doryus. It's the evilest luck there is to have a female on a boat, unless she's a windworker."

Calwyn said nothing. Did that mean that if the pirates found out she had no gift of windcraft, they would throw her overboard? She asked suddenly, "Are you truly a windworker?"

The girl shrugged again. "I'm still here. I s'pose I must be."

"What's your name?"

The girl hesitated, then said, "Mica."

They both looked up together as there came a sudden shout and the thud of running feet on deck. "Gettin' under way again," observed Mica. "They'll come and get me soon. They'll be headin' back to Doryus now, but the wind's in the wrong quarter."

Sure enough, there was a thumping at the cabin door and the noise of the bolt being drawn back. One of the sailors, his cap dangling by one ear, poked his head inside and growled, "Come on, witch. You're needed on deck. Not you." He pointed at Calwyn with a warning finger. "You stay here. One of you's enough for now."

"Even one of us is too much for you to handle," retorted Mica rudely, but she got up and allowed herself to be hustled outside, and the door slammed on Calwyn once again. Presently she heard the creaks and groans of the ship moving under sail and felt the familiar motion as it cut through the waves. Mica did not come back, and at last Calwyn leaned back on the hard bunk and fell asleep.

She was woken by the return of Mica, with a bowl of stew in one hand and a large hunk of bread in the other. "You might as well eat, I s'pose," she sniffed. "Move over, can't you."

For some time there was silence while the pair mopped up the thick stew with the dry bread. Calwyn was ravenous, but it was obvious that there would be no more. Mica tossed the empty wooden bowl away into a corner and pulled her feet up onto the bunk, staring at Calwyn again with those disconcerting golden eyes.

Calwyn tried to look back at her calmly, as Marna would have done. "Don't they need your arts any longer on deck?"

"They've caught a true wind now to take 'em north. They keep me locked up in here, 'cept when they need me."

"That must be a dull life for you."

Mica shrugged. "Better here and alive than burned like the rest of my village was, when the slavers came — Where're you from?" she asked suddenly.

"Antaris."

"Where's that?"

"In the mountains, beyond the riverlands and the plains of Kalysons."

"The western lands?"

"Antaris is the westernmost land of Tremaris. Beyond it there's nothing but mountains and forest, as far as the eye can see."

"That must be a dull life for you," Mica mocked her. But Calwyn wouldn't let herself be provoked. Mica reminded her of the little girls who were chosen sometimes from the outlying villages to train as priestesses. Some would weep with homesickness in the first days, but some would be angry and rude, disguising their own hurt by hurting those around them.

She asked, "Where did you learn to be a windworker?"

Mica gave a derisive laugh. "You can't *learn* windwork. It's in the blood, or it ain't. I took the gift from my grandma. She were a famed weatherworker on Emeran. That's in the Isles of Firthana, if you don't know."

"I thought you must be from Doryus, like the rest of the crew."

"Not me!" Mica spat. "I ain't no Doryan. I'm a daughter of the Isles, I am — I seen your ship," she added abruptly. "They're towin' her behind. What were you doin sailin' in such a little boat so far out from the westlands?"

"We were caught in a storm."

Mica stretched her arms above her head and entwined her fingers, then let them fall into her lap. "The captain's got plans for you. He's got a buyer who'll pay good coin to get hold of a windworker. There was someone tried to buy me, see, but the captain wouldn't sell. Windworkers ain't so common that he could throw me away. In my grandma's day, it were different," she added. "She always told me, when she were a little girl, every fisherwoman in the Isles could sing up a wind. Not now."

"Where is your grandmother?"

"Dead," said Mica shortly.

"Oh." Slowly Calwyn tucked her feet beneath her, so that she and Mica were sitting cross-legged, face-to-face. Thinking that it might make a bond between them, she said, "My mother is dead too."

"Was she killed by slavers and your home burned while you stood by?"

"No. She died of a winter fever when I was very young."

Mica sniffed. There was a short pause. Then Mica said, "Your friends are still alive. They're on your ship."

Calwyn's heart skipped; she longed to know what had become of Darrow, whether he was badly hurt. "Have you seen them?"

But Mica shook her head.

"Do you know what will happen to them?"

Mica shrugged. "The captain'll sell 'em in the slave market in Doryus Town."

"And me?"

"No. He'll try to find the man who offered that good price for me. That were days ago, he could be anywhere by now. But *he* thinks it's worth lookin'."

"But I'm not a windworker," said Calwyn.

"I know," said Mica. "But you don't want to go tellin' *him* that."

Calwyn's heart was beating hard, but she tried to keep her voice level. "What will happen if you tell him? Would he sell me in Doryus Town with the others?"

"Don't think you'll all be kept together," said Mica sharply. "Don't think *that*. And he might decide it ain't worth keepin' you at all, for the bad luck you bring. He might just toss you over the side."

Calwyn said, "It would only take one word from you."

"I know," said Mica simply. "I'm thinkin' about that, ain't I." Then there was silence in the cabin for a long time.

They cleared out the top bunk as well as they could, making just enough space for Calwyn to lie down if she kept her legs curled up and ignored a stiff fold of sail that dug into her back. Calwyn thought she would never get to sleep, her mind churning over what had happened and what might happen. Long after night fell she lay in the moonlight, listening to Mica's steady breathing, before she too slid uneasily into sleep.

Thumping at the door woke them; a pearly half-light at the porthole showed that it was just before dawn. "Get up, girl! The wind's died. Captain needs you on deck!"

"Give me a breath!" shouted Mica, sitting up, her hair all tousled, and pulling on her shoes. A fat sailor flung open the door.

"Hurry yerself, can't you?"

Mica stood up. "She can come too," she said, nodding toward Calwyn. "I'm all worn out from blastin' your ship along. If *he* wants a wind, she'll have to help me."

"Please yerself," grumbled the sailor.

Calwyn was frozen with doubt, but Mica beckoned her down with an impatient gesture. "Just do the same as me," she murmured in Calwyn's ear, so that the sailor couldn't hear. "We'll fool 'em between us."

Filled with unease, but grateful to be out of the stifling little cabin at last, Calwyn followed Mica and the sailor through the maze of cabins and narrow passageways and ladders, up onto the deck. The sky was gray with the cold, clear light of early morning; two moons hung like shining baubles just above the horizon. Calwyn's heart leaped at the sight. Two moons, close together, the Swollen-Belly Moons: a good omen for the birth of partnerships and joint endeavors. The Goddess surely smiled on her and Mica, and whatever plan it was that Mica had. She turned around quickly and caught sight of poor broken *Fledgewing*, limping some distance behind the pirate ship at the end of two immense ropes. There was no sign of movement aboard. But Mica tugged her onward, up some more steep steps to a higher deck, where the captain stood near the wheel with a few of his men. They were all staring gloomily up at the enormous square sails hanging limp and lifeless in the still air.

"What's this?" asked the captain as soon as he caught sight of Calwyn.

"Two windworkers are better'n one," said Mica. "We can work together."

"One windwitch is too many for me, and two worse than one," muttered the helmsman.

"We'll go back below then, will we, and leave you with your calm?" flared Mica.

The captain looked displeased. "Stop your chattering! Hold your tongue and make haste. We've been long enough without a breath of breeze."

Mica led Calwyn to a place on the upper deck where they stood facing the flapping sails, with the helmsman and the captain behind them. "Just follow me," whispered Mica. She raised her arms, and Calwyn raised her own. And although she hadn't meant to begin a chantment, she could feel the tingle in her hands and behind her eyes that signaled the power of the Goddess stirring. The ship rose for a moment into a wave, and she could see again the pale spheres of the moons coming into view and feel the cool, fresh air on her face like the Goddess's own perfumed breath. Then Mica's clear voice rang out in a chantment of her own craft, and although Calwyn didn't recognize the words she sang, the power that thrummed through them was plain. She felt herself slipping into that dreamy state in which magic was wrought, almost a trance, all her senses clear but somehow distanced from her, and she found that she could hear and copy Mica's words almost as soon as she sang them. So they stood, side by side, as the sun rose, with Calwyn's chant following close on Mica's, threading in and out of it, rising and falling with the rhythm of the waves themselves, and slowly she began to feel the stirring of a wind. The two squares of canvas billowed out before them, bellying fatter and fatter as they sang, until every inch of the sail was stretched taut as a drumskin, and the huge ship was racing along so swiftly that *Fledgewing*, bobbing behind, flew out of the water at the crest of every wave.

"Steady! Steady!" cried the helmsman. "I can hardly hold her!"

"I asked for a wind, not a hurricane!" shouted the captain, and Calwyn let her voice die away so that Mica sang alone. The wind lessened, and the ship settled back to a steady speed. The freshly risen sun was warm on Calwyn's cheek, and she exalted. She hadn't thought she would be able to do it. Truly the Goddess had smiled upon them both.

But it was clear that the captain was not happy to have them both on deck at once, and before long she was hustled below, back to the little cabin.

Mica came back partway through the day to eat her midday meal. The captain never allowed her to eat with the crew; he was afraid of her making friends, though most of them avoided her in any case, thinking her very presence on the boat unlucky. "They'll want me again afore long," she said, tearing hungrily into the bread and fish that had been brought to them. "Leastways, they'll want one of us. Why'd you tell me you weren't no windworker? I thought we'd trick *him* into sparin' you. But then the gale came up, and I knew it weren't no trick of mine."

"I've never learned windcraft," said Calwyn. "But I have other arts. I was as surprised as you. It must be all one: the power of the Goddess." Marna's words came back to her: *All the chantments are but aspects of that one unknowable mystery, just as each face of a jewel strikes light in a different direction.*

"I don't know nothin' about no goddess," said Mica matter-of-factly, wiping her nose on her sleeve. "All I know is how to raise the wind at my fingertips, and the words my grandma taught me, back in Emeran. But just the words ain't enough."

"Not enough in themselves," agreed Calwyn. "But they are necessary. Quickly, teach me, so I can take your place this afternoon."

Mica laughed, the first laugh that Calwyn had heard from her, and it was a rusty little sound, as if she had not used it for a long time. "I can't teach you all the words of power in the space of a meal! I couldn't teach 'em all to you in the turnin' of the moons." She took a sip of water from the beaker, considering. "But I could teach you the words we used this mornin'. They'll want to keep northbound for a long time yet." She eyed Calwyn doubtfully. "The words ain't too easy. You sure you can learn 'em right off?"

But Calwyn was well used to memorizing difficult words and tracts of lore and long chants. All the rituals of the sisters were learned by heart, and she was soon able to hum the notes and repeat the words of power back to Mica without a stumble.

"You're quicker'n I ever was," said Mica at last. "My grandma had to give me ginger biscuits to make me keep still. 'Course, I were only a little girl then," she added loftily, though it seemed to Calwyn that she was barely more than a little girl even now.

When the sailor came to fetch the windworker, it was Calwyn who went with him, and Calwyn who kept up the steady chanting that drove the ship northward all that day. She and Mica took it turn and turn about, the next day and the next, and in the brief periods when they were confined to their cabin together to eat, Mica taught her more and more of the craft of windworking. In return, Calwyn tried to teach Mica some of her own skills, but even when Mica succeeded in repeating the words of chantment exactly, she couldn't summon up the magic of ice-call. "It's no good, it ain't in my blood," said Mica with a shake of her head. "You must've had someone from the Isles back in your history, to sing up the winds like you do."

And then Calwyn was silent, wondering who her father might have been. Perhaps Mica was right, and he had been a man of Firthana or Doryus. It gave her a strange feeling to think that they might even now be sailing toward his home, perhaps the very place where she had been born. But Mica nudged her out of her thoughts. "Show me the ice again, Calwyn."

Calwyn never forgot the look of astonished delight that spread across Mica's face when she first sang the water in their wooden beaker into a solid block of ice that she could slide out and hold in her hand. Mica had lived her whole life on the scorching islands and warm seas around Doryus; she had never seen ice before and never tired of begging Calwyn to repeat the chantment. "*They* ain't never seen nothin' like that!" she'd say with satisfaction.

Mica spoke of the pirates always as *they*, never *we*. She was not sure how long she had been on the ship: maybe three seasons, by Doryan reckoning, maybe six. That meant half a year, or a year, or somewhere in between. "I've growed since the slavers took me, that's all I know," she said, peering at the length of brown arm that stretched beyond the end of her sleeve.

Calwyn said, "When we get back to *Fledgewing*, I'll give you some clothes." She spoke with more confidence than she felt.

But Mica shook her head, and her face closed in on itself. "My grandma stitched this for me," she said, and she hugged her arms about herself, holding the faded jacket tight against her skin.

All the while, Calwyn was trying to think of a way to rescue the others, who were still trapped on *Fledgewing*. Once or twice she thought she caught a glimpse of someone at the portholes, but she could never be certain. There were still pirate sailors aboard the other boat. Calwyn would have given up all her newly learned craft to go across, just once, to see that Darrow and the others were all right. But she and they were too closely watched for any chance of that.

Then one morning Mica came below with a grim, sour look. "They've had a sight of land."

Calwyn strained to see out of their single tiny porthole. "Land? What land?" Far away on the horizon she could see a dark, indistinct smudge; it might have been a storm cloud, or a shadow.

"That's Doryus," said Mica. "We'll be in their harbor afore nightfall."

Blood Moon

The massive peak that lay in the middle of the Isle of Doryus rose up, stark, sullen, and brooding, a black shape stamped against the yellow sky, the pivot around which all the little islands wheeled, the point to which every eye was drawn.

All day long the sailors had been sniffing the air, as the distinctive sulfur stench of the island drifted across the waves toward them and seeped below the decks into every cranny of the ship. With each breath, Calwyn imagined a yellow stain furring her nostrils and throat; the air was thick, tainted, metallic. She couldn't believe that people lived and walked about and ate their meals in this overpowering stink.

The two ships had dropped anchor at one of the many small, rocky islands that lay sprinkled around Doryus. This was the pirates' base, the place where they counted their coins and fought and fished and repaired their boats, where they grew their slava and kept their women. Like all the Doryan islands, it was a fierce, hot, and lawless place. There were few tall trees; the huts that huddled by the shallow harbor were built of stones and thatched with wild sea grass. Slava bushes struggled up, stunted and rusty-looking, from the cracks between the rocks, and the acrid stench of slava mingled with the smell of sulfur. Greenish stains of slava spittle were spattered all over the ground.

Even after the sun went down, the air inside the cabin was hot and stifling. The sounds of the pirates' carousing drifted in from the shore, and the lanterns strung up along the water's edge sent sickly yellow light flickering over the roof and the walls. Softly Calwyn began to sing, a quiet chantment that sent a cool breath into the air, and then Mica joined her voice to Calwyn's, chasing the coolness into a gentle breeze that sighed across their bunks.

Presently Mica said, "Tomorrow *he's* takin' your friends to the slave market in Doryus Town." *He* was the pirate captain.

Calwyn's song faltered, but she made no reply.

Mica sat up on her elbow. "Calwyn, did you hear me? And while he's there, he'll be askin' about for that trader with the empty ship, so's he can sell you too."

Calwyn broke off her chantment. "What did you say? What empty ship?"

"Empty as a slava-chewer's head. I seen it myself. Plague ship, *they* was sayin'. All his slaves must've gone over the side. The one that tried to buy me, that's who I mean. Back at the time of the Whale and the Two Brothers — half a turn of the moons ago," she amended, remembering that Calwyn's way of reckoning the moons was different from her own. She leaned back with her arms behind her head. "He might think it's cheaper to buy one windworker than a whole galley-full of slaves, but it won't be, not if *he* gets the price he's askin' — What's wrong with *you*?"

Calwyn let out a long, shuddering breath. "I know him," she said. "He's no trader. He's a prince of Merithuros, and a sorcerer. He moves the oars of that ship with chantment, not slaves. He — he killed our friend. Back in the Westlands."

"Well then," said Mica flatly. "There's a good reason not to get sold to him."

Calwyn was silent.

Mica said sharply, "Ain't you listenin' to me? This is our only chance, now, tonight! We got to get out of here while *he's* ashore drinkin' and the rest of 'em chewin' slava. We got to get onto your friends' boat."

"It's not so simple, Mica!" said Calwyn. Thinking about Samis again brought back all the feelings of the last days on *Fledgewing*, the despair, the fighting, their hopelessness. She said dully, "Even if we get off this ship, we'll all be in bondage again soon enough. Bondage to *him*. Who knows, it might be better to stay where we are."

"What are you talkin' about?" demanded Mica. "Are you sick? You talkin' in your sleep? Don't you *want* to be free?"

Calwyn was silent for a time. Then, slowly, with many hesitations, she told Mica about Samis, and his ambition to be emperor of all Tremaris, his plan to master the Nine Powers, and how he had already mastered at least five of them. "We had a quest to stop him, my friends and I. But that's all finished now."

"Since you was captured."

"No. No. It was over before that."

"I don't understand you," said Mica, and her voice was small and hard and cold. "This sorcerer, he's a cruel man, a bad man?"

"Yes. Oh, yes." Calwyn thought of the white figure of the falling priestess in the courtyard, of Xanni's long lashes against his pale cheek as he fought for breath on that long, dreadful night, of the look of greedy triumph on Samis's face as he stretched out his hand for the Clarion.

"And if he gets his way, there'll be hurt for people? People killed?"

"I should think so," said Calwyn drearily.

Mica sat up. "It seems to me, them that sees an evil thing unfold, and don't do nothin' to prevent it, are just as bad as them that does the evil. If I could've fought the slavers when they came to Emeran, I would've done it. I *have* fought *him* and his crew, when I could, and paid the price for it too. But I were just one against many. *You*" — she jumped off the bunk, waving her hand toward the sea to indicate *Fledgewing* — "you and your friends is many against one. What excuse have *you* got?" Her voice was mounting in fury as she spoke, and her last words were almost a shout.

Calwyn sat up too and stared at her. Mica's round, golden eyes gleamed with anger, and with something else too: disappointment.

Calwyn said, "He's very strong. He's stronger than any of us." But her words were feeble, and she knew it.

"Better to be brave, and try, and be beaten, than creep off to some *corner* and die of shame and fear, like — like a *snail!*"

Mica's words bit her like bee-stings. Wasn't that just what she'd said to Darrow long ago in Antaris? She had despised him for giving in to his despair. But that was before she'd seen Xanni killed, she argued with herself; everything was different then. But as quickly as she framed the thought, the answer flashed back, firm as the beating of a gong: *Xanni would want us to go on fighting. Or else his death will be for nothing.*

For a time there was no noise in the cabin but the unsteady songs of the sailors, already drifting into a haze of slava.

Mica said, "You're thinkin' how to get out." It was a statement rather than a question.

"Are you a thought-reader now, as well as a windworker?"

"You ain't goin' without me!" said Mica fiercely. "You can't get off this ship without me. You wouldn't last five breaths on this island."

"Hold your peace," said Calwyn. "I'm not going to leave you behind."

The bonds of the captives on *Fledgewing* had been removed long ago, but the hatchway to the deck was kept securely fastened, and there were always three or four pirate sailors standing guard. The snug cabin was almost unrecognizable; the captain had ordered his men to search it, but they hadn't found anything they counted as treasure. Even the cushions on the benches had been slashed, but spilled out nothing but feathers; the lockers had all been emptied and their contents taken away to the pirates' ship. The three sat gloomily among the wreckage as they had done for many days.

"It'd be easy enough to surprise them and throw them overboard," said Tonno, for perhaps the hundredth time.

Trout, also for perhaps the hundredth time, looked dubious. "And once we've thrown them overboard, what then? We can't escape without Calwyn. And we can't go anywhere without a new mast."

"Now we are by land again, that is not so large a problem as it was." Darrow looked through a porthole toward the cluster of huts on the shore. "This is where the bandits bring their ships to be repaired. There must be new masts somewhere on this island. See, Tonno, there, they have set some out to season and strung up lanterns from them."

"Not bad. Yes, one of those would do."

"Except that we're locked in here, and the poles are out there on the shore!" said Trout in exasperation.

"We must take our chance while we can." Tonno spoke urgently to Darrow, ignoring Trout. "They could come and take us off to a slave-trader's yard at any time. If we lose *Fledgewing*, then we're lost indeed. We must take back the ship before anything else. Whatever happens after — whatever happens, we must get out of the clutches of these bandits."

"But what about Calwyn?" said Trout.

Darrow said, "Tonno is right. If we have *Fledgewing* in our own hands, we can try rescuing Calwyn. But if we try to rescue Calwyn without *Fledgewing*, we are all in greater danger than before."

"Lucky she's not here to hear you say that the boat's safety comes before hers," muttered Trout, so low that he thought Darrow wouldn't hear him.

But Darrow's ears were keener than he realized. "No one thinks more of Calwyn's safety than I do," he said sharply. "But Calwyn would agree if she were here. *Fledgewing* first. When we are all together again, you can ask her for yourself."

It seemed that half the night had gone before the two girls heard someone moving sluggishly about in the passageway outside their cabin. Mica began pounding on the bolted door. "Hey! *Hey!* You out there! Bring us some water, can't you? We're parched in here!"

A dismissive muttering was the only reply, but Mica banged even harder on the door. "*Hey!* You deaf? Some water!"

At last the door was thrown open, and a bleary-eyed sailor appeared with a jug in his hand. "Shut your mouth! Do you want to wake the whole ship?"

"Why not? You and your dogs of friends've been keepin' us awake with your so-called singin' ever since the sun went down," retorted Mica. Calwyn began to sing, as if in mockery of the tuneless songs they had been hearing all night. The sailor merely grunted, shoved the jug into Mica's hands, slopping out half the water, and retreated through the doorway. Calwyn and Mica looked at each other. They could hear him struggling to push the bolt back. At last he managed to shoot it halfway into the hole in the door frame, grunted, gave up, and shuffled away.

Mica brought her hands together in a quick, fierce clap of delight. Calwyn's song was not really a mocking imitation; it was a small chantment, singing up a tiny chunk of ice to partly block the bolt-hole. Now she crouched by the doorway and sang softly, coaxing the small block to grow, little by little, slowly easing the bolt across.

"Quick, quick!" urged Mica in a whisper.

"I don't want to make a noise."

"There ain't no one to hear. Hurry!"

At last, with a creak that sounded like a thunderclap to Calwyn's ears, the bolt slid free. Mica gave the door a gentle push, and it swung open.

At once Mica was racing through the maze of passageways; Calwyn saw the flash of her bare feet as she ran, like pale fish darting through murky water. The passages twisted and turned, walls loomed up in front of her face; she didn't know the way as well as Mica, who could have run it blindfolded. Calwyn held out her hands as she stumbled forward, trying to keep up.

Here at last was something familiar: the rungs of the ladder that led onto the deck. She grabbed the solid wood and pulled herself up, eager to poke her head out of the choking darkness, into the clear moonlight. But on deck it was still dark. Only one

solitary crescent moon sailed close to the horizon, glowing an uncanny red. The lanterns along the shore had burned out too, although muted lights still shone from within some of the huts.
The great peak of Doryus loomed over them, black against black.
Calwyn shivered.

Mica tugged at her arm, grimacing at her to hurry, and pulled
her through the deepest pools of shadow toward the wheel deck.
Here and there sailors lay sprawled and snoring, seeking some
cool air rather than stifling below; stupefied with slava, they didn't
stir as Mica and Calwyn tiptoed lightly past.

Like little mice, Mica's feet pattered swiftly up the ladder to
the high wheel deck at the stern of the ship. Calwyn followed, re-
hearsing in her mind the chantment she would need. She was going to build a bridge of ice between the two ships so she and Mica
could cross, and then bring it crashing into the sea before anyone
could follow them. It would need raised sides so their feet
wouldn't slide off; the ice would have to be strong and thick so
that it didn't melt in this humid air. She knew there were pirates
on *Fledgewing* still, but she was sure that she and Mica could deal
with them — She came up with a bump against Mica's back in
the thick dark.

"What is it?"

"Look, look!" Mica ran to the rail. "They're gone! Fine friends
you've got. They've gone without us!"

Calwyn pushed her aside. It was true. The two long ropes that had fastened the ships together were dangling limply in the water. *Fledgewing* had disappeared.

Trout knew he would never get to sleep. He was far too hot, for one thing, and he was nervous. It was all very well for *them* to speak so lightly of throwing pirate sailors overboard, a great burly fellow like Tonno, and Darrow, a vagabond without a homeland, who must have picked up a few shifty tricks in his time. But he, Trout, was no fighter, and he had seen enough fighting in this company already to last him the rest of his days. It was odd, he thought, that he'd spent his whole life in Mithates, learning how weapons worked, inventing improvements to them, studying the sharpness of steel and the trajectories of catapults, but never until now had he seen actual combat, and bruises, and broken bones, and blood. Before Xanni, he had never seen anyone die. He hadn't really thought about it before, what the weapons and war machines were *for*; he'd only thought about passing his exams. Would he be able to go back to the haven of his workshop without thinking of those things every time he picked up a blade or an arrow or a model of a war machine? Restlessly he turned over again, pummeling his pillow.

"We'll wait until just before dawn," Darrow had said, "when the watch are at their sleepiest. Best to get some rest while we can." But Trout lay awake, watching the lantern lights from the shore play over the roof of the cabin as the others slept.

Tonno was stretched out on his back, snoring with a steady rhythm; Darrow slept sitting up, a faint frown on his face, as though even in his sleep he was still wrestling with some problem that had to be solved. Trout rolled over onto his other side but found it no more comfortable. How could these Doryans bear to live under such heat? No wonder they took to chewing slava to dull their misery. If he had some of the disgusting stuff on hand, he might almost try it for himself.

Just then he heard voices up on deck, the mutterings of the sailors on watch. Someone was coming aboard. "Hey lads."

"You come to relieve us?"

"Better'n that! This way you can enjoy yerselves and follow the captain's orders at the same time. Take a look, I've brought you some slava."

There was a murmur of appreciative laughter, sounds of back-slapping, and then a period of concentrated silence as the pirates settled down to enjoy their shipmate's gift. Trout lay in the dark, listening and thinking hard. He didn't know much about slava; it was forbidden in Mithates on pain of exile, but there were always one or two students in every term who risked smuggling some of the stuff up the river from the traders who called at Mithates Port, and he had seen people under its influence, dull-eyed and stupefied. And that was in Mithates, where the only slava available would be weak stuff, adulterated with who-knew-what weeds and other rubbish. But this was Doryus, where the bushes grew, and the leaves would be pure and potent.

He struggled up out of his bunk and woke the others with a finger on his lips, gesturing toward the deck above. "They're chewing slava," he hissed.

Darrow was awake in a moment, alert as if he had never been asleep. Tonno was more difficult to rouse, but when he realized what was happening, it was all they could do to restrain him from rushing on deck at once. The three of them waited in the dark, straining their ears as the slow moments slid by, waiting until the slava should take its full effect. One by one the sailors slumped against the side of the cabin. Cheerful murmuring turned gradually into drowsy grunts, and finally into silence, broken only by an occasional deep sigh followed by sluggish spitting, as the spent wad of slava was discarded and a fresh one groggily pushed between the chewer's teeth.

At last Darrow nodded and sang a single low note. Slowly, easily, the hatch at the top of the companionway swung open. Darrow was through it in a moment, closely followed by Tonno. Four sailors sprawled, nearly comatose, about the deck. Only one of them looked up as Darrow leaned over him. "Wha — ?" he began, but Darrow laid a finger to his lips and sang a series of low, growling syllables. It seemed to Trout, watching open-mouthed, that invisible hands plucked up the sailor by the scruff of his collar and the belt of his trousers, levered him up through the air, and deposited him neatly on the jetty, where he rolled over and began to snore as comfortably as though he were lying in his own hammock. Tonno swiftly bound the hands of the other pirates with their own long caps, and Darrow used the chantment of iron to lift them off the boat and onto the wharf.

Trout clutched at the rail with clammy hands. He had always believed that there was no such thing as magic; he was sure he'd seen nothing on that last night in Mithates that could not be explained by the laws he'd been taught. And yet here were men flying through the air and doors swinging open without the touch of any hand or machine. It could not be, and yet it was.

"Simple," grunted Tonno.

Trout found his voice, though it was somewhat cracked and unsteady. "All right, we've the boat back, but how are we going to move it?"

Darrow was singing once more; this time the ropes that held *Fledgewing* fast to the stern of the pirates' ship were loosened and flung back into the water with two soft splashes. "We are in shallow water here, I can move us as far as we need. The more important thing is to get us a new mast."

Now his hands were a blur of swift movement, and a stream of guttural song flew from his lips. One of the spare masts that lay in a pile on the shore gave a jerk, then lifted itself. At once the string of yellow lanterns draped over the poles collapsed, and the flickering lights blew out. The whole harbor was plunged into darkness; Trout had trouble seeing his hand in front of his face. The pole hurtled through the air toward the boat, while the boat itself moved steadily away from the shore. Tonno called to Trout to come and hold the tiller. Now the mast clattered down onto the deck, narrowly missing Trout's foot. Darrow gave him an apologetic glance; evidently he had too many things to juggle to be precise about where he dropped the pole. Trout ran to the stern and gripped the tiller.

"Just keep her heading away from the shore." Tonno clapped him on the shoulder. "Darrow'll take care of the rest." And then he was off, leaping across the deck and dashing down below to fetch the spare sails.

Darrow sang rapidly, the notes tumbling from his mouth faster and faster. Trout could barely see what was happening, but he could hear the stump of the old mast cracking at its base, little by little. Still *Fledgewing* moved, slowly, steadily, farther and farther from the shore, slipping away unnoticed in the darkness. *Where are the moons?* Trout wondered suddenly. There was one: a reddish crescent behind them in the southern sky. *A blood moon,* thought Trout, and shook himself. There was no time for superstitious nonsense like that now.

The old mast stump was fallen; the new pole rose up silently where it had been. Tonno had lugged the sails up on deck, but Darrow shook his head. Beads of sweat flew from his brow as he heaved for breath. "No, not yet. I cannot —"

Trout saw the tall spear of the new mast slowly topple to lie flat on the deck again. Darrow's magic couldn't stretch to do it all: keep the ship moving, fix the mast in place, and hold up the sails, all at once. Trout's heart sank; were they going to leave Calwyn behind after all? But still *Fledgewing* was sliding away; the pirates' ship was far behind them now.

"Where are we going?" called Trout, no longer bothering to keep quiet.

"Around the island a little," replied Darrow. His teeth were gritted with effort. "The waters are shallow, I can keep her moving a little longer. We won't need the sail just yet."

They were almost out of the harbor. "We can rest soon," said Darrow, but he spoke in such a low voice, Trout couldn't tell whether he was reassuring them or himself.

Mica was quicker to move than Calwyn, who stood frozen in disbelief, staring at the smooth place in the water where *Fledgewing* had been. "Come on!" She plucked urgently at Calwyn's sleeve. "Never mind about them now. We got to get away while we can!"

Get away to where? But already Mica was running silently across the wheel deck, disappearing down the ladder, swallowed up by the darkness. Calwyn followed her.

The red moon watched them, a half-closed eye, as they darted across the deck. One of the sailors stirred and called out something, slurred with sleep and slava, but Mica sang a quick little chantment to send a cool breeze playing over his hot face, and he fell back again into his stupor. She found the place on the lower deck where the gangway reached out to the crude wharf and pulled Calwyn across it. They both staggered; even on such a large ship there was some sea motion, and their legs were not accustomed to solid ground.

"This way," whispered Mica. "Quick, past the houses. I know a place we can hide. There's an old fishin' hut 'round the other side of the island."

And what then? Calwyn wondered. They couldn't hide for long on this tiny island; they were bound to be discovered. Without *Fledgewing* to run to, there was no reason to leave the ship at all. She wanted to tug at Mica's sleeve and drag her back across the plank. But she couldn't have caught her. Mica skipped past the huts, dodging around the faint cracks and squares of candlelight cast from inside. Calwyn heard just once the unsteady murmur of voices and a tinny clatter as something, a jug or a goblet, was knocked over. Was that the captain's voice? She froze, listening hard, but Mica pulled her on.

What could have happened to *Fledgewing*? She couldn't believe the others would have sailed away without her. Could Samis have found them somehow and spirited the ship away, or destroyed it? A sick feeling clenched in her stomach as she thought of her friends, trapped in the cabin, water rushing in. "Mica," she hissed suddenly, "why is it so dark? What's happened to the moons?"

They had already come out of the village, if the haphazard cluster of stone huts by the water could be called a village, and begun to climb the steep and rocky hill that rose behind the harbor. It was so dark that they had trouble seeing where to tread; pale stones slipped and skidded away under their feet.

Mica stopped and looked up at the sky. The red moon swung low above the horizon, and its reflection left a bloody stain on the sea, but there was no spangle of stars flung across the darkness as there usually was when only one moon shone. "Must be a storm comin'," she said with a shrug. "There's clouds all over the sky." Her voice was curious rather than concerned; she was too excited by their escape to be troubled by anything.

"I didn't know it was the time of the Blood Moon," murmured Calwyn, unable to shake off her unease.

"You call it that too, up in your mountains?" Mica scrabbled for a foothold among the shifting stones. "There's always storms in Blood Moon season."

"I don't think it's a storm."

"What then?"

"I don't know," said Calwyn, but she began to scramble more quickly up the slope. There was a strange stillness in the air as well as the unnatural darkness; no bird chirped, no breath of wind stirred the boats at their moorings. She shivered, though the air was as sticky as ever. Mica was ahead of her, silent and climbing sturdily, eyes down. Neither of them looked down to the stretch of sea below, nor the boat that lay there, out of sight of the harbor, a boat without a mast.

On *Fledgewing,* Tonno turned to Trout. "Get me that tube of yours."

Darrow, slumped wearily by the tiller, looked up at Tonno. "What is it, what can you see?"

"There, on the island." Tonno squinted and pointed at the two tiny dark figures moving against the pale rocks. "It looks like Calwyn."

Trout reemerged from the cabin, breathless, with the looking-tube in his hand. "It can't be. She's with the pirates. And you can't see from here, it's too far."

"Why do you think I asked for your tube?" Tonno held out his hand for it impatiently. After a moment he said, "She's not with the pirates anymore. She's with that other girl we saw on the deck, the little Doryan girl, the windworker."

"There's no such thing as a windworker," muttered Trout from habit, before he remembered what he had seen that night. He shot a quick glance at Darrow, but he wasn't listening.

"Tonno, look there, at the bottom of the hill, behind them. Do you see another person?"

Tonno was silent for a moment. "Yes — no. I'm not sure." He lowered the tube and rubbed his eyes fiercely. "This thing'll send me blind."

Darrow snatched the tube. "It's the captain," he said after a moment. "The pirate captain. He's gaining on them."

"We have to warn her," said Tonno. "Trout, go below again, fetch me a lantern."

"But what if she's looking the other way?"

"Do as I tell you for once!" roared Tonno, and Trout backed away, then turned and fled down into the cabin. *A light's no good,* he thought stubbornly as he rummaged in the wreckage of the stores and lockers. Calwyn might not see it until it was too late. It would be better to make a noise. But they had nothing to use to make a noise. Tucking the lantern under his arm, he scrambled back up onto the deck.

                                    *   *   *

"Mica, wait!" Calwyn grabbed Mica's jacket.

"Time enough to catch our breath when we get to that old hut. We got to hurry. I don't want to get caught in no storm."

"I don't need to rest. Stop a moment. Listen."

Reluctantly Mica stopped a little farther up the slope. "What? I can't hear nothin'."

"There's someone behind us — someone sliding on the rocks. There! You must have heard that!" There was a skittering of pebbles somewhere far behind them.

"Better hurry then, like I said." Mica turned away indifferently.

But the next moment there was no doubt that they were being pursued. Faintly there came the sound of someone yelling, and then the rattle of rocks dislodged by scrambling boots. Mica stiffened and clutched at Calwyn's arm. "That's *him* — the captain! Quick, quick!"

Calwyn ran after her, sliding on the loose stones, but her heart was filled with dread. They couldn't hope to evade the captain now; even if they reached Mica's hut, they would soon be found. *Fledgewing* was gone; she herself would be sold to Samis. There was no hope. But still she stubbornly struggled up the hill, feet skidding, her heart hammering.

And then, from somewhere ahead and below in the darkness, from far out on the sea, there came a sound unlike any she had ever heard. It was the blaring of a trumpet, and the wild cry of an eagle, and the sweet music of a choir, and the clear chime of a hundred bells pealing out, echoing through the night. For the space of ten heartbeats the sound hung in the air, pure and bright, and there was no other sound, no other movement, nothing in the world but the shining glory of that note. And then slowly, sweetly, it began to fade, dying away into stillness, a silence so deep and calm that Calwyn heard her own blood roar in her ears like a rising storm.

Then it all began.

First there came a fierce grumbling from the depths of the earth beneath them; the loose stones on the hillside began to roll and slither down the slope, and Calwyn heard the voice behind them, the captain's voice, shout out in fright. The ground shook so violently that she and Mica were almost knocked off their feet. They clung to each other as the ground heaved beneath them. This was no spell of seeming, thought Calwyn; this was a true earthquake. The slope buckled and bent like the ocean in a storm; at any moment it would tear itself into pieces. Mica put her mouth close to Calwyn's ear. "Look, look there!"

As they watched, a banner of flame was flung across the darkness, from horizon to horizon, lighting up the world below, dim and reddish as though fires burned in the clouds themselves. Calwyn could see Mica's face flush with the crimson glow, the white stones stained pink and strange at their feet, and the great expanse of the ocean like a sea of dark blood spilled out before them. And far off, across the sea, the shadow of the peak of Doryus was glowing with its own fire, golden bright, a crown of light at the summit of the mountain.

Once again the ground trembled under their feet with the growling roar that was not thunder, the sound rolling around the bowl of the horizon. "The mountain — the mountain's wakin'!" cried Mica, and her voice was filled with awe. They both stared at the great peak of Doryus that loomed over all the islands. A tongue of fire glowed at the summit. As they watched, it spilled over the rim like a boiling stew overflowing a cauldron, and poured, with a dreadful, deliberate slowness, down the side of the peak. "A fire-flood!" Mica clutched at her, more excited than afraid. "Just like the stories!"

Now the reddish light was fading from the sky. The rising sun glimmered behind a veil of sooty steam, casting an eerie metallic light over the sea, the boats in the harbor, and the cluster of huts. Slava-dazed people began to stagger outside, shaken from their stupor by the tremors, milling about the waterside in confusion. Calwyn could hear their scared cries borne through the still, hushed air.

Across the water, on Doryus, slowly, stealthily, the tide of fire crept down the side of the mountain, an inexorable river licking its way toward the sea.

"May the Goddess protect us," whispered Calwyn. And she shivered as she placed her fingertips lightly on the marks of the moon that were etched on her arm, for this was stronger magic, more ancient and terrifying, than anything she had ever witnessed.

But Mica was not looking at the fire-mountain now; she was staring back down the slope behind them. The captain was draw-

ing closer, his face clearly visible now in the sickly light. The gold
threads woven through his beard glittered, and sweat shone on his
brow; he was climbing toward them at a great rate, his face contorted with rage and terror. He was still shouting, and his words
carried to them clearly. "This is witches' work! You won't escape
me. When I catch you, I'll have you tortured till you beg for
mercy! When I'm done with you, then you'll wish you'd perished
on Emeran with your witch of a grandmother!"

Calwyn was tugging urgently at her arm. "Mica, I can see
Fledgewing. The others are waiting for us — quickly!"

But Mica stood where she was. She raised her hands, threw
back her head, and began to sing.

"Mica, there's no time!" Calwyn could see *Fledgewing* clearly
now, battered and mastless but free, and the three figures on
board. Someone was standing on the cabin roof, waving his arms
to and fro, with a lantern in his hand. She swung around. The captain stumbled up the slope, yelling and cursing and waving his
fists. But as she watched, the wind of Mica's chantment caught
him full in the chest. He stopped and doubled over as though he
had been punched by an invisible fist. Then a look of horror
spread over his face as he found himself lifted off his feet, up and
up into the air, higher and higher, far above the slope and the huts
by the harbor. The wind carried him, twisting him as lightly as a
straw, out over the water where Mica's arm pointed arrow-
straight. She stood tall and scornful, singing out her spell, and
then with a sudden gesture she dropped her arm. He was too far

away for anyone to see him fall, or to hear any sound as he struck the water.

"Let him drown!" cried Mica, wild-eyed, but Calwyn had seized her hand and they were running, running down the hill toward the sea, toward *Fledgewing*, half-falling down the slope that still shuddered under them. Her feet thudded in time with the rapid beating of her heart. They were at the bottom of the hill now, running along a beach of smooth gray pebbles. There was *Fledgewing*, there was Trout, still waving madly, and Tonno.

Calwyn cupped her hands to her mouth. "Bring the boat as close as you can! And hold her steady!"

Tonno nodded; then Calwyn caught sight of Darrow seated beside him in the stern, as upright as ever, but pale and grim-faced. Her heart jumped. The boat drew nearer to the rocky shore. Calwyn sang the words of chantment and called up the bridge of ice she had intended to make earlier. It was not easy; the little boat bobbed about on the water, and the ground where she stood was not too steady, still trembling as the mountain of Doryus stirred and roared. But she blocked out every distraction, just as the priestesses had taught her, and called up the bridge, weaving it across the gap one handspan at a time, until an arc of ice joined the pebbled beach and the deck of *Fledgewing*.

"Mica, quickly!" Calwyn ran across first, not letting herself think how slippery the ice felt beneath her feet. She had tried to make it as rough and safe underfoot as she knew how, but as she held out her hand, she could see how Mica wavered and hesitated, placing one foot gingerly in front of the other. "Quick, quick!" But Mica had never walked across ice. She could not be quick, and even as Calwyn reached for her hand, she almost fell. Calwyn caught her just in time and hauled her bodily down the slope of the bridge to tumble on the deck. Calwyn was on her feet again in a flash and rapidly singing the words of undoing to melt the ice.

Darrow was beside her. "If I lift the new mast, can you fix it fast? We must raise sail."

Calwyn nodded. "Mica is a windworker," she said, and that was the only introduction Mica had before she became one of the crew.

They were drifting now toward Doryus, through the scattering of rocks and islands that made up the archipelago. The fire-mountain still belched and roared, and Trout, clutching the tiller, could scarcely tear his eyes from the sight. But everyone else on *Fledgewing* was frantic with activity. Darrow raised up the new mast. Swiftly Calwyn sang a firm foundation to bind it in place, a solid block of ice at its foot to hold it upright. With Darrow's help, Tonno hauled up the spare sail and held it steady. And Mica raised her hands and her clear, young voice, and from the still air drew a wind, gentle at first, but growing slowly stronger, to fill the sails and drive them steadily away from the islands, farther out into the open sea, leaving Doryus and the mountain behind them.

In the weird half-light, the peak stood out starkly against the boiling clouds of steam and smoke, its summit outlined in bright red-gold. As they watched, a jet of steam and ash and rock suddenly shot high into the air and rained down on the island, spattering and hissing into the waves. One fragment hit the deck of *Fledgewing* near Trout; he bent to pick it up, then dropped it hastily, shaking his fingers. "It's hot!"

Calwyn turned to Darrow. "Will Doryus Town be destroyed? Is there anything we can do to help the people?"

"I wouldn't shed no tears if Doryus Town *was* destroyed, with its slava, and its pirates, and its slave market," said Mica with venom, and spat over the side of the boat.

Tonno gave an approving chuckle. "Don't you fret over them, lass. They won't burn, nor drown. See there, the fire-flood's moving to the east, it'll flow into the sea. If they stir themselves, they'll come to no harm."

"Can't we stay and watch a little longer?" Trout was staring at the peak. "I've heard tales about the fire-mountain of Doryus. But I never thought to see the river of liquid rock with my own eyes."

"*Liquid rock?*" said Mica with frank derision. "How can a rock be liquid, like water? Don't make no sense."

"How can water be solid?" retorted Trout. "But you saw it turned to hard ice just now. It's the same with rock. If it's made hot enough, it melts."

"But what made it hot?" Calwyn swung to Darrow. "Was it chantment? What was that sound, did you hear it, before the fire began?"

"Hear it? The whole of the Isles must have heard it," said Tonno.

"That was the Clarion," said Darrow quietly. "The Clarion called up fire from the earth. It could have been nothing else."

"So Samis — " Calwyn stared at him, wide-eyed.

Darrow turned his head toward the south, where rags of fire still hung across the sky. "He is there, somewhere. Testing his strength. Seeing what the Power of Fire can do."

"We have to go after him!" Calwyn's eyes blazed as she grasped Darrow's hands, half-beseeching, half-commanding. "We can't just let him go! There are three of us now, three chanters united. We must try! I've told Mica everything, and she agrees. Don't you, Mica?"

Darrow looked from one face to the other: Calwyn's dark eyes burning; Mica's sharp, mistrustful but eager little face; Trout, wary, blinking behind his lenses, but holding the tiller firm as he'd been asked to do. At last he turned to Tonno. "What do you say, old friend? This is your vessel. Where shall we take her?"

There was silence for a breath or two, while the mountain roared and hissed behind them.

"We need provisions," Tonno said.

"There's the Small Isles, half a day from here," said Mica quickly. "There's good folk on Eo, no friend to pirates. They helped me once. Reckon they might help me again."

Tonno gave the smallest of shrugs. "South then. If that's where he is."

Darrow found Calwyn's eyes; her face was lit up with a smile of pure joy. "So," he said in a low voice. "The hunt goes on. Calwyn, I believe you have saved me again."

"It's you who have saved me, this time."

For a moment they gazed at each other, their hands still clasped together. Then, gently but firmly, Darrow pulled his hands from hers. Swiftly she let them go, suddenly embarrassed.

Darrow looked at Mica. "Can you give us a wind to take us south?" She nodded. "Then let us go now. I would like to catch him up. Can you do that?"

"I can help," said Calwyn quickly. "Mica's been teaching me windcraft."

Darrow raised an eyebrow, but he said nothing. All at once Tonno was the captain in command, bellowing orders. "Trout, keep your hands on the tiller and stop your eyes from wandering, or I'll give you something better than a fire-mountain to look at. Darrow, those cleats look none too firm. Calwyn, your ice is melting in this heat, look to it, if you please. And you, little lass, what did you say your name was? Mica, you say you can summon us a wind, then let's feel it!"

Soon the boat was leaping across the waves out in the open sea, leaving the Isle of Doryus and its fire-flood to grow smaller behind them.

Presently Calwyn found a moment to stand beside Trout. "I expected you to argue about following Samis," she said. "I thought you'd want to go home."

Trout shifted his hands on the tiller. "Could you take it for a breath? I'm getting cramp in my fingers — oh well. I've failed this term now anyway. Missing lectures without leave, smuggling girls into the college, going off like that without a word to anyone. They'll probably have me tried as a spy when I get back."

"You didn't seem worried about that before."

"When we were all locked up in the cabin, I started thinking. And I thought, well, it's not *so* wonderful in Mithates, is it? And besides, if I'd stayed in Mithates, I never would have seen *that*." He nodded behind them, to the tiny gold-and-red fountain of flame against the bone-bleached sky.

"I'm glad you're staying," said Calwyn. "I think we may need you."

Trout blushed as red as the moon had been. "I can take the tiller back now," he said shyly.

"And I should be helping Mica," said Calwyn, getting up.

All that day, with the double breath of chantment in *Fledge-wing's* sails, they followed the trail of the fire in the sky, the scarlet ribbons flung across the horizon, like the most vivid of sunsets, even though the sun blazed its own path above their heads.

It was sinking toward the sea, an immense orange ball, by the time they glimpsed Samis's ship. Calwyn caught her breath at the familiar shadow against the sky: the square sail, the banks of oars, the high serpent's head of the Gellanese prow.

Darrow lowered the looking-tube. "He has stopped the ship," he said. "He waits for us."

"Will we blow him out into the sea, like I did with the captain?" asked Mica fiercely.

Darrow held up his hand. "Wait!" he barked. "I would speak with him."

"Samis is stronger than your captain, Mica," whispered Calwyn, and Mica's thin, brown hand crept into hers and squeezed it.

Before long they could all see him: the still, menacing figure in the empty boat. His large, shaggy head was poised and watchful above broad, bulky shoulders, and the ruby of the great square ring gleamed on his finger, catching the light of the sunset. He stood with folded arms, utterly motionless; only the gray cloak fluttered behind him.

Trout swallowed hard and tried to turn it into a cough. Tonno raised his hand to Calwyn and Mica, and they fell silent. *Fledgewing* stopped; the two ships rocked on the waves.

"Hail, Samis!" cried Darrow.

The sorcerer stood impassive, as still as carved stone, waiting.

Darrow called across the water, "We have all seen now what the Clarion can do. But we have more chantments between us on this little boat than you can cram into one voice. We shall see what powers will be summoned in the final reckoning. Take heed, Samis. Pride has always been your weakness, and it will prove to be your downfall yet, if you persist in this course. It is not too late. Not too late for you, nor yet for me."

For a long moment there was silence, but for the slap of the waves. Samis stood motionless in his ship; but the curl of his lip communicated utter contempt.

Darrow tried again. "I know what you think. How can he dare to challenge me, with his ragbag of witchlings and his broken fishing boat? But *there will be a reckoning.* We are stronger than you imagine. *I* am stronger than you imagine."

Slowly, deliberately, Samis tipped back his head. Now, surely, he would reply. But instead he raised his hands, and the powerful throat-growl of chantment echoed out across the water. The rows of oars dipped together and pulled; the galley swung about and began to pull away.

Darrow's face was a mask.

"What now?" Tonno stood scowling at the tiller. "After him?"

"How can we? We still don't even have the mast fixed properly!" Trout snatched off his lenses and rubbed them frantically on his shirt.

"We'll lose him," said Calwyn softly.

The golden light of the sunset dazzled off the water, turning all the sea to a sheet of gold. Already the small dark shape of Samis's ship had been swallowed up in the brightness.

Darrow shook his head. "Let him go."

"We don't know where he's going," said Tonno.

Darrow half-smiled. "I know where. He has told me."

"But he didn't say nothin', not a word!" cried Mica.

"You forget that I know him. I know his plans. I was his friend, he told me everything. He is ready to try the reach of his power, and he goes south. South, to Spareth."

Calwyn shot a questioning look at Tonno, but he shook his head.

"Spareth," said Darrow. "The Lost City of the Ancient Ones. The birthplace of all chantment. They say that in Spareth, chantments had ten times the force that they have now. The farther we have moved from that homeland, the more our chantments have diminished. Samis told me, in Gellan, that he would go there, when the time came."

"So where is Spareth?" asked Trout.

"No one knows for certain."

"South," brooded Tonno. "Through the Southern Straits? But there's nothing beyond that but the Wildlands."

"And after the Wildlands?" There was a gleam in Darrow's eye, though whether it was amusement or something more grim, none of them could tell.

"After the Wildlands — why, nothing." Tonno frowned.

"The coast is unknown. That is a very different thing from there being no coast at all," said Darrow.

Calwyn could have stamped her foot. "You're speaking in riddles, Darrow!"

Tonno turned away. "Let him have his riddles. I've a ship to sail and a port to find. Mica, you know these waters, lass. Which way to Eo, by your reckoning?"

The others began to move about the boat, and presently they were under way again, this time heading a little to the northeast, where Mica said the island of Eo lay. But Calwyn stayed beside Darrow. He was staring over the rail into the southern waters, where Samis had vanished.

"Why didn't we try to fight him just now?" she said. "We're all here. Why did we wait?"

"Chantment is stronger in Spareth. We will have a better chance of defeating him there."

"But if chantments are stronger in Spareth, then he will be stronger too."

"I have my reasons, Calwyn. This is not the time." Darrow's face was stern, hawklike.

"He let you see where he was going. It's as if he *wanted* us to follow. Why would he do that? Could it be a trap?"

Darrow made no reply.

"You said, 'It's not too late for you, nor yet for me,'" she persisted. "What does that mean? It sounds almost as if you want to beat him at his own plan!"

"That is enough questions for one day," said Darrow. "Even for you."

"Darrow!" She reached out her hand, but he turned aside. She let her hand drop. At the very moment they'd begun to draw close again, he was shutting her out, as though there was room only for Samis in his thoughts now. Without another word, he limped along the deck toward the cabin and went below.

For a long time Calwyn stayed where she was, staring after him with her eyes narrowed and the line of a frown between her brows. Then she reached behind and shook out her hair, and began to replait it, strand by smooth strand, until it was all neat again, two smooth dark ropes hanging down her back, just as they should be.

The Song of the Trees

For many days they sailed southward, into the Southern Straits, which Mica called the Sea of Sevona. Every day Tonno peered through the looking-tube, scanning the horizon for some sign of Samis's ship, but he never saw it. "He must have rowed far ahead while we were at Eo."

"No! We must be quicker than he is," said Trout, oddly proud, watching Mica and Calwyn as they sat side by side singing up a steady wind to send the boat flying across the blue sea. "I think *we've* passed *him*. No one could go faster than *Fledgewing*."

Gradually the cultivated lands petered out, and they left far behind them the silver streams and flat, dusty fields. They sailed past the very fringe of the lands that could be called Kalysons, where farming had been abandoned long ago. Ruined windmills pointed forlornly to the sky, and here and there a line of trees still straggled to keep the pattern of their planting, but the Wildlands had triumphed. The land was barren here, a tide of rocks and scrub too strong to be beaten back with farmers' plows and hoes.

There was a chill in the air now, and at night the sun set more slowly, drawing dusk across the sea like a gray veil. With every day that passed, they sailed deeper into autumn, deeper into the Wildlands.

As they rested at anchor one evening, Calwyn sat in the prow, watching the blue smoke of Tonno's pipe curl over the railing and into the dusky sky. Trout was stretched out against a coil of rope some distance away, crunching on an apple. The only other sounds were the soft slap of water on timber and, far off, from the shadowy shore, the rhythmic cries of night darts as they came out to feed and flit about in the strengthening moonlight.

At the other end of the boat, Darrow shifted his weight from his twisted foot, which often began to ache at nightfall, and sat back against the cabin wall. Mica was beside him, mending a fishing net; she began to sing a song from Emeran, and the notes floated up to Tonno and Calwyn. Mica's voice when she sang the songs of her childhood was quite different from when she sang the chantments of windwork; it was huskier, and there were tears buried in it.

Tonno gave a contented grunt. "I like to hear the little lass sing. She puts me in mind of our Enna. Like a little lark, she was, always chattering and laughing and singing away. Mebbe this one'll be the same, once she gets a bit of happiness in her." He sucked at his pipe and gave Calwyn a shrewd look. "You seem troubled."

Calwyn stared up at him in surprise. She wouldn't have expected gruff Tonno to notice her unease, or to care. She hesitated before she answered. "It's nothing."

He shook his head. "Something's eating at you, lass. Let's have it."

Calwyn looked up to be sure that no one else could hear. In a low voice she said, "It's Darrow." Nervously she glanced at Tonno, but he was expressionless, chewing at his pipe stem.

"Aye. What about him?"

"It's only — you heard how he spoke to Samis, when he said, *it's not too late*, and *I am stronger than you think*. He *almost* made it sound as though he wanted to be the Singer of All Songs himself."

Tonno frowned. "Mebbe he said that to throw him off guard. Until now Samis has taken his time in going about this plan of his. But if he thinks we're racing him to the prize, why, then he might stumble, be careless."

"Yes, perhaps. But —"

"Speak your mind, lass. I never could abide a time-waster."

Calwyn spoke slowly, cautiously, glancing over to where Darrow rested with his eyes closed. "I'm sure this doesn't mean anything, and at the time I didn't even believe it, but — when I met Samis in Mithates, he told me it was *Darrow's* idea to collect the Nine Powers. That they only quarreled when Darrow realized Samis was a greater sorcerer than he was."

Tonno snorted. "I thought better of you than that. To believe the words of one like *him!* "

"I'm not saying that I believed him," said Calwyn hastily. "But at the end, when Samis sailed away, letting us follow him — perhaps he wants Darrow to join with him again. And Darrow seems — changed. He doesn't speak to you anymore. Or to me. Perhaps — perhaps he *is* thinking of going back to Samis."

"You don't know him as well as me, lass, and that's a fact," said Tonno bluntly. "The only thing he's thinking of is how to stop that rogue. Aye, he's thinking hard. Too hard to talk to you and me about what's for dinner, or whose turn it is to swab the deck. I wouldn't expect anything different. And nor should you."

Calwyn was silent, playing with the end of her plait.

Tonno knocked his pipe out on the side of the boat. "Foolishness," he said, and that was the end of that conversation.

They sailed on, close to the shore, close enough to see the barren wastelands, with their cover of gray scrub, through Trout's looking-tube. Once they saw a great beast grazing on the bushes; it lumbered from one plant to the next, tearing at the branches with its massive jaws.

"It must be near as big as the pirates' ship," said Mica in wonderment.

Trout shuddered. "Then its jaws must be large enough to snap this boat in two and swallow us all without chewing."

"It is an eater of plants," said Darrow. "It would not be interested in chewing on us."

"All the same, I'd rather we didn't land *just* here," said Trout. "If no one else objects."

The next day they saw a herd of the shrub-grazers, and the

sound of their mournful bellows carried across the water. They had a favorable wind to take them south, and Mica was able to spend all morning at the railing, gazing at the creatures. "You sure we can't land?" she asked wistfully. "Look at 'em, Trout, gentle as kittens. Wouldn't you like to have a look up close?"

"No, thank you," said Trout firmly, and later that day something happened to convince him he was right.

They were eating the midday meal on deck when Calwyn caught sight of a flock of birds, wheeling and turning, a crowd of black dots between the boat and the shore.

"What are they? Too big for gulls — Trout, where's the looking-tube?"

"Here," said Tonno, raising the tube to his eye.

"Comin' closer," said Mica. "Must be gulls, after scraps."

Suddenly Tonno sprang to his feet, knocking his plate of food aside. "They're no gulls. Darrow, quickly, look! Have you ever seen creatures like these?"

Darrow took the tube, and his eyebrow raised. "I have heard of them, but never seen them. I had thought they were creatures of legend."

"Let me see," demanded Trout, even though he could never manage to see through the tube as clearly as the others. But Mica was quicker.

"They're coming closer," said Calwyn. The shapes that had been mere dots a moment before were now clearly creatures with long, straight wings, swooping and riding the wind like kites. Their cries rang across the water, sharp, fierce, high-pitched calls. Mica passed the tube to Calwyn, and said just four words: "Look at their teeth."

Calwyn put the tube to her eye with a hand that shook. There they were, suddenly clear and huge, enormous flying beasts, not birds, far bigger than any bird, and without feathers. Their wings stretched like sails from scaly bodies to clawed feet, and their heads turned as they flew so that Calwyn could see their small, hooded eyes and their long jaws, lined with row after row of sharp, gleaming teeth. She held out the tube to Trout.

"They speak of these beasts in the ancient tales of Merithuros," said Darrow in a calm, interested voice. "They were known as the guardians of the Wildlands. Some call them the flesh-eaters."

"Flesh-eaters!" Trout's voice was a squeak.

"I think," said Tonno, with admirable steadiness, "that we should all go below."

Trout was already clattering down the companionway.

Eagerly Mica asked, "Tonno, you want Calwyn and me to call up a wind and hold 'em back?"

"No," said Darrow. "Let them be."

"Calwyn could put up a shell of ice to protect us," said Tonno. Calwyn gave him a sharp look.

"We do nothing unless it is needful," Darrow said sternly.

"These creatures belong to this place, they have every right to defend it. If we show them that we mean them no harm, they will leave us alone. Once we start to fight them, they will have all the more reason to attack us."

"You speak as if these were people, with reasoning minds, not blind and stupid beasts," said Tonno. "Do I ask permission of the fish before I haul it out of the sea? Do I beg the pardon of the rabbit before I set the trap?"

"Perhaps you should," said Darrow, with a faint smile. "Mica will tell you that the people of the Outer Isles beg permission of the fish every year in their great ceremony."

"Please," said Calwyn. "If we're not going to fight them off, then let's go below!"

The creatures were very close now. Their harsh cries and the eerie whistle of their wings grew louder on the wind. The rest of *Fledgewing's* crew hastened down the companionway, and Tonno pulled the hatchway firmly closed behind them.

"Can they open latches?" asked Trout, white-faced, peering out of the porthole. "With those jaws, they must be able to. They look like vices — or pincers —"

"For the last time, these are mere beasts!" said Tonno in exasperation.

"The legends say they are as intelligent as any man or woman," said Darrow. "It's said that they are masters of the ninth Power, the Power of Tongue — though of course they have their own language, different from ours."

"If no one can speak it, how do they know it's a language?" Even shaking with terror, Trout couldn't stop himself asking.

"If it is a language, it's not one I want to listen to," said Tonno, with a shake of his big, curly head.

Mica edged closer to his side. "You think the sorcerer sent 'em? Is he spyin' on us?"

"I dunno, lass. Mebbe." Tonno looked at Darrow.

"It is possible," he said impassively. "He may be capable of anything now."

"They're here!" cried Trout, and in the next moment there came a terrible noisy chorus as the creatures perched on the decks and the mast and the roof of the cabin, the sound of a hundred sharp talons rasping, fifty pairs of scaly wings folding. It was a sound to send chills down the spine. Suddenly the cabin darkened as the creatures settled, screeching, in front of the portholes. Hastily Trout hauled at the curtains. "I don't want them looking in at us with their little beady eyes."

Mica was huddled in a corner, her usual bravado quite vanished, as the creatures clamored all around them. Even Darrow, though still resolute, looked a little apprehensive. Tonno picked up Darrow's walking stick and tapped it against the edge of the table, muttering something that might have been a curse, or a plea to the gods for protection.

Then Calwyn closed her eyes and began to sing. She sang softly, no louder than a murmur, the quiet soothing song that she used to sing when the bees swarmed in Antaris. As the familiar words rose from her lips, she was aware that the others in the cabin fell silent and listened. She let her voice grow stronger, the words clearer in the gentle lulling melody that Damyr had taught her long ago.

"Listen — listen — they can hear her!"

"Ssh!"

Beneath the steady rhythm of her song, Calwyn heard Mica whispering and Darrow hushing her. The song was carrying her now, the words themselves drawing her onward. And then she knew that the creatures were growing still on their perches, their wings silenced, their cries muted. They could hear her; they were listening just as the bees used to listen. Sometimes in Antaris the bees would become utterly quiet, as though she sang them to sleep, and sometimes they would sing in their turn, an answering murmur, so that she and they sang together, an easy, peaceful melody.

And now she heard them, softly at the fringes of her hearing, a barely audible rasping chorus, as the creatures whispered in answer to her song. For a long time Calwyn and the terrible creatures sang together, and then all at once there came a great rustling of wings, and the boat lurched as the flock took flight, pushing off together with their sharp claws. The cabin grew light once more. The creaking of the great scaled wings sounded around them and diminished, and then there was silence but for Calwyn's clear voice rising and falling. Then the song ended, and everything was quiet. She opened her eyes.

The others were all staring at her, wide-eyed. Mica gave a loud sobbing gasp, as though she'd been holding her breath all the while, and then tossed her hair out of her eyes and pretended she had never been frightened at all.

"How did you do that?" Trout's voice shook.

"I sang the old song, the song to the swarm," said Calwyn. She felt a little dazed, as if she were waking from a dream. Her fingers were tingling. She stared down at them as though she had never seen them before, then, suddenly understanding, looked up at Darrow with a question in her eyes.

"Yes," he said quietly, though she had not spoken. "It is the eighth Power, the Power of Beasts. Whatever you used to sing to the bees, these creatures understood it too."

Tonno asked gruffly, "Will they leave us alone now?"

"If they don't, she can sing to 'em again, can't she!" Mica's golden eyes shone with pride as she nudged Calwyn in the arm.

"I don't think she will need to do that," said Darrow, and as he stood to go back up on deck, he laid his hand briefly on Calwyn's shoulder. It burned there like a brand for the space of a heartbeat or two, like the ice-brand that had marked her arm when she became a novice. Even after he had lifted his hand and limped away, she felt the shadow of its burning, and all that day she felt it burning still.

That night, as Calwyn lay sleepless in the little cabin that she now shared with Mica, she overheard Darrow and Tonno talking in low voices.

"Didn't you once tell Xanni and me that it was so difficult to master one craft, it could take a lifetime?" Tonno was saying. "And that was what made Samis dangerous, that he could master two or three Powers so easily?"

"I remember." Darrow's voice was low.

"And yet she comes to us an iceworker, learns windcall in a day or two, and now it seems she can tame the beasts as well."

"It is interesting." Darrow's voice became more lively, and Calwyn heard the knock of his boots as he stretched out his lame foot. "Perhaps I should have guessed it when I saw her with the bees in Antaris. That Power, the eighth, is the one that all the scholars thought was lost. Maybe it's carried in the blood, in the depths of memory, passed on without knowing, the way beasts themselves know how to sing, and build their nests, and hunt, without being taught. Or the priestesses of Antaris have been guarding those chantments without knowing it, as well as the craft of ice-call. Interesting—"

"You've always called Samis such a marvel. Such a mighty sorcerer. And here's this lass with her plaits down her back, with the same gift, mebbe. Mebbe stronger than his, for all we know."

"Maybe." The word was breathed so low that Calwyn barely heard it.

"Mebbe *she's* the one, not him — the Singer of All Songs. Think of that! I'd like to see his face if he knew it, to be trumped by a slip of a lass, not even in skirts." Tonno's rare, deep laugh rumbled through the cabin. "Aye, I'd like to see that day!"

"There's one day I would not like to see," said Darrow. "A day when the two of them joined their powers together."

"She'd never do that." Tonno's reply was instant, dismissive.

"He can be very — persuasive. He is not easy to refuse. And she would have power over all the world. Empress of Tremaris. Better than being a mere High Priestess of Antaris."

Tonno laughed again, uncertainly, as if he didn't know whether Darrow was making a joke. "Aye, well, who can say if any of us would say no to all that, eh?" Calwyn heard the scrape of his chair as he stood up.

"Good night, friend."

"I'll wake you for the second watch."

She could hear Tonno climb the steps onto the deck, where he would keep watch. But she heard no sound from Darrow; he sat at the table for a long time, lost in thought, and by the time he stirred, she had fallen into a troubled sleep.

The next morning she found a reason to sit by Darrow at the tiller. The strange beasts had not come back; the skies were clear and the sailing brisk. They'd come round the southernmost cape of the unknown coast; *Fledgewing* was heading westerly now, away from the morning sun. The scrubby landscape with its herds of huge shrub-grazers had gradually given way to a grimmer vista of high, bare cliffs and peaks.

Darrow did not greet her or even look at her; it was as though she wasn't there. Calwyn sat in silence, watching the dark line of the shore. Her throat was tight, as if a string were tied around it and wouldn't let her voice out.

At last she said, "Am I really so unnatural?"

Darrow said, "Uncommon, perhaps. But not unnatural." He'd known she was there all the time. He glanced up at the sail and shifted his hand slightly on the tiller. "I wondered whether you had overheard us."

Calwyn's face flushed, and she said quickly, "Then you should have been more careful with your words. You must know that I'd never do anything to help Samis."

"Mind what you promise, Calwyn. Whatever arts we may possess, not one of us can see into the future."

She stared at him, white now with hurt and anger. "I think I can safely promise *that*! Can *you*?" The words shot out before she could bite them back, and he flinched as though she had struck him.

In a low voice, he said, "If anyone had come to me five years ago and said to me that my dearest friend would become my fiercest enemy, that he would try to kill me a dozen ways, that I would rather see him dead than —" He stopped, staring across the waves, and was silent. "We cannot know what lies ahead," he said at last, his voice shaking. "But one thing I do see clearly. We will fail in this quest, unless we can trust each other." He turned his head and looked at her with his keen gray-green eyes.

For a long moment they stared at each other, while the sound of the sea rushed beside them, and the clear, high thread of

Mica's song hung in the air, bright and thrumming as a golden wire. And she saw that he knew about her own doubts, her fears, and even her feelings for him, and their misgivings were mirrored, each in the other's face.

For some reason she thought of Marna then. *Do not be enemies.* It would be all too easy to allow doubts to grow into mistrust, mistrust into bitterness, bitterness into hatred. And then Samis would have won, without ever lifting his voice against them.

The angry light died in Calwyn's eyes, and the hard line of Darrow's mouth relaxed. She held out her hand, and he took it and pressed it briefly against his cheek. Then he turned to the tiller again, and the distant mountaintops that gleamed with caps of snow. "Look, Calwyn," he said. "These are your mountains. If you followed the range north, you would come to Antaris."

Calwyn gazed at the silent peaks with an odd feeling in the pit of her stomach. Somewhere, far to the north, life went on in Antaris as it always had. The autumn ceremonies would be underway, the leaves of the blazetree in the sacred valley turning scarlet. Then the leaves would fall, and at midwinter moondark, under the bare branches, she would have been made a full priestess. Soon, perhaps, she might have taken over from Tamen as Guardian of the Wall. Now that would never be.

She looked about at the shining sea and the clean stretched canvas of *Fledgewing*'s sail. She looked at the eager face of Mica as she pointed to a school of leaping fish, and at Trout, almost overbalancing as he tried to net the fish because they were a kind he had never seen before, and at Tonno's strong, stern gaze as he watched them. And at last, she returned Darrow's grave smile. And she knew that, even with the menace of Samis all about them, she would rather be here on *Fledgewing* than anywhere else in Tremaris.

At last the mountainous shore grew less forbidding, the slopes more gentle. Trees appeared, at first just a light scattering of green, but then more and more, clustering thickly right up to the water's edge, until there was nothing to be seen but dense forest. Mica's eyes were wide with wonder that there could be so many trees in the world. In the Isles, it was rare to see two trees growing side by side; to see a hundred, or a thousand, with barely a hand's gap between them, was a marvel beyond belief.

Through the looking-tube they saw bright flashes of color: the glimmer of birds' wings, blue and yellow, and trees in fruit, with globes of heavy red and gold hanging from their branches.

"We should land as soon as we see a river," said Tonno. "We need to fill the water barrels."

"And I can't wait to taste fresh fruit again," said Mica longingly. "I swear, next plate of bean and fish stew I see, I'll chuck over the side. Though it's the best bean and fish stew I ever ate," she added hastily, seeing a scowl on the face of Tonno, who was responsible for producing the meal they ate most days.

It was Trout who saw the harbor first. The wind had slackened, but not quite died; they were debating whether it was worth Mica or Calwyn summoning up a breeze when Trout gave a cry. They all gathered at the boat's side, silently watching as they came around the promontory, and Calwyn caught her breath, for every tree that lined the inlet was a blazetree in full autumn colors. The narrow cove was an extraordinary sight, a splash of scarlet against the dense green of the forest. Calwyn had only ever known the one solitary blazetree of the sacred valley in Antaris, but here hundreds thronged along the water, like a crowd of people all dressed in bright crimson and scarlet, pressing eagerly forward to glimpse them as they glided by. The blazeleaves stirred and rustled in the breeze with the whispering she knew so well, but magnified a thousandfold, so that a sighing chorus reached out to them across the water. She whispered, "The trees are singing—"

"It's a song of welcome, then," said Tonno briskly, practical as ever. "There's a stream flowing into the cove. Fresh water. Darrow, help me haul in the sail, if you please. We'll anchor here."

While the others were busy dropping anchor and readying the dinghy and the water barrels to be filled, Calwyn remained at the rail, looking out toward the trees. When Mica touched her elbow, she jumped.

"You bewitched? You been starin' at them trees ever since we first came round the point."

Calwyn shivered. "I have a strange feeling about this place."

"Bad feelin', or good?"

"Not a bad one," said Calwyn slowly. "But it's as though the trees were calling me. Do you hear it?"

Mica paused, and listened, her tousled head on one side. "I can hear 'em rustlin' all right," she said at last. "Noisiest trees I ever heard, and no mistake. But I can't hear no callin'."

"It's just a fancy," said Calwyn, giving herself a shake. "Perhaps it's the strangeness of seeing so many blazetrees in one place."

"You comin' ashore with Tonno and me, or you want to stay here?"

"No. I'll come."

The nearer they rowed the little boat toward the pebbly beach, the louder grew the song of the trees.

"Careful!" Tonno shook himself as Calwyn splashed him.

"I'm sorry. I was listening. I can almost hear the words —"

Tonno looked skeptical, but merely said, "Well, watch your oar."

They unloaded the water barrels, rolling them up the beach to where the stream flowed between the trees. The whispering of the leaves was almost deafening now. It made even Tonno and Mica uneasy to move about in the lively rustling that drowned out their own speech. But it was stranger still for Calwyn to stand there in the scarlet grove, surrounded by the trees she held most sacred, and hear them call to her in words that she strained to understand, while she performed such an everyday task, rolling the water barrels and filling them in the clear water, just as if they'd landed at any ordinary stream. Suddenly she let go of the end of the barrel she was balancing with Mica.

"What? What's the matter?"

"Over there, did you see?"

Mica stared toward the shadows beneath the trees. "Can't see nothin'."

"There was someone standing there — someone watching us."

"What's the delay?" called Tonno impatiently from the edge of the stream.

"Calwyn thinks she saw someone, under them trees."

Tonno carefully set upright the barrel he had just filled and came over to where they stood. "There are no people within twenty days' sail of here, Calwyn. You must have seen a forest beast. Unless — was it Samis?"

Calwyn shook her head vehemently. "It was a man, but not him," she said. "Standing by those trees and watching us. I saw him. He was tall, and he had strangely colored skin, like tarnished brass."

Tonno's face was wary. "You haven't forgotten, he can make himself look like anything, to deceive us."

As if she could forget that! "It wasn't him," said Calwyn passionately. "I know it. If there was a chantment of seeming at work here, I'm sure I'd feel it. It was someone else, a man, watching us."

Mica peered at her anxiously. "Calwyn, I know it's turned you wrong side up to be in all these trees, but we'll go soon —"

"I'm not upset!" exclaimed Calwyn. "I'm not — I'm quite all right." She scanned the space beneath the trees, but there was nothing but shadows. The trees' song filled her ears, calling her, calling her — She shook off Mica's hand and began to walk hesitantly toward the trees.

"Calwyn! You be careful! What if it were a beast you saw?"

"Then she'll tame it, no doubt, like she did to the others," growled Tonno. "Let her be. When she sees there's nothing there, she'll come back and be more useful than she is now. Come on, Mica. We fisher-folk can manage between us; we can do without the dreamers."

Calwyn kept walking until she was under the canopy of the trees. It was cool, the ground damp underfoot. She closed her eyes and let the song of the trees wash over her. Now she knew what it reminded her of: not just the lonely whisper of the blazetree in the sacred valley, but the ancient songs that the priestesses sang there at moondark, calling the novices into the sisterhood. She took one step forward, then another, and found her lips moving to the words she knew by heart, the words she had heard every year at the turn of the season for as long as she could remember, the calling song. Tonno was right, it was a song of welcome. The trees were welcoming her, deeper and deeper, embracing her, calling her home.

She opened her eyes.

A young man of about her own age was standing before her, the same man she had seen waiting and watching at the edge of the forest. He was tall and very thin, thinner even than Darrow, and his skin was dark, with the almost metallic sheen she had tried to describe to the others. His long hair was tied back from his face, and he wore a simple robe of woven fibers. Elaborate tattoos spiraled up his arms and across his chest. Her eyes flew at once to his wrist, and as if he knew what she was looking for, he held it out toward her so that she could see the three moons branded there, in the same place as on her own arm, the mark of the Goddess. He smiled, and although no words left his lips, she heard his voice inside her mind. *Welcome, sister. Welcome to Spiridrell.*

"I don't believe you," said Trout flatly. "There are no people here! How could there be? No traveler has ever crossed the Wildlands."

"But I've seen them," said Calwyn. "Or one of them, at least. I didn't expect you to believe me, Trout." She turned to Darrow and asked him directly, "Do you doubt my word?"

"Not your word," said Darrow slowly. "But I do not trust this forest. I think it may have thrown some chantment over you, to make you see what is not really there."

"Perhaps it was Samis," suggested Trout. "Lurking in the trees, singing up visions to trick us. We'll wander off into the forest and never come back."

"She says not," said Tonno.

"I saw a man," said Calwyn. "*Not* Samis. He means us no harm. He says he's been waiting for us. He's not afraid of us, and we shouldn't be afraid of him. Darrow" — she turned toward him imploringly — "you must believe me!"

After a moment, Darrow said, "Yes, I believe you. I'll come ashore with you. But the rest of you may stay here, if you wish."

There was an uncomfortable pause. Then Tonno said, "I'll come with you. I wouldn't leave you to face danger alone."

"I'll come," said Mica in a flash. "I'm not feared."

"Then I suppose I'll have to come too," grumbled Trout. "I've got no wish to sit here by myself and wait for you all to be killed together."

At first it seemed that Trout's and Tonno's doubts were right after all, and Calwyn's eyes had been playing tricks on her; when they stepped ashore there was no sign of life. Even the birds were silent and invisible. The breeze had dropped; the whispering of the blazetrees was hushed. It was as though the forest held its breath. But Calwyn's feet were steady as she led them alongside the stream.

"She might be leading us into an ambush," Trout whispered to Mica.

"If Calwyn and Darrow says it's safe, then it's safe," she whispered back fiercely. "And Tonno won't let nothin' hurt us."

Presently Calwyn stopped; they were standing in a grove marked out by a circle of blazetrees. Ringed by white trunks, with the scarlet and crimson canopy of leaves overhead, they might have been standing under a great tent. The air was very still and cool. Calwyn held up her hand. "He's coming."

Trout gave a start as he saw a man materialize, in perfect silence, out of a dark place between the trees. He swung about, fearing that more men might appear, that they might indeed be caught in a trap. But there were no others, and the stranger was holding out fruit and flowers, not a weapon.

Welcome, friends. Welcome to Spiridrell. I have been waiting for you, waiting for our sister to arrive.

Darrow turned a startled face to Calwyn. "Does he mean you?"

Again the unvoiced words sounded inside their heads. *I was told of your coming by the arakin.*

"The arakin?" said Darrow.

The ones you call the flesh-eaters. They told me one was coming, a singer of songs.

"They talk to you, those creatures?" Trout grimaced. Who knew what other frightful beasts this strange young man might be in communication with?

They are the guardians of Spiridrell. The stranger stepped forward and presented a piece of golden-skinned fruit to Darrow. *It is time for you to follow now.*

He turned and walked away silently between the trees. Darrow and Calwyn followed.

"Wait!" said Trout. "We're going with him, just like that?"

"It may be that these people dwell in Spareth, that Spiridrell is their name for the Lost City we seek," said Darrow. "Perhaps they are the direct descendants of the Ancient Ones."

"There's nothing to fear, Trout," said Calwyn gently. Her eyes were shining. "Come."

The man had paused and was waiting for them, but as soon as the crew of *Fledgewing* began to follow, he turned and moved swiftly and unerringly through the forest. Behind them, the blaze-leaves whispered in the breeze, a sibilant song of farewell.

The stranger set a rapid pace, flitting nimble and light-footed from shadow to shadow. It was difficult to keep up, and they stumbled along, cracking twigs underfoot and brushing past leaves and vines. Once Calwyn turned to Darrow and saw that his lips were folded tight, and sweat gleamed on his brow, but he swung his stick swiftly, without faltering, and she didn't dare offer him her arm or any other help.

They followed the course of the stream, moving gradually up-hill, until Calwyn was startled to see the jagged crimson stain of the blazetree cove far below them and *Fledgewing* tiny as a toy on the blue-green water. The day was passing like a dream: the soft sounds of the forest, the cool shadows of the trees, and always just ahead of them the figure of their guide, fleet-footed, darting silently between the leaves and flowering vines. Her head was drowsy with the scent of the flowers, sweet and wild, and she moved her feet mechanically, one step after another, following the stranger who led them on, deeper and deeper into the forest, trac-ing an invisible path. She had no desire to speak, and the others were silent, as if the forest itself had laid hands on their shoulders and hushed them.

They came at last to a small clearing, and the stranger stopped, utterly still. *Wait!* came the command into their minds.

Now that they were no longer moving, Calwyn could hear the tiniest sounds of the forest: the faint calls of birds, the shifting of unseen forest creatures, the gurgle of streams, even the distant whisper of the blazetrees and the sea lapping on the shore. But when the tall figures of the other forest people appeared silently between the trees, she heard no sound, no footfall, not even a breath. It was as though they rose out of the forest like a mist, or as if the shadows solidified into human form and came to life. Where there had been no one and nothing but the trees, suddenly there was a band of a dozen men and women, all dressed in the same simply woven cloths and with the same intricate tattoos as the young man who had led them from the grove.

But these people, still and silent as the trees themselves, were not holding out fruit and flowers, and their faces were stern and unwelcoming. Calwyn was aware of Trout behind her shuffling a little nearer, and Tonno's hand moving surreptitiously toward his belt, where his sturdy fishing knife hung in its sheath. One of the strangers stepped forward, a woman with her hair scraped back and oiled and piled up high on a carved wooden comb. She faced the man who had led them through the forest.

Go back. Take them back to the water. You cannot come any farther.

The young man did not move. *They are friends to us, not enemies. The arakin foretold their coming. I must take them to Spiridrell.*

They are not welcome in Spiridrell. The Elders will not see them. Take them to your own place, if they are of your kind. The woman turned her head and looked them up and down contemptuously.

Darrow said, "We intend no harm to you. We are travelers."

But at the sound of his voice, all the forest people backed away; some clapped their hands to their ears.

They may not come to Spiridrell! The woman's eyes were gleaming with fear and anger. *Take them away. We want no Voiced Ones, no singers of songs here. Take them to your own place, and take the harm they bring upon yourself alone!*

For a moment the young man stared back at her, then without replying he turned and beckoned the crew of *Fledgewing* to follow him back through the forest. Calwyn saw that his dark eyes were shining with unshed tears, and impulsively she put her hand upon his arm. He did not smile, but he looked at her steadily, acknowledging her touch, then slipped through the trees the way they had come.

"What's this?" muttered Tonno to Darrow. "Are these people fighting among themselves?"

"We cannot expect them to agree on everything, any more than the other peoples of Tremaris."

It is more than that.

The young man did not turn around, but it seemed to Calwyn that his back was stiff as though he had been beaten and was trying not to show his pain.

They have cast me out. The Elders will not suffer me to live among them. I must live apart from Spiridrell.

"Why's that?" asked Mica.

I speak with the beasts and understand them. And I have other skills, skills that others do not share. The People have no love for me.

"They fear you," said Darrow quietly. "They fear what they do not understand. It is the same everywhere. There's not one of us who could not tell you the same story. Everyone who works with chantment knows what it is to be feared, and to be hated."

"How do you speak with the beasts if you have no voice?" asked Trout, puzzled as usual over a practical question. The young man turned around at that, smiling at Trout.

I speak with them as I speak with you.

Suddenly he raised his arms high at his sides and threw back his head. Calwyn heard no call, no chantment, but at once they were surrounded by a whirring of wings, and from everywhere there swooped and fluttered dozens of the bright forest birds that they had glimpsed before. This time they did not dart away into the cover of the trees but answered the silent call of the young man; they settled on his shoulders, his outstretched arms, his head and back, even clinging to the fibers of his robe with their claws, so that he was covered from head to foot in their jeweled feathers, a living garment of iridescent color, with just his proud, serious face visible between the curving wings. Mica clapped her hands and laughed in delight.

Again the young man gave some silent signal, and the birds flew away, all but one bright green-and-yellow bird that remained perched on his shoulder.

Come. We are almost there. And as though nothing out of the ordinary had happened, he turned and walked on through the forest, with the little bird looking back at them, still chirruping quietly.

At last he halted. *We have arrived.*

They were standing in a grove with tall trees on all sides. A dense canopy of leaves cast a deep veil of shadow over the forest floor; a stream gurgled over a bed of smooth stones with a sound like laughter.

Then Mica thought to look upward and gasped. Far above their heads, partly hidden by the thick cover of foliage, was a large platform, like a raft sailing on the sea of green leaves. A rope ladder dangled down to rest on the ground just in front of them.

Darrow looked inquiringly toward their guide. The stranger nodded and put his foot to the ladder, and in a moment had run up the rungs as nimbly as if they were an ordinary flight of steps. Trout gulped. Tonno said, "I don't know if that contraption will bear my weight."

"There is only one way to be sure," said Darrow. He tested the first rung with his boot, then began the laborious process of hauling himself higher and higher, trying not to put too much weight on his crooked foot. The others followed him.

Calwyn was the last to pull herself up onto the platform. She stood for a moment blinking in the flood of sunshine that greeted her, for the structure was level with the treetops, bright and warm with sunlight, floating above the shade below as a boat floats above the depths of the sea. It was a large, flat, wooden deck, sturdily built, and hemmed by the treetops so it seemed that a hedge of green grew along its edges. A ladder led to a smaller platform, higher in the tree. Flowering vines spilled untidily over the smooth planks, filling the air with a dizzying perfume.

Welcome to my home. The stranger regarded them solemnly. *My name is Halasaa.*

Darrow stepped forward and spoke each of their names in turn. Halasaa bowed, then fetched a carved wooden cup. Calwyn took it and inhaled a strange wild scent like the flowers. "Careful!" she heard Trout hiss at her side. But she tipped the cup; the sweet drink left her lips and tongue tingling. Halasaa handed the cup to each of the others. Only Trout would not drink; he sniffed the cup, and sneezed, and set it down.

Halasaa gestured to them to sit. He watched as Darrow lowered himself awkwardly, holding his foot out stiffly before him.

You are hurt.

"An old injury, long healed. It no longer gives me pain."

But it impedes you.

Darrow gave a wry smile. "Yes, at times."

Let me see it.

Darrow hesitated for a moment, then unlaced his boot and stretched out his twisted foot. Halasaa looked at it carefully, then laid his brown tapered hands on it, closed his eyes, and began to move his fingers up and down rapidly, gently pinching and tapping in an elaborate rhythm so quick that Calwyn could hardly follow the flickering movements. A shiver traveled down the back of her neck. Once again she had the sensation, as she had when she stood beneath the blazetrees, of hearing a song half-remembered, half-understood, but just out of her reach. This was chantment, but a strange, silent chantment, without words or music. She could not understand it, but she knew that whatever Halasaa was doing, it was as magical as any song. She heard Darrow take in a sharp breath and saw his hands press hard against the planking, the knuckles white and bloodless. Halasaa shifted his hands, and the rhythm of his movements slowed to a firm, kneading pressure. Then the chantment ended, and Halasaa opened his eyes and lifted his hands away. Darrow's long, thin foot rested on the floor, as straight and whole as if it had never been hurt.

Mica gasped, and Tonno shook his head in wonder. Quietly, Darrow said, "I thank you." He took his foot between his own hands and felt it quickly all over, then without fuss reached for his boot and pulled it on.

Trout gaped. "How——?"

Halasaa smiled. *My father taught me the old craft. He was as I am. He taught me how to dance with the force that binds and flows in all living things, in you and me, in the trees of the forest, in the birds and the arakin and the creeping beasts of the ground. All of the world sings, and dances too. All is one, all are joined in the great river.*

"The fourth Power," breathed Calwyn. "The Power of Becoming."

Yes. He taught me that there is no ending to the river, only a ceaseless changing flow. Nothing leaves the river, and nothing remains the same within it. All is change, all is movement, yet the river is always the river.

"How can you heal what's broken?" asked Tonno.

When a rock or a tree branch is placed in a river, the water's flow is altered a little. Have you not seen this? Our dances are pebbles and twigs, we make a lit-

tle ripple in the great stream, that is all. *Nothing leaves the river. This is how heal-ing is accomplished.*

"You say that nothing leaves the river," said Tonno, and now his voice was harsh. "But what about the dead? Is it in your powers to bring back the dead?"

"Tonno," said Darrow softly, warningly.

Calwyn felt a quick, eager rush of hope. But Halasaa was shak-ing his head, gazing sorrowfully at Tonno. *You have suffered a great grief. I too suffered when my father left me. But the one you have lost cannot be restored in flesh.*

"Some other way, then? Is his spirit, his life force, whatever you like to call it, is he still in this river you speak of?" Tonno could not look at him; there was a terrible angry hope in his voice. Halasaa laid a hand upon his arm.

His spirit is there, yes. But we cannot call it back. The spirit is always part of the river, just as your own spirit is. After the great change that we call death, the spirit mingles joyfully and disperses in the great stream. All is change, all is movement, yet the river is always the river. Halasaa's words were very gen-tle; Tonno bowed his head and did not speak for a long time.

Darrow got to his feet and walked slowly about the platform, gingerly testing his weight on his newly healed foot. "It feels strange indeed to walk on a straight foot after hobbling so long on a crooked one." He paused by the railing and looked over the tree-tops. Halasaa and Calwyn joined him there, and Calwyn gazed out toward the glittering band of blue that was the ocean, jewel-bright in the light of the declining sun. But Darrow was staring the other way, deep into the forest, and then Calwyn saw it too, far off across the trees. The platform on which they stood was not the only one perched high in the roof of the forest. In the distance were others, a flotilla of rafts buoyed by the treetops, a whole city riding high above the ground, linked with narrow rope bridges and broader walkways. She could see the tiny figures of people moving about on the platforms; men sat in groups, one woman combed out another's hair, and children swung nimbly up into the branches of the trees and ran about as easily as though they were on the ground.

Darrow turned to Halasaa. "You know so much about us. Is that the place we seek, the Lost City of the Ancient Ones? It is not as I expected."

Halasaa tipped back his head in a soundless laugh, and the little bird on his shoulder gave an indignant cry and flapped away to preen itself. *That is Spiridrell, the Place of Trees.* He sobered suddenly, and when he looked toward the city, his face was sad. *I know the place you seek, but it is not here. My people are the Tree People, not the Ancient Ones you speak of. They were here long before the Voiced Ones ever set foot upon this world. But I know the Lost City. My father took me there when I was a child.*

Darrow's grip on the railing tightened. "Do you know how to get there? There is one who we must meet in that place, a sorcerer—"

Halasaa frowned. *The arakin have told me of another, a singer of songs also. This one chased them from his ship with his magic and tormented them.*

"That sounds like Samis," said Calwyn ruefully.

Darrow asked urgently, "Was he ahead of us, or behind?"

The arakin did not tell.

"We must reach Spareth before him," said Darrow. "Can you take us there?"

If you wish it, I will take you.

"Then let's go now!" Tonno jumped to his feet. "We've wasted enough time here already!"

Be still. You are too impatient. All is as it should be. You will rest here tonight, and tomorrow we will sail for Spareth.

The Desolate City

Calwyn lay on her back watching the dappled play of green leaves, layer against layer. Sometimes the white light of the sun lanced through them and made her blink, but mostly the pattern was transparent green, a shifting dance of light and shadow, pale and silver and dark. She could almost imagine herself back in Antaris, lying in the orchard and staring up at the sky through the leaves of the apple trees. But the trees in the orchard would be bare now; after the fruit, the leaves would have turned to gold and fallen. The younger novices would be shoveling them up for the bonfires the men would set alight, chasing one another and shouting.

Did winter ever come to this part of the Wildlands? She had asked Halasaa, and he had assured her it was so, and put pictures into her mind, images of the Tree People making their long, yearly trek to caves in the mountains, children and elders gathered close about a fire in the darkness, and hungry men and women searching all day in the bitter cold for food. His face had clouded. *Many Spiridrelleen die in the hungry season. It was not always so. When the Voiced*

Ones came, the Tree People were driven from the warm lands of the north, where we could dwell in the forest all year round.

"I'm sorry." Calwyn hadn't known what else to say.

There are fewer of us every year. And now that my father is gone, I am the last to know the dances of healing. There is no other.

"Then they should cherish you all the more—" Calwyn had stopped. The priestesses of Antaris had cherished her. But when Halasaa had spoken of being shunned by his people and feared by them, she had understood.

They like to keep me close by, in case they need my skills. If someone is hurt or ill, then they come to me, but in secret, after dark. But they will not eat with me, nor let me teach the dances to the children. When I am gone, it will all be lost.

"It's the same everywhere. Look at Trout. Even when he sees and hears chantment before his eyes, he still tries to find a way to disbelieve it. Perhaps magic is dying all over Tremaris. That will make it easy for Samis, if we can't stop him." And how exactly would they ever stop him? she had wondered, not for the first time.

Halasaa had seemed to hear her thoughts and had placed his warm brown hand reassuringly over hers. *Do not fear. This life is a dance, and not a battle. We are all part of this world, not masters of it. Tremaris dances hand to hand with the moons and the stars. The ocean embraces the river, and the sky breathes in every song. The sorcerer should know this, and we must remember it too.*

Looking up at the leaves, Calwyn remembered his words and smiled. Though she had no idea what they might mean, she found them comforting. It was peaceful here, and pleasant to rest after so long at sea. Today they would sail for the Lost City. Tonno and Mica had gone with Halasaa to collect eggs from the water-birds that nested by the stream, and Trout had been taking apart the pulley that hoisted a basket up to the platform, to see if it was better than the ones he had constructed in Mithates. She didn't know where Darrow was; he was so impatient to be off that she wouldn't have been surprised to find him already waiting for them on *Fledgewing*, pacing the deck.

"May I come up?" Darrow's voice broke into her thoughts.

Calwyn sat up, flushing at the unexpected sound of his voice. "Of course."

He climbed the ladder as nimbly as a boy, and Calwyn laughed. "It's good to see you so light on your feet!"

"I had forgotten how good it feels to run." He brushed the hair back from his face and grinned at her. "But to sit quietly is a good thing too."

She smiled back at him, and they sat side by side in comfortable silence on the edge of the platform, their feet dangling among the leaves. Calwyn looked away, across the rustling sea of green that stretched as far as the horizon. To the north somewhere, invisible, was the shadowy line of the mountains where she had grown up, the place she had always considered her home, the place she might never see again. Supposing they did defeat Samis, what would happen then? Would they go back to Kalysons and help Tonno with his fishing? Or would she make the long journey home through the mountains, to Marna and Ursca and the others? Would Mica come with her? She smiled at the thought of quick-tempered Mica training in the quiet ways of a priestess of Taris. Tamen would find her even more difficult to handle than Calwyn herself had been. Half-regretfully, she put the idea out of her mind. Besides, she knew for certain now that the Wall of Antaris would never again be able to contain her own restless spirit. Perhaps they could all come back here and live in peace among the trees. But the Spiridrelleen would not welcome them.

She sighed and looked at Darrow, at his hawk's profile outlined against the leaves. He had spent so many years in companionship with Samis, then in rivalry, then pursuit. Once this chase was over, there would be a great emptiness in his life. How would he fill it? Wistfully she remembered the image that Samis himself had suggested to her in Trout's workshop: she and Darrow, wandering the world together, seeing all kinds of marvels, side by side— She shook herself. This hunt was not ended yet; she couldn't know how it would end. And if they weren't strong enough, if they couldn't manage to defeat Samis, all of them together, three chanters and Halasaa? Calwyn left the thought unfinished.

She turned to Darrow. "Will you leave your walking stick behind, now that you don't need it anymore?"

Darrow looked at her steadily. "A gift is not thrown away so lightly. Especially a gift from a friend. No, I will keep it, to remind me that not all friendships need to end in bitterness."

Impulsively Calwyn laid a hand on his sleeve. "Sometimes

friendships end in other ways. They can change — into something more . . ." Her face grew warm. Would he understand her? She stammered, "As Halasaa says, *all is change*. . . ."

For a moment Darrow looked puzzled. Then his face cleared, he flushed, and he laid his warm hand on top of Calwyn's. "There are things that you and I must say to each other, Calwyn," he said, and there was a tenderness in his voice that she had never heard before. "When this is finished —"

But before he could say anything more, Mica's clear shout rang up from below, sending a handful of the red and green fruit-birds fluttering into the air. "Hey, you two, come down! We got enough eggs for a hundred omelettes! And Halasaa says it's time to go."

Darrow gave Calwyn a regretful, apologetic look before he scrambled to his feet. The quest still came first. But Calwyn sensed that he was not as eager to be under way as he had been before. Perhaps Darrow too had his doubts about what awaited them. All the calm certainty about their task now seemed to belong with Halasaa; it was as though he had been waiting for them all his life and knew exactly what must be done. Looking over the edge of the platform, Calwyn could see him, still and straight as a sapling, his face turned upward, his eyes bright, a little bird on one shoulder and a woven basket of fruit slung over the other.

Come. It is time to leave.

Calwyn couldn't help comparing the look of serene joy on Halasaa's face with Darrow's stern, set frown. Quickly she seized his hand and pressed it between her own.

"When this is finished," she said.

He nodded and gripped her hand. Their eyes met and held, and in that look there was a promise.

They spoke little in the next few days of swift sailing along the southern coast, as though the silence of the Tree People had seeped into their bones. They moved about the boat with quick, deft actions when it was necessary, or stood motionless at the tiller or the prow, scanning the horizon. The shore slid by, the endless forest gliding past them; from time to time the noise of birds or the rustle of leaves would call out to them like whispers of encouragement. But not once did they catch sight of Samis's ship, either before or behind them.

The arakin came sometimes to Halasaa, not in the great flock that had descended on the boat before, but one or two at a time. Trout still flinched at the sight of them swooping toward the boat and took himself hastily below, but Mica stood bravely by Halasaa, willing herself not to move out of range of their sharp-toothed beaks. The arakin would speak to Halasaa in that language that only he could understand, and then flap away on their scaly wings. Every time the message was the same.

They say they cannot see the one you seek.

"Perhaps he's hiding himself with the Power of Seeming," said Calwyn.

"Perhaps he's sailing beside us *right now*," said Trout.

At once Mica snatched up an egg from the basket and hurled

it at the place where Samis's ship might be, but the tiny splash as it dropped into the empty waves did not wholly reassure her.

Darrow's face wore the grim look all the time now, and once a whole day went by without his speaking a word to any of them.

They turned northward, and it was then that the rains began, softly at first, a silver curtain falling between *Fledgewing* and the shore, reminding Calwyn of the days in Antaris when the rains fell in a dull roar over the Dwellings. Then the novices would sit by the hearth, weaving and spinning and listening as the priestesses told the long tales of Taris and the other gods, and the Ancient Ones and their adventures. There were no Tree People in those stories. There were no tales that told how they had been chased from their lands and driven deep into the wilderness, no stories of their hunger and cold, nor of their own silent dancing magic and the secrets of becoming. And what were the stories that the Spiridrelleen told of the Voiced Ones, the people who had driven them away? She did not like to think what horrors those tales would hold.

Day after day the rains fell as the landscape of the shore changed before their eyes. The blanket of dark solid trees gradually gave way to a coverlet of more slender trees with pale trunks and silver-gray leaves. The land shimmered with delicate light, so that it was hard to see where the boundaries between the sea and the rain and the trees began and ended. During the day, the rain blurred the light of the sun, but this was also a time when all three moons were at their fullest, the Three Lanterns of the Goddess shining bright. Even at the depth of night, a silvery glow shone through the mists, and the lines between day and night were blurred too. The sound of the rain washing against the decks and sighing into the sea was like soft music, and droplets of water clung to the ropes and the sails like diamonds.

On they sailed through this indistinct world of blues and greens and silvers. Calwyn gave up all tasks on the ship and stood unmoving at her place in the bow, barely eating or drinking, rarely sleeping, consumed by the faint, steady call of the place that waited just beyond the horizon: the abandoned city of the Ancient Ones, the heart of all magic, the breath behind every song. Her serious dark eyes were always fixed at some place in the mists beyond the dipping of the prow, but it seemed to the others that she was listening rather than watching.

At last, at a time that could have been early morning or silver dusk, she heard what she had been waiting for. She turned her head. "Mica, still the ship."

Obediently, Mica broke off her song. The sails drooped; there was a sudden silence, but for the lapping of the sea and the ever-present murmur of the rain.

"What is it?" said Darrow.

Halasaa's quiet words sounded in their minds. *This is the place.*

Calwyn stood with her hands gripping the rail, and as the mists thinned, the others saw a wide cove spreading before them. And there was Samis's ship, his Gellanese galley, the long rows of oars stilled and silent, the single square sail furled against the crossmast.

Trout groaned; they all felt the same sickening despair. Tonno took up the looking-tube. "No one there that I can see," he said, in a voice more subdued than usual.

"He's not on the ship," said Calwyn, with certainty. Since she had met Halasaa, she had become aware of a flickering sense she hadn't recognized before, a sense of the presence of life. It was neither seeing nor hearing, but some other ability that had lain long dormant inside her. It was like being able to close her eyes and still see the imprint of a candle flame, flickering against the dark. Now she could turn her mind toward Samis's long ship and know in an instant that it was empty. She was even, very faintly, aware of someone, Samis himself, enclosed in the expanse of shimmering forest on the shore.

"If he has gone ashore," said Darrow, "we should follow him."

Tonno and Darrow took the oars of the dinghy, and the little boat slid through the mist. When the water became too shallow for rowing, Trout took the rope and waded the last few steps onto the pebbly beach. Calwyn was the last ashore and stumbled as she left the boat. Mica steadied her.

"You all right?"

"Yes, but—" Calwyn looked around at the slim trees that stood like a crowd of silent witnesses all around them. "There's something about this place, a doomed feeling."

There was a great slaughter between the Tree People and the Voiced Ones here, all around the Lost City. Halasaa's face was taut with sadness. *The land remembers.*

Calwyn closed her eyes, and for a moment it was as though she could hear the cries that had rung through the trees on that day so long ago, and the clash and whistle of weapons, and see the terrified faces of the fleeing people, and the stain of blood spreading slowly, slowly, a dark tide across the land, tinting the pale pebbles of the beach with scarlet, the blue-green sea soaked with red. So many bodies, so many, the land heaped with the dead and dying, and the stench of killing everywhere. She took a sharp, sobbing breath.

A firm hand gripped hers; Calwyn opened her eyes, expecting to see Mica, but it was Halasaa who stood there.

Come. This is the way.

The trees of this forest, unlike the trees of Spiridrell, were not tightly packed together. Light and rain filtered between them in a pale mist that subdued the sound of the crew's footsteps and their hushed voices. Halasaa led the way, then Calwyn and Darrow. Mica and Tonno followed, close together, with Tonno's big hand resting protectively on Mica's shoulder, and reluctant Trout last of all, snatching off his misted lenses every few steps and rubbing them on his shirt. The earth was damp underfoot, covered in soft, muffling moss that squelched where they trod.

After a time the trees thinned out further, and lumps of stone jutted from the ground. In a few places the stones made an island of paving, surrounded by moss.

"This must have been a road once," muttered Trout to himself.

Now they followed the line where that ancient road had been.

Once it had been a broad avenue; now the trees had reclaimed it, their slender trunks reaching up through the stones, as though they too were walking with slow determination toward the city.

Suddenly Mica clutched at Tonno's arm. "What's that?"

"Just the wind, lass," murmured Tonno uneasily. But they could all hear it now: an uncanny cry that echoed through the forest, a howling that grew clearer at every moment, until it resolved itself into a human voice, into human speech.

"What does it say? What does it say?"

They had all halted, listening. A chill ran down Calwyn's neck as the unearthly sobbing rose and fell around them.

Darrow's face was pale. "Heron," he said. "Heron, I summon thee to thy fate."

The call died slowly away. Shivering, Mica wrapped her arms around herself; Tonno made a surreptitious sign to ward off evil. Trout said, "Heron? What does that mean? I haven't seen any."

"Heron was Samis's name for me, long ago." Darrow turned away, shoulders hunched.

"Was that — that voice, was that *him*?"

"He is close by," said Calwyn quietly. "Very close."

Come. We must not linger here. Halasaa set off, stepping lightly across the ruined paving stones. Trout hung back, thrusting his hands miserably into his pockets. Surely it was madness to obey that uncanny call. Walking with their eyes open, straight into a trap. He followed the others, but lagging farther and farther behind.

The attack came without warning.

From nowhere the ravens swooped down in a black flurry of wings and savage beaks, cawing in wild triumph. Halasaa took the worst of it; helplessly he threw up his arms against the fierce beaks that thrust and thrust again at his eyes. As fast as one bird was brushed away, another dived to take its place, vicious, relentless, so that Halasaa was invisible in the midst of the dark storm of beating wings.

Darrow leaped into the fray, striking out blindly at the whirling ravens, but he could not beat them back; Tonno ran forward, tearing off his jacket and flailing it in front of him. "Calwyn!" he roared. "Sing! By all the gods, why don't you sing?"

Calwyn's mouth was dry. She stepped back and swallowed hard; her mind was blank, not a single word came to her. The ferocious birds swooped and crowed, merciless; Halasaa had fallen to his knees, his arms wrapped about his head. Calwyn pressed her hands together and began to sing. At first only a hoarse croak emerged, but soon her song was strong and clear. This was different from singing to the bees, or even to the arakin. That was companionable, friendly, one voice to another. But this was a fight, her song a weapon to drive the birds back, and she felt the chantment strike through the air like the slash of a sword blade.

The ravens dodged and cawed; for a moment they whirled above Halasaa's head in confusion, a black storm cloud, then they streamed away and vanished among the trees.

Tonno helped Halasaa to his feet. *Do not fear. I am unhurt.*

Halasaa's eyes were bright as ever, though his hands were shaking. *They would not listen to me.* He seemed bewildered, his serenity disturbed for the first time. *They would not listen.*

"We must be on our guard," said Darrow grimly. "This is not a friendly place."

"And we must stick together!" barked Tonno, glaring at Trout, who had just caught up to them. The attack had been over in the space of a few breaths, and Trout had seen nothing.

"What? What's happening?"

"Never mind that. Just stay close." Tonno shook him roughly by the arm; he looked ready to clip him over the ear, but Trout broke free.

"All right, all right! There's no need to get *violent.*"

"I'll show you violent, if you wander off again."

"Please!" cried Calwyn. "Let's keep moving." The awareness of Samis close by, and the presence of power, made her head throb unbearably. She pressed her hands to her temples. "Come on."

They continued along the broken road, with Calwyn leading the way. Rebelliously, Trout fell behind again, keeping out of Tonno's sight; he preferred to risk Tonno's predictable wrath than the unknown dangers that lurked up ahead.

As they walked deeper into the forest, Calwyn moved more and more hesitantly. At last she stopped. There were no more paving stones to mark the road to the city. "I can't — I can't find the way." She rubbed her wrists against her forehead. "It's too — there's too much *noise.*" Under the trees it was as silent as ever; the cacophony was inside her mind. She appealed to Halasaa. "Do you know the way?"

But Halasaa shook his head. *It is dark to me now. I cannot see.*

Tonno gave a sudden, sharp cry. "*There!*" He plunged forward and disappeared between the trees.

"Tonno! Come back!" cried Mica in alarm. As they'd walked, the mist had been imperceptibly thickening. With two strides, Tonno had now vanished completely.

Then they heard his voice ring through the grove. "This way! Come on!"

"Tonno, wait!" Darrow chased after him; when the others caught up, he was gripping Tonno by the sleeve. Tonno tried to charge away.

"I saw him, I saw him, I tell you!" he panted. Sweat shone on his forehead, and his eyes were wild. He gave another desperate lunge; it was all Darrow could do to hold him back.

"You saw Samis?"

"No!" Tonno shook his burly head so vehemently that drops of sweat flew from his hair. "Not Samis — *Xanni!*"

"Tonno, Tonno, listen to me!" Darrow shook his friend, but it was like trying to reason with a maddened ox. "It is an illusion! Xanni is dead."

"In this place, who knows? Magic has more power here, you said. Mebbe the dead walk in these forests — *Look there!*" And with a wild cry, he broke from Darrow's grasp, his arm outstretched. They all turned. Calwyn gasped. There stood Xanni, a little way off; Xanni, with his mop of curling hair and his lopsided cheeky smile, reaching out a hand to Tonno.

"My brother, my brother!" Tonno charged toward him, but the figure turned and dodged through the trees. An echo of laughter hung in the air where he had been, and Calwyn took a shuddering breath: surely it *was* Xanni. There was Xanni's grin, Xanni's laugh — But there was no time to think. Already Tonno had vanished under the trees, and Halasaa sprinted after him, with Darrow following.

Calwyn seized Mica's hand. "Quick! We mustn't lose them."

"We ain't gettin' lost if I can help it, not here!"

The two girls ran on and on between the ghostly trees, their feet silenced by the moss. They could hear Tonno blundering ahead, crashing into branches, imploring the phantom figure of his brother to slow down, to wait for him. Calwyn and Mica ran until they were fighting for breath, and the mist had grown so thick they could hardly see the way ahead.

After a long time, Tonno began to slow down, and his shouts became less frequent and more despairing, until they heard no more. Then they called to him, and elsewhere in the forest they heard Darrow crying out his name, and the silent call of Halasaa.

They stumbled across Tonno at last, collapsed onto a fallen log, his head in his hands. Mica fell to her knees and took both his hands in hers. "Tonno, Tonno —"

Tonno looked up, his face streaked with tears. "I saw him," he said dully. "I saw him."

Mica wrapped her arms around his curly head and hugged him roughly to her. After a moment, Tonno put his arm around her. "You'll have to be my family now, lass," he said gruffly.

"All right, then," said Mica, and her tone was so offhand, Calwyn had to smile, though she could see in Mica's face how pleased she was.

She heard a footfall behind her; it was Darrow. "Halasaa!" he called. "They are here!" He turned to Calwyn. "Where's Trout?"

"I haven't seen him since the birds attacked us." Alarmed, Calwyn looked around as if Trout might fall from the treetops.

Halasaa materialized out of the mist. *He is here.* He was propelling Trout before him with one brown hand on the boy's shoulder.

"For pity's sake!" said Trout irritably, shaking him off. "I wish you'd all leave me alone."

"I think, in truth, you wouldn't like to be left alone here," said Darrow, unsmiling.

"Well, maybe not," admitted Trout. He shivered. "What now? We're not going to camp here all night, are we?"

Calwyn stood very still, her head tilted, and her eyes shut tight with concentration. "I know the way."

Steadily, she began to walk. There was no confusion in her head now; the source of power called to her, clear and insistent, and very close. And Samis was there too, an unmistakable presence stamped on her awareness. She was conscious of the others, close on her heels, but they were faint sparks compared with the bright, terrifying flame that was Samis.

Suddenly the trees thinned out, and they were on open ground. But the mist still pressed against them from all sides, thicker than ever; they could scarcely see their hands in front of their faces. Calwyn stopped. The light that guided her had snuffed out, as if the choking mists swirled inside her mind.

Mica raised her hands and sang a spell for a breeze. Her voice rose clear and small in the dead silence, and the fog that eddied around them tore into shreds and was whisked away.

Mica lowered her hands, gaping in awe. They were standing in a ruined square; strange structures rose on all sides. There were slim silver towers, their tops hidden in the thinning mists, low silver domes that gleamed softly in the muted light, and broken-down stone walls, lined with moss. Slender trees thrust up between the paving stones. The place was eerily silent, abandoned.

This is Spareth. This is the Desolate City. Here the Voiced Ones dwelled, and from this place they fled at last. Halasaa bowed his dark head. *Here my people died.*

"Amazing," breathed Trout. Wide-eyed, he trotted across the empty square to the nearest of the polished domes, and Mica ran after him.

"I ain't never seen nothin' like this before, have you?" she whispered.

"Never." Instinctively, they both kept their voices hushed.

"What's it all made of?"

"I don't know. It looks like beaten metal, but —" He brushed one hand against the silver wall. The surface was cool and smooth;

he could see his own puzzled face shining dimly back at him. "I don't know."

"Look out!" Mica caught at his sleeve. "Calwyn's off again, come on!" She ran after the others, bare feet flying across the crumbled stones.

"Coming," said Trout distractedly, but he lingered by the wall, knocking the burnished metal with his knuckles. Everywhere that stone had been used to pave roads or build walls, it lay crumbling and overgrown with moss. But the strange silver towers and domes still shone untarnished, untouched by time.

When at last Trout turned to follow, the others were about to vanish down one of the ruined streets. He scampered after them as they strode past buildings with gleaming silver walls and no roofs, down one street, then another, and across another smaller plaza.

It was hard to imagine that these broad, silent streets had ever teemed with people. What kind of people had the Ancient Ones been, to design such structures, and what kind of equipment could have built them? They must have had extraordinary talents indeed — Deep in thought, Trout almost missed the turning that the others had taken, but he spotted them at last on the far side of another vast, empty square.

They were all standing at the foot of one of the soaring towers, so high that its top was invisible in the tumbling mists. Darrow gazed upward, frowning. "In here?"

Calwyn nodded. "He's inside." She put her hands to her head;

the awareness of power, close at hand, confused and very, very strong, almost overwhelmed her. She could see from the look of strain on Darrow's face, and from the way Mica reached out a sudden hand to Tonno, that they could sense it too. Only Halasaa was unperturbed, staring up at the tower with a look of wonder, but no dismay.

"Where's the door?" said Trout.

Tonno growled, "Can't see one."

"Of course not," said Darrow sharply. He held out one hand to the unbroken wall and sang three notes, deep and commanding. Silently the wall shivered, and a circular opening appeared. Darrow threw back his head and strode inside. Halasaa darted in behind him.

"Quick, in case it closes up again." Tonno seized Calwyn and Mica's hands and pulled them through the round doorway.

"What if we're trapped in there forever?" moaned Trout. But he was more afraid of being left alone outside than of going in with the others, so he scurried after them.

The doorway did close; the wall sealed behind them. They were standing in a curved, low-ceilinged corridor made from the same burnished material as the outside walls. Light glowed softly from an unseen source; their own blurred and startled reflections shimmered on the silver walls, like images seen through water.

"What now?" Tonno whispered, and his voice echoed around the walls, chasing itself up and back until they could hardly tell where the sound was coming from.

Trout held out a hand to the curving wall and tried to keep his voice steady. "This room must run right around the foot of the tower." — *of the tower* — *of the tower* — "How do we get to the top?" — *to the top?* — *to the top?* — came the soft mocking echo.

"No," said Calwyn firmly. "We must go down, not up." — *not up* — *not up* —

"What difference does it make?" said Mica, loud and defiant. "There ain't no steps goin' up nor down!" — *nor down!* — *nor down!*

Trout fumbled in his pocket. "We should mark the place where we started out." He kept his voice low, but an unintelligible murmur rippled around the walls. Trout's pockets were always crammed with odds and ends: pieces of string, nails, the fragment of fire-mountain that had fallen from the sky, a filthy handkerchief, a pocketknife, a slingshot, a fishhook. All these things tumbled out onto the floor, as well as the stub of chalk he sought. But as he bent to gather them up, Darrow shot out a hand. "Look there!" — *there!* — *there!*

The little piece of chalk was rolling slowly away down the corridor. Even as they stared, it disappeared around the curve, but they could still hear the faint noise of its progress. "The floor slopes!" cried Trout. "*That's* why there aren't any stairs, the whole tower is a ramp!" — *a ramp!* — *a ramp!*

But Calwyn didn't stay to hear his speculations. She had already set off down the silvery corridor, her plaits whisking behind her, drawn toward the source of humming power. Her hands were tingling and clammy with fear; the sense of strong magic pounded in her temples like the beating of a great drum, ceaseless, terrifying. But she was compelled to go on, to draw closer.

The others followed, treading cautiously on the slippery floor, down and down, gradually but inexorably descending. Trout was right. The entire tower was one spiraling corridor, narrow at its top and broad at its base. But now they followed the spiral down below the base, beneath the ground, each spiral wider than the last. After a while it seemed to Mica that they had been walking forever between the same curving walls, stretching on and on. She put out her fingertips to touch the smooth surface on either side, and her shadowy reflections reached out their wavering hands to touch their fingers to hers. The hum of power intensified as they went deeper; even Trout and Tonno could feel it now.

"Like walking through mud," said Tonno between gritted teeth; beads of sweat stood out on his brow.

Halasaa looked over his shoulder and nodded, grave-faced. He was walking as light-footed and silent as ever, never missing a step.

Trout came last, his hands thrust into his pockets, clutching at the reassuring solidity of the objects he carried. He tried not to imagine what waited for them at the end of this everlasting corridor. Calwyn and Darrow were so far ahead that he could no longer see them. What were they rushing toward so eagerly? There was the little piece of chalk lying on the floor, run out of momentum at last. He bent and picked it up; its powdery roughness was comforting after the smooth featureless silver of the curved walls. Actually, it was *one* wall, strictly speaking, since he couldn't see any joints anywhere. . . .

Voices. Bright light and some indefinable force that made his head ache. It was the end of the corridor at last, and the others had all gone on, into the vast cavernous room that opened up ahead. But Trout hung back in the shadows, peering from the shelter of the corridor, to see what would happen next.

The others were standing at the edge of a huge round chamber filled with dazzling light. The spiraling corridor formed the outside wall of the tower, and its inside was hollow and open to the sky, like an immensely tall chimney. But the blinding light was not coming from the aperture at the tower's top. Floating in the center of the chamber was a large silvery sphere, spinning languidly, as if it had been flicked by a giant finger. The light and the intense hum of power that filled the chamber radiated from this sphere. Calwyn, shielding her eyes, was reminded of the hum of the Clarion when it flew to Samis on the riverbank; but this was a hundred times stronger.

Samis. The floating sphere was so bright, the force that emanated from it so powerful, that she hadn't even seen him at first. He was standing directly beneath the sphere, arms outstretched, head thrown back. The square stone of the ruby ring burned fiercely on his hand with a bloodred light almost as bright as the sphere itself. The hood of his cloak had fallen back, and his eyes were wide open, unblinking, as he stared upward. It took Calwyn a moment to realize why they looked so unnatural, but then she saw that they had been drained of color by the strong light from the sphere. His eyes, which had been so dark and piercing, were white now, like a blind man's.

The sorcerer spoke, and his deep voice resonated around the huge chamber.

"So, my Heron, my old friend. Have you brought your *reckoning?*"

Calwyn shivered, but Darrow's voice rang out clearly over the hum of the sphere. "I am your friend no longer."

"Yet you followed me here, all the way to this lost place. The ties that bind us are not dissolved."

"I expected to find you striding among the gods by now. What are you waiting for?"

"*Aah*—" It was a long sigh, of regret, or of triumph. "Did you think I would finish it without you? We made our plans together, you and I. Have you forgotten?"

"I have forgotten nothing." Darrow stood very straight; his hands were clenched at his sides, as if he held on to something very tightly. "I have not forgotten the day you stood on the bridge in Gellan and said that you would rule over the whole of Tremaris, that you would be emperor of all the lands, and crush the empire of Merithuros into dust, and the rest of Tremaris too, if you desired it."

"Yes. I said that," replied Samis. "And I said that I would do it with your help or without it. And you knew then that I did not need you any longer, that my gifts were stronger than yours and always would be. And it was then, only then, Darrow, that you turned against me. It is envy, and jealousy of my power, that has driven you to oppose me. The only reason you wish to tear me down is because you wish that you had the strength to stand now in my place. Is it not so? Is it not so, Darrow, old friend? You know I am right. You know as well as I do that this pitiful divided world needs one strong leader to put an end to its petty squabbles."

Majestically, the sorcerer swept his arm to include them all in his grand vision, and as he spoke it seemed that pictures formed and dissolved before their eyes. "You know, you all know, that every corner of this sorry world is stained with hatred and fear. You, windworker, daughter of the Isles, you have seen the slave markets and the terror that the pirates bring. You, fisherman, would you not like to see the seas swarm thick with fish again, and the farms golden with grain? Then no child would die of the wasting fever for want of good food —"

Tonno gave a low cry and clenched his hands, and Calwyn knew that he was thinking of his dead sister, Enna. Now Samis turned to Halasaa.

"You, son of the forests, you see your people hidden away in the trees and caves, sickly and afraid. Together we can bring them a new beginning, restore their ancient strength, their ancient wisdom. And you, my dear, my little priestess —" The white eyes burned now into Calwyn's, and his voice dropped to a caressing whisper. "You remember the promises I made to you, yes? We will open the lands of Taris to the wide world. There will be no more outcasts, no more runaways. You would like that, wouldn't you? To break down that mighty wall?" Then he turned to Darrow. "And you, Heron. You cannot deny that the great empire of Merithuros trembles on the brink of collapse and chaos, all because of the stupidity of its princes and the blindness of its emperor. And when Merithuros collapses, the whole of Tremaris will shudder."

Darrow did not answer. He stared straight ahead, not looking at Samis, or any of them, tense as a hawk who waits at the cliff's edge to fall into the arms of the wind.

"Imagine if all the lands, all the peoples, were united in peace and plenty, singing with one voice!" Samis's words rang, strong and authoritative, through the chamber. "The Nine Powers shall be One Power, and the Nine Songs shall be One Song!"

"You call yourself the Singer of All Songs," said Darrow quietly, and his voice was cold and hard as ice. "Very well then. Will you stand here now before us and sing every chantment you've learned? Or have you failed before you have even begun? *You do not have the Nine Powers.* I challenge you to sing the chantments. Sing for us now, *old friend!*" The last words bit as viciously as a lash.

For a long moment there was silence but for the restless hum of the bright spinning sphere. Then Samis began to laugh, a chilling laugh that filled every corner of the chamber before dying away.

"So, you challenge me? Keep your challenge, Heron. It is too late." A look of greedy exaltation appeared on the sorcerer's face. "You still believe that the Singer of All Songs must sing every kind of chantment with his *own* voice. But you are mistaken. I have discovered the truth. The one who will unite Tremaris is the one who can *command* every chantment to be sung. Then the prophecy will be fulfilled: all songs will be one. Here is the place where it can be done, in this city, in this building, within these very walls. *And it is more than half-done already.*" Once more the soft laughter chased around the chamber, echoing up and back.

Darrow whispered, "No —" But his face was gray.

"When I called to you, Heron, in the forest, that was the Power of Tongue. When the little priestess drove off the birds, that was the Power of Beasts. There were no birds; the Power of Seeming is stronger here in Spareth, is it not? Is it not so, fisherman?" He turned and leered at Tonno. "When you saw your brother under the trees, that was the Power of Seeming also. When the child blew away the mists —" He nodded toward Mica. "That was the Power of the Winds. And Darrow, *old friend*, when you opened the door to this tower, that was the Power of Iron."

"No!" cried Calwyn in despair. It couldn't be true. Had they been *helping* Samis all this time?

Coldly, Darrow said, "This is trickery. You are no master of chantments. You have no right to call yourself the Singer of All Songs, any more than you have the right to the Ring of Hathara on your finger."

Samis closed his hand over the great ruby stone, and the queer white eyes narrowed. "And yet I do hold the Ring. And yet I will be the Singer."

"You have summoned only five of the Nine Powers. What of the four that remain? You must know that we will not be tricked again."

"Aah —" Samis's voice sank to a sibilant whisper. "I will need no more trickery. You will give me your help, and give it freely, for the good of all Tremaris."

Suddenly Samis wheeled about and pointed to where Tonno and Mica stood close together, Mica's hand wound tight in Tonno's jacket. Before Calwyn realized what was happening, the growling throat-song of chantment rang out across the chamber. Mica screamed; Tonno's arm grabbed her close. A silver net was rising up around the pair, woven of loose, shining mesh; pin-points of light flashed as it enclosed them, and Calwyn saw that each knot of the mesh was tipped with a needle-sharp barb. Samis sang, and the net was drawn tighter. Mica cried out again as one of the barbs bit into her flesh; a red gash tore across her arm. Tonno bared his teeth like a dog snarling. Samis smiled and let his song fade into the silence.

"The Power of Becoming," he said, in that soft, menacing voice. "The power of quickening, and growth, and change; the power of the journey into death. Your power, son of the forests. Will you sing for me, or must I summon up the chantment with the death of your friends?"

Horrified, Calwyn stared at Halasaa. He was very still, his gaze fixed on the dark figure at the center of the chamber.

Do not fear. His words sounded clear and calm in her mind, and she knew they were for her alone. *Remember what I have told you. This life is a dance, not a battle.*

Calwyn pressed her hands to her mouth. She had never felt so helpless, so despairing. What use were fine words about dances and battles now? There was no hope. She could see from Darrow's pale, unhappy face that he felt it as keenly as she.

"Do as I bid you!" hissed Samis. "Or would you see your friends slashed into ribbons before your eyes?"

"Don't do it, Halasaa!" cried Mica. Tears were streaming down her face. "Let him do his worst! We're not feared!"

"Foolish girl!" Samis tipped back his head, and the light glinted in his white eyes. "You think to thwart me with your bravery? Understand this: your deaths will summon up the Power of Becoming as surely as your friend's song. There is nothing to gain by defying me."

"Do as he says!" Darrow bit the words out.

Halasaa looked at Mica and gently shook his head. He raised and lowered himself on his toes, like a forest bird about to take flight. And then he began to dance.

Slowly at first, he spread his arms and began to twirl and spin, stamping his feet in a wild rhythm. Round and round the chamber he leaped and wheeled. His burnished skin glistened, his long hair flew free from its binding. Even through her despair, Calwyn marveled at the power he summoned with his wordless magic, the craft of the Tree People. She could feel the power thrum through her own body as he danced, the spark of awareness and hunger for survival that struggled in every being, the force of never-ending change: birth, and growth, and decay, and death. She began to sway with the beating of her own heart and the pulsing of her breath; she felt the murmuring force, the burning flame that animated each of them in that ancient tower.

As the dance went on, her awareness broadened and heightened, and she could sense the powers of the beasts that crawled and flew through the forest, the powers that beat slowly through each tall tree and flickered more quickly than she could measure through the tiniest mosses and blades of grass. And as Halasaa's dance grew stronger and more confident, the pulse of becoming throbbed through the chamber, the rhythm of every breath of every person in Tremaris, crowding there all around her: the Spiridrelleen, the peoples of Mithates and Antaris and Doryus and Gellan, and far off across the ocean in Merithuros and Baltimar, and peoples beyond whose existence she had never imagined. And out and out, flickering faintly from the stars themselves, distant worlds and beings that she had never dreamed of, humming about her like a cloud of bees, brushing her with innumerable tiny wings. It was all woven together; she felt herself, a minute stitch in an immeasurably huge fabric, tiny, tiny, spinning, dissolving. It was exhilarating, terrifying, yet somehow comforting, all at once.

Samis raised his arms high and cried out in triumph. Above his head, the silver sphere spun faster than before, the light shone from it still more brightly, and the hum of power grew louder.

"Chantments of tongue and beasts and seeming, I command

thee! Chantments of winds and iron and becoming, I command thee!" Samis's voice rose to a shriek. "Power of Fire, *obey me now!*"

He reached inside his cloak and drew out the Clarion of the Flame. For a moment he held the little golden horn in his hand, then he raised it to his lips.

As the wild, unearthly song of the Clarion rang through the chamber, a ring of fire licked out from the hem of Samis's dark robe, flames of red and gold, purple and green and blue, the eerie cold fire of the stars and the reflected light of the moons. Wider and wider the sea of flame spread across the floor of the chamber, until it lapped at Calwyn's own feet. She cried out and sprang back, but the fire came no nearer. Tonno and Mica still clung together as the flames writhed around their woven cage; at its base, the silver mesh glowed red-hot. Halasaa whirled on, leaping through the flickering tongues of fire so swiftly that he hardly seemed to touch the ground. But Darrow — Calwyn spun around and saw that he was surrounded by the flames. With a cry of pain, he threw up his arms and stumbled back, but the fire pursued him. A smell of burning flesh and cloth reached Calwyn's nostrils, and she saw Darrow's face contorted in a silent scream of agony.

"Little priestess." Samis's voice was in her ear, soft and deep. "Save him. *Put out the flames.*"

She didn't stop to think; in that instant nothing mattered but the terrible danger to Darrow. She forgot that in doing Samis's bidding, she might give him absolute power. She forgot her misery and despair, forgot that they had come here to defeat Samis, and yet at every step he had tricked them into helping him. Everything left her mind but the need to save Darrow.

She raised her hands, threw back her head, and sang. The craft of ice-call was deep in her blood, she had been learning it longer than she could remember, and to exercise it now was as simple and effortless as curling her hand to grasp a cup. She sang the ancient chantment, slow, inexorable, precise, older than fire, older than life, the power of cold and darkness and death.

As she sang, shadows appeared in the chamber. Between the bright tongues of flame there grew deep pools of pitch blackness, as black and fathomless as the spaces between the stars on a night of moondark. Wreaths of cold air crept across the ground, and breaths of mist rose where the flames met the darkness. Faintly, as if in a dream, she heard a voice shouting her name, calling her to stop. But she could not stop. The flames still writhed around Darrow, and she must put them out. Swaying, her eyes tight shut, she sang.

"Power of Ice, I command thee! All of the Powers, the lesser and the greater, obey their master!" The hum of the spinning sphere rose to an unbearable scream as Samis's voice echoed through the chamber. "I call upon the first Power! The Power of all that is, and everything that is not, the Great Power, the unknown and unknowable, the mystery that lies beyond our understanding —"

But before the sorcerer could cry out the final words *I command thee!* there was a deafening explosion as the great silver sphere burst apart. Calwyn's eyes flew open. A flood of brightness, of light and song mingled, erupted above their heads. Calwyn gave a cry and thrust her hands into the air, just as she had done when she was a little child in Antaris, running out to greet the first snowfall, holding up her face and her hands to the sky in sheer delight.

With a roar that shivered through the ground, the tower split outward like the cracking of a seedpod. Silver segments peeled back, curving slowly out and down to the ground, silver arc after silver arc, thrusting the floor of the chamber upward, so they stood at the heart of a great gleaming flower.

Calwyn saw that it was night. The mists had cleared, revealing the sky spangled with stars and the three moons shining down on the ruined city. And now she felt the light and the shadow and the song and the silence raining down on her, soaking into her being. And when at last it died away, she lowered her face and looked around at the others, and she saw the same uncomprehending happiness on their faces that glowed on her own.

The cage that trapped Tonno and Mica had fallen away, and Mica leaped to Calwyn and threw her arms around her. Dazed, Calwyn hugged back. Trout stood nearby, looking sheepish, a slingshot dangling from one hand.

Tonno said, "Samis —"

Calwyn had forgotten about him, but now she saw the fallen figure in the center of the chamber. The mighty sorcerer lay crumpled and diminished, all power gone out of him, an ordinary man. Darrow knelt by his side.

Calwyn rushed over. "Is he — ?"

"Dead," said Darrow abruptly, and he drew the gray cloak over the face that gaped up toward the sky, hiding the blank, staring eyes. One hand protruded from the cloak, the golden ring with its square red stone glimmering dark as blood. Darrow eased it from the lifeless finger and held it up. "The Ring of Hathara," he said softly, and slipped it into his pocket. He saw Calwyn's shocked look. "It never belonged to him. It is an ancient object of power, from the first days of Merithuros. I will take care of it, for now."

"What happened?" Tonno shook himself like a dog coming out of water.

"I think it was me," said Trout shyly. He held up the slingshot. "You were all acting so strangely, seeing things that weren't there. Tonno and Mica were in that net thing. And then Calwyn was singing, and she looked — well, the way she looked, it was the end of everything. And so *someone* had to do *something*. And there was only me. And this was all I had —"

"It was the fire — Darrow would have been burned alive —" stammered Calwyn.

Trout shook his head. "I did see the flames when *he* blew the Clarion. But they weren't going to hurt anyone. They were — well, they were *beautiful*, I suppose." A dreamy look drifted across his freckled face.

Tonno grunted. "You didn't think of shooting Samis, instead of that silver ball?"

Abruptly Trout stuffed the slingshot back in his pocket. "No. I didn't want to do that. I mean, that was the logical thing to do. But it didn't seem right. And anyway," he added candidly, "I'm not that good a shot, and the sphere was a bigger target."

"The sphere was the focus." Darrow looked up. "It bound the chantments together. You chose wisely, Trout."

The Voiced Ones used this place in ancient times. Halasaa had flung himself to the ground, exhausted, but glowing with joy and exertion. *Here they called upon their gods. The sorcerer knew this.*

"Trout," said Darrow. "Come here a moment. You say that we saw things that were not there? But you didn't see these things? Calwyn, sing a note, if you please. The highest note you can."

Obediently Calwyn sang.

Trout shook his head apologetically. "I can't hear it. I'm a bit deaf, you see. There was an explosion in my workshop about a year ago, and it hurt my ears. I can't hear anything really high, like whistles, or insects."

Darrow caught Calwyn's eye and gave a small smile. "So you will never hear the chantments of seeming, the highest pitched of all the chantments."

"No wonder you never believed!" Calwyn began to laugh, weak with relief and happiness. Her head still swam with the memory of Halasaa's dance, and the chorus of life and being that it had summoned into her awareness. She felt dazzled, as if sparks still darted across her inner vision. Even the departed glow of Samis's life seemed to echo somewhere in her consciousness. It would take some time before this new sense of hers lay quiet and harmonious again.

Mica jerked her thumb at the body that lay covered in the gray cloak. "What Trout did — that killed him?"

Unexpectedly, Darrow said, "Even without Trout, I believe he would not have succeeded."

"What do you mean?" exclaimed Calwyn.

This life is a dance, not a battle. Halasaa's eyes were closed, but the look of exaltation had not left him. *The Powers cannot be fought or conquered. We must dance within their bounds. There can be no conqueror.*

"Speak plain, can't you?" growled Tonno.

The sorcerer thought himself stronger than the Voiced Ones of ancient times. But he was overreaching himself.

"His own greed would have been his undoing," said Darrow. "He was not the Singer of All Songs, and he knew it, for all his fine words. If he had called upon the Great Power at the last, it would have consumed him."

"Are you certain?" Calwyn cried. "Is that why we followed him here, why you wanted to wait? You knew he would destroy himself —"

Darrow passed a hand over his eyes. "I guessed, and hoped. But I am glad that, in the end, that hope was not put to the test." He turned his back on the still and silent shape. "Enough. Let us leave him here."

"Aye," said Tonno. "Leave him. He's gone where Xanni is." And a look of pain crossed his face.

Halasaa opened his eyes. *Do not envy him. Change will come in its own time. It is happening now, all the time. Let it flow as it should. You too will join the Great Power, when your day comes.*

Quietly, one by one, they moved away from their circle, to wander slowly between the curved silver petals that had formed the tower, or to sit on the fallen stones nearby.

"Look! The Clarion!" Trout pounced on the little battered horn where it had rolled away across the stones. For a moment he hesitated, holding it in his hands; he looked to Darrow for guidance, but Darrow had walked away by himself. Trout said to Calwyn, half-defensive, half-defiant, "He did steal it from me, you know."

"You found it, Trout," said Calwyn. "Back in Mithates, before Samis ever did. If anyone has a right to be its guardian, surely it must be you."

"Perhaps," said Trout, a little shyly, and he tucked the horn deep inside his shirt, next to his heart.

The air was cool and fresh on their skin, everything washed clean and bright in the moonlight, as if a storm had passed. There was a fountain on the far side of the square, filled with rainwater. Calwyn and Mica wandered away from the others to take a drink, and Mica washed the blood from her arm where the barbed net had scratched it.

Calwyn said, "I think I understand it now. I think Samis never learned the chantments of ice-call in Antaris, after all. Perhaps Marna was right, and no man can sing them."

"Then how come he could sing seeming? Them chantments are higher'n yours," said Mica.

"Darrow explained that to me. He could lift his voice out of the ordinary pitch. But that's not a natural way of singing. He could sing the very highest chantments of seeming like that, but perhaps not the songs of ice, which are meant for women's voices. Or perhaps the priestesses wouldn't teach him. But, you see, *that's* why he kept luring us on."

Mica's eyes widened with comprehension. "It were *you* he needed! All along, it were you, not Darrow —"

"All of us," said Calwyn soberly. "He needed all of us."

"'Cept Trout." Mica giggled suddenly. "He'd be sorry Trout ever came along!" She swung her feet at the edge of the fountain. "Does Darrow know, d'you think? 'Bout *him* not knowin' ice-call?"

"I don't know. Perhaps." One day she would ask him. But not yet. There was plenty of time. *There are things that you and I must say.* A slow and private smile crept across her face.

Mica nudged her. "Look at Trout!"

He was marching about the tower, studying the material, taking off his lenses to peer at it more closely. They saw him run up to Darrow and ask some question, and Darrow's dismissive reply.

"I think he'd be happy to stay here forever," said Calwyn, "exploring this strange place, studying its secrets."

"Darrow called it the Lost City. Better it stays lost," said Mica sharply. "What good's a place that's all full of pain and bad memories? If I was Halasaa, I wouldn't come nowhere near it, not if you paid me a bagful of coins. Best to forget it."

"We can't make right the evils of the past by forgetting that they happened," said Calwyn. "That's not the way. Samis was partly right. There *is* healing to be done in Tremaris, though he was wrong about the way to do it. One person can't control everything. All voices will be one voice, he said. That's wrong. True power lies in many voices. But singing together, helping one another, as we have done — that's where strength lies."

"So," said Mica. "Where're we goin' to start?"

Calwyn looked at Trout, prowling about eagerly with his measuring string and his quick curiosity, and the lump under his shirt that was the precious Clarion. She looked at Tonno, silent and sad, carrying all the grief of a world that had seen too much sorrow, too much waste, and too much poverty. She looked at Halasaa, curled in a sleep of sheer exhaustion, an outcast from his people, yet the wisest of them all.

Lastly she looked at Darrow, the one she had known the longest, the person she knew the least. He was staring down at the gray-shrouded body; his hand was hidden in his pocket, fingering the ruby ring. She couldn't guess what thoughts were passing through his mind. Was he remembering the days when Samis had been his friend and companion? Or thinking of their long chase to follow him here? Or was he pondering, like Mica, what they would do next?

Calwyn turned to Mica, with her bright, impatient eyes, her swift temper, and her unswerving loyalty, as she sat waiting for her answer.

Samis's vision of Tremaris, peaceful and prosperous, was a persuasive one. There would always be scars; no deep pain could be readily forgotten. But the everlasting changes of the river and sea, of the great Powers and chantments, must be wrought to begin the long, slow healing.

She moved her fingers in the water of the fountain. All the lands, like the fingers of one hand; all different, but all connected, all part of the beautiful wounded world on which they spun together beneath the three moons. The mark of the Goddess on her wrist was blurred under the water. She imagined handmaidens of the Goddess, warriors of Merithuros, the silent Tree People, even the pirates of Doryus, all the peoples of Tremaris, at peace, not quarreling and suspicious, but exchanging their magic and their stories, their songs and dances, their food and their handicrafts, all their different wisdom. She pulled her hand from the water and dried it on her jacket. There was something in her pocket. She drew it out: the little wooden globe, the model of Tremaris that Darrow had carved for her so long ago. She closed her hand around it.

"I'm not sure exactly where to start or how to do it," she said. "But we must. And it will be hard work."

"Hard work don't scare me!" Mica tossed back her mop of tawny hair.

Calwyn stood up. "Then let's begin."

The two girls ran across the wide ruined square, past where Halasaa lay dreaming. Trout, bent over his measurements, did not look up, but Darrow turned his head and watched Calwyn as she ran with Mica, the two girls hand in hand, toward the line of trees where Tonno stood locked up in his sorrow, waiting to be comforted.

About the Author

KATE CONSTABLE grew up in Papua New Guinea, without television but within reach of a library where she "inhaled" stories. She studied liberal arts and law at Melbourne University, then worked part time at a record company while beginning her life as a writer. She now lives in Thornbury, Australia, with her family. *The Singer of All Songs* is her first novel.

Look for Book Two in The Chanters of Tremaris Trilogy

The Waterless Sea

Heben knew that he was dreaming. He curled himself deeper into sleep, to make the dream last.

He was at home, on the lands of the Cledsec, in the north of Merithuros. The glorious curve of the sands swept out before him, sculpted by the wind, the same wind that whipped across his face as he spurred the *hegesu* into a gallop. The twins whooped with glee, crouched on their own beast: Gada in front, with Shada clinging on behind, her eyes shining.

They were racing to the top of the dune. Heben heard the soft *splat, splat* as the *hegesu*'s feet thudded into the sand, and the huffing protest of its breath as he urged it on, and he felt the matted woolly coat under his hands.

At the crest of the dune, Heben saw the whole of his father's lands spread out below: the swell of bronze and golden sands, and the silver flashes of the water pools. Far off, a low cluster of tents and flags marked his family's homestead, where they lived in the old way, under canvas. Flocks of *hegesi*, brown and milky dots, shifted slowly across the sands, and above it all spread the taut canopy of the silken blue sky.

The twins were just behind him. Gada stumbled up the dune, dragging the reluctant *hegesu* on its tether, and Shada ran up to tease him —

"Out of the way, you stinking desert dog!"

A sharp kick in the ribs woke Heben. He cried out and tried to roll over, hunched against the pain. Except that he couldn't roll over. He was roped to the prisoners on each side, and none of them could move. His neighbor, a heavy Gellanese whose red face dripped sweat, eyed Heben with displeasure.

"Keep still, can't you," he growled between clenched teeth. "You'll have us all thrown overboard!"

Heben blinked and struggled to sit up.

"I beg your pardon," he said, from force of habit, but good manners were equally unwelcome. The Gellanese curled his lip contemptuously and turned his head away. Heben tried not to grimace at the stench of his companion. After five days without washing, he probably didn't smell very sweet himself.

The pirate's ship was a long galley, with a snake's head for a prow, like all Gellanese vessels. But the pirates, rather than feed the hundred slaves they'd need to haul at the oars, preferred to move under sail, and the benches below the deck were packed with treasure and prisoners, not slaves. About a dozen captives were tied with Heben up on deck, roped at the ankles and wrists, and crammed into a space barely large enough to hold four men.

It was five days since the ship on which Heben had been a passenger was captured and sunk, and he had almost given up wondering what would happen to him. At first he'd thought he might be held hostage for a ransom from his rich father, the head of the Clan. The pirates weren't to know that his father had disowned him, and forbidden him ever to return to the lands of the Cledsec. But the pirates had shown no interest in his parentage. Nor did they ever ask why a wealthy young Merithuran lordling might have gone to sea, when it was well known that highly born Merithurans loathed everything to do with the ocean, and never went near it except from dire necessity.

"They'll sell us for slaves in Doryus Town," muttered one of the prisoners, but instead of turning to sail south, toward Doryus, the stronghold of all piracy in the Great Sea, the serpent-headed ship kept its course to the north. The mutterings grew darker. "Taking us to the tallow pits of Firthana . . . no doubt about it. . . ."

"What are the tallow pits?" Heben asked.

The prisoner on his other side, a bald and bony sailor who had been the cook aboard Heben's ship before it was scuttled, gave an ominous cackle. "Don't they talk of the tallow pits in them deserts of yours? The tallow pits is where the pirates take them they don't need, and them they wants to be rid of." He drew his finger across his throat. "Spit 'em, blood 'em, skin 'em, melt the fat down for candles. You never heard of a dead man's candle? They can burn for a whole turn of the moons without losing the flame."

"They won't get much fat off you," sneered the fleshy Gellanese.

The cook gave Heben a nudge and nodded over the side of the boat. "Looks like we might be nearly there."

Heben strained to see. Sure enough, the ship was drawing close to one of the little islands that dotted the straits. It was a strangely beautiful sight to someone who'd never known anything but the desert. The sheer rock of the cliffs reared out of the sea, and the deep green of trees fringed the shore. A gull soared overhead, a white flash against the blue. It had rained in the night, and the morning was washed fresh, with a tang of salt that could be tasted on the tongue. The sky shone blue and unblemished, like a glazed bowl filled with clear light.

If this was truly to be the last day of his life, thought Heben, at least he would die in a place of beauty. He hoped he could face death as a Merithuran warrior should: unblinking, straight-backed, so that the ancestors who waited on the other side of the curtain to greet him need not be ashamed.

"Boat ho!"

Heben saw a little dinghy bobbing on the water. A scruffy-looking boy was at the oars, and sunlight flashed on the two round glass lenses that he wore perched on his nose. A strange device, thought Heben.

There were two others in the little boat. One was a tall, thin, young man who looked about seventeen,

Heben's age. He had dark burnished skin, and tattoos spiralled across his face and chest. And there was a young woman about the same age, with a long dark plait over one shoulder. The man with the tattoos was half naked, but the boy and the woman wore sturdy, plain-colored shirts and trousers, the clothes of people who worked hard with their hands.

Fisher folk, thought Heben. This must not be the place after all; death would be postponed. He gulped in the cold air with relief. His ancestors would have to wait for him a little longer. To be honest, he was not looking forward to meeting them. They would probably disapprove of him, just as his father did, and the thought of an eternity spent with ancestors pursing their lips and shaking their heads was not a prospect he relished.

"Hello!" muttered the Gellanese, yanking Heben sideways as he craned to see what was happening in front of the ship. "Pirates won't like this! Can't they see where they're goin'?"

The boy with the strange lenses was rowing directly into the path of the much larger pirate ship. Sailors leaned over the rail and shouted through cupped hands. "Out of the way! Hey, boy! Out of the way!"

"That boy'd better look to his oars," observed the Gellanese. "This ship won't turn aside for him."

"We'll smash 'em like a twig!" The cook rubbed his hands together in glee.

Heben stared. What were the three in the little boat thinking? Still the boy pulled steadily at his oars, without ever looking over his shoulder. He might have been alone on the whole wide ocean, from here to the coast of Gellan. The other two seemed equally oblivious.

The dinghy was right under the serpent's head now, in the ship's black shadow. Heben braced for the collision. The pirates raced up and down, waving and cursing, for even though their vessel was so much larger, the little rowing boat still might damage it.

Then the woman with the dark plait did something that made Heben sit up with a jolt, and draw in a breath so sharp he almost choked. Slowly, she stood up in the center of the little boat, balanced despite the dip and sway of the dinghy. She raised her hands and opened her mouth. And she sang.

Heben felt her song before he heard it. A blast of icy wind hit the galley, so fierce and unexpected that the whole row of roped prisoners was thrown back sprawling. The ship lurched and tilted, and prisoners and pirates alike slid helplessly across the deck. Then another blast of wind roared from the opposite side of the ship and tilted it back the other way. From where he was caught in a tangle of ropes and flailing feet, Heben saw two of the pirates topple overboard and splash into the sea.

The huge vessel plunged back and forth like a toy in a bathtub, gripped by a childish hand. The sky was still a cloudless blue, the sea unruffled by any hint of storm. The gulls still shrieked and swooped, riding the currents of the air on their own errands, untouched by the mayhem below.

The serpent-headed ship was in chaos. Some of the pirates struggled to furl the sails, to reduce the amount of canvas the winds could catch, but the rigging swung about so violently that the task was impossible. The string of prisoners came to rest in a corner beside the wheelhouse. Heben was stuck fast in a pile of heavy bodies, but his head was free so he could see what was going on.

"Sorcery!" shouted one of the other prisoners, too close to Heben's ear. "This is bleeding sorcery, that's what this is!"

The ship gave another mighty lurch, and Heben could see that there were two little boats besieging the galley, one on each side. He caught a glimpse of a burly dark-haired man at the oars of the second dinghy, and another girl, golden-eyed, a year or two younger than the first, with a wild mop of sun-bleached hair. Like the other girl, she was standing, with her mouth open and her hands raised. Then the ship rolled back, and Heben lost sight of them.

"Windwitches!" howled the prisoner who had cried sorcery. But the rolling was less violent now, the pitching of the ship less extreme. Individual pirates were being picked off, and the whole crew was in a state of utter, gibbering panic, running this way and that in a vain effort to escape the ruthless winds.

The pirate captain had enough presence of mind to lash himself to the foremast with a length of halyard. Now, over the terrified shouts of the crew and the clatter of rolling water barrels, above the whip and crack of ropes and canvas, he shouted, "Stop! A parley, a parley! Witches, hold your song!"

Then Heben heard it clearly: a high, melodious song that threaded back and forth across the ship, carried by the voices of the two girls. It was an unearthly sound, like the faint moan of the wind as it thrummed in the rigging. Or, he thought, like the eerie call of a far-off desert storm as it whipped across the sands. The hairs on the back of his neck stood up, and his fingers twitched in a gesture to ward off evil. Then the song died away, and there was quiet.

The serpent-headed ship rocked slowly into balance on the waves. The few remaining crew, frightened almost out of their wits, clung to the railing. Heben saw a hard-bitten, much-scarred man weeping with terror, and desperate cries and gurgles echoed up from those in the water.

The dishevelled captain yanked at the ropes that entangled him. The dark-haired young woman stood quietly in her little boat and waited, one hand shading her eyes against the sun.

"Come aboard," demanded the captain, as he flung aside the last loop of rope. "Come aboard, and we'll parley."

"There's nothing to parley about," said the young woman. "Do you surrender, or must we throw you overboard as well?"

"No! No!" The captain rubbed his hands up and down on his stolen embroidered coat. "Wait on. Let's discuss this sensibly. No need to act like barbarians, is there?" He gave them a nervous grimace that was intended as a mollifying smile.

"Surrender!" A girl's voice rang out from the other boat. "Surrender, you murderin', thievin' son of a dog, or you'll find yourself flyin' over the Sea of Sevona afore you can draw another breath!"

The cook let out a long cackle from under the pile of prisoners. "You let 'im have it, witch-girl!"

"The witches of the Isles," said the prisoner who believed in sorcery. "It's them, by all the gods. I heard tales, but I never thought to see 'em — no, nor hear 'em, neither!"

Heben swallowed. He felt the same way; he could scarcely believe what he'd witnessed. Perhaps this was the dream, and what he'd taken for a dream was reality. But then someone kicked out a foot and caught him under his rib, and he gasped in pain. This was no dream.

The older girl with the dark plait raised her hands again and sang one clear note. The captain's hands were suddenly manacled, encased in a lump of some stuff that glittered like diamonds in the sunshine. Heben had never seen ice before. The captain gave a yelp of fright and leapt backward.

"It's cold!" he spluttered.

"Do you surrender?" asked the girl patiently. "Or shall I imprison your whole body in ice?"

The captain staggered for a few steps, regarding his trapped hands with horror. "I surrender, I surrender!" He sank to his knees and began to thump the block of ice against the deck. But it was impervious and wouldn't even crack.

"Very good," growled the burly rower. "We'll come

aboard. You — you with the beard — let down a ladder. And don't think about any tricks."

But the whole crew were so cowed by what they'd seen that they were incapable of thinking up any tricks of their own.

The pirate ship was soon transformed. The pirates were disarmed, trussed up, and herded to the stern of the ship, where the burly man stood guard, his thick eyebrows drawn into a fierce scowl. Those who had been blown over the side were hauled aboard to join their fellows, shivering and chastened. The prisoners were freed. Heben and the others were untied, and those who had been locked up below were released, blinking, into the sunlight.

Briskly, as if she'd done this a dozen times before, the tall young woman took charge. "Where is your wind-worker?"

The captain shook his head. "Don't have one."

The other girl snorted. "Pirates, with no windworker? S'pose you ain't got no sails to your masts, neither!"

The captain turned pleadingly to the tall girl. "She ran off. With my second mate, half a turn of the moons ago. We haven't found a new one. There aren't as many wind-workers for sale as there used to be."

The younger girl laughed. "Cos we got 'em all on our island!" she crowed.

"Never mind," said the dark-haired girl. "We did come to free your windworker, but there are plenty of other things to do."

The pirates were set adrift in rowing boats, with suffi-cient provisions to take them back to port, but no more. The serpent-headed ship was handed into the control of the sailors whose own ships had been sunk by the pirates, and the stolen goods returned to their proper owners.

"But you ain't just lettin 'em go?" objected the Gel-lanese who had been roped to Heben. "What about cut-tin their heads off? Or even their hands?"